Property Of

cp smith

Acknowledgements

Thank you to my family for supporting my work. I love you to the moon and back. To my friends who lift me up and keep me going and to the readers who reach out and let me know how much they enjoy my stories, thank you!

I hope you enjoy Dallas and Nicola's story set in the hometown that I love.

Dedication

I dedicate this book to these lovely ladies: Angela Shue, Kasey Austin, Janeane Dee, Kristina Marie Kozak, Taryn Rivers-McCullough, Lisa Kerns Flanagan, Sian Davies, Rosemarie McKenzie, Brynne Hounsell, Melissa Webster, and Stacy Lynn White-Cline. Your names helped build wonderful characters and I hope I did them justice. Thank you for sharing them with me . . .

"Life imitates art far more than art imitates Life." — *Oscar Wilde*

One

Everyone thought romance novelists had exciting sex lives—if they only knew . . . I needed a hero first.

To date, I have published twenty historical romances filled with *danger, passion, humor, and huge hulking heroes that take your breath away.* That, incidentally, was a quote from a review of my novel "Highlander's Woman." I, of course, wouldn't have a clue about huge hulking men who took your breath away. I just created them.

My name is Nicola Grace Royse—though I write under the pen name Grace Martin—and I'm a romance novelist slash romance junkie slash eternal believer that love conquers all. I have been since I was old enough to understand a woman swooning would capture a knight's attention. I'm also a tiny bit dramatic in my thought process. For example, a purple flower is not a purple flower, but a violet colored masterpiece given to man from God in order to capture a lady's heart. As I said, I'm dramatic.

As a child, I played with dolls and dreamed up magical lands where Prince Charming carried Barbie away on his trusty steed. As a teen, I didn't date much because of my overprotective twin brothers. I had to satisfy my need for romance by devouring passionate novels where Barbie finally graduated to Guinevere and Ken became the Knights of the Round Table. Then, one day, I picked up a book about Scottish Highlanders. They were big, they were bold, and they wore a kilt with nothing underneath. If I could have transported myself back in time to the Highlands of Scotland and those sexy Scottish clansmen, I wouldn't have hesitated. The mere thought of being manhandled and thrown over the shoulder of a gigantic Scotsman with a sexy brogue . . . well, it damn near occupied my every waking dream.

My love for the past earned me a bachelor's degree in education, with a focus on medieval history. My love for history and the romance of it all, along with a healthy appetite for reading, found its way onto a word document one boring weekend in June when I was twenty-two. And the rest, as they say, was history.

All those years I played make-believe, read historical romances, and daydreamed about the perfect man who one-day would sweep me off my feet had translated into a bestseller by the time I was twenty-five. Unfortunately, for me, though, my strapping Highlander, Lowlander, or plain old Prince Charming had never made an appearance.

I'm thirty-two, and never been married—hell, I'd never even been close. Which, by the way, was a sore spot with my mother. She liked to blame my single status on the unrealistic characters I'd written about in my books.

"Nicola Grace Royse," she always said, "men like that don't exist, for goodness sake."

I'd like to point out that my brothers still weren't married either, yet she never seemed to worry about their single status.

"They'll marry when they stop being boys and start being men," she explained. I, however, had my doubts on whether or not they'd stop being boys.

My brother's aside, I held out hope that one day I could prove my mother wrong. You see, like all good daughters in their twenties, I knew more than my mother did. Now, in my thirties, my biological clock ticked away, and the only thing I had to show for the last ten years was my books. Sadly, I'd come to the frightening realization that my mother, in fact, may have been right all along.

Part of the reason I haven't found a man who appeals to me is because men aren't raised to be men anymore, in my opinion. Gone are the take-the-bull-by-the-horns, never-say-die men legends are made of.

So, I write my own legends.

Men who are fearless, handsome, great between the sheets, love their women with all their hearts, and take care of them or die trying—Scottish Highlanders.

***

"Broderick gently laid his precious Rebecca on the dewy grass. The sun shone on her golden tresses, creating a halo around her head. Her eyes were hooded as she reached toward her husband, for she had but one thing on her mind.

"Are you my Laird or my husband in this moment?"

"I am one and the same, wife."

"'Tis true. But right now, I prefer the gentle hand of my husband than that of my Laird."

"Aye, you'll get my gentle hand and my strong back, my love, as I drive into ghaeahtabaejt'appppppppppppp ppppppppppppppp

"Oh, come on. Get off the keyboard, Snape!" I shouted at my feline child.

Snatching the offending orange tabby (who reminded me of Garfield on a good day) off my desk, I placed him on the floor just as the sound of liquid spilling and glass breaking grabbed my attention. My other cat, Simi, who was solid gray in color with big green eyes that reminded me of emeralds, had taken Snape's place on my desk, knocking over my cup of coffee.

"Seriously, guys? I only had one coffee pod left and that was my favorite mug, you annoying cats." Simi's responding meow caught my attention so I answered, "Yes, I'm talking to you. Who else would I be talking to, huh?"

Lifting Simi into my arms, I kissed the ornery cat as I stood up to grab some paper towels. My office was located off my kitchen in the three-bedroom house I'd bought and renovated with the help of my brothers. Nestled in a quiet older neighborhood in midtown Tulsa, the Arts and Crafts bungalow had once been the home of my favorite romance author's distant cousin. On his father's side, twice removed—or so I'm told. Of course, hearing that, I just had to buy it. The large wraparound porch on the quiet street was a huge selling point as well. I could see myself sitting on a porch swing with a cup of coffee and a notebook plotting my novels as I watched the sun set in a clear Oklahoma sky.

When I hit the bestseller list, everyone thought that I'd take off for New York or Chicago. But there was no way I'd ever leave my family. Born and raised in a state where the skies are blue, people look you in the eyes when you walk down the street, and hold God, family, and country close to their hearts, I knew I'd never be happy in a fast-paced big city. So I stayed, even though my agent recommended that I move.

Speaking of why I stayed—brothers only a sister could love.

Just as I walked into the kitchen to grab some paper towels to clean up Simi's mess, my side door banged open and my brothers, known to all as Bo and Finn, came walking in. They treated my house as their own and came over unannounced whenever they felt like it. They owned their own construction company, specializing in home renovations, and had a large crew they supervised. This gave Bo and Finn the freedom to work when they wanted, and ample time to keep tabs on me, which, for some reason only known to them, they thought was necessary.

"Do either of you know how to knock?"

Bo, who liked to call himself the oldest of our threesome, responded with, "If we knock, we lose the element of surprise."

"Element of surprise for what?" I asked, confused.

"Really, Nic?" Finn sighed with exaggeration as if speaking with a small child. "How else can we kick some guy's ass for messing with our baby sister if he has fair warning?"

"Explain to me again why I put up with you two?"

"It's the fraternal bond," Finn explained, "and the fact that we're so damn charming."

Did I mention that not only were they my twin brothers, but I also happened to be born at the same time? Finn and Bo liked to refer to themselves as the twins since they're identical, and that I just came along for the ride. Technically, we're triplets, though most days I don't claim either because of their behavior.

I rolled my eyes at my frustrating, but lovable, brothers and grabbed a handful of paper towels. I wasn't about to agree with either of them—it would only feed their egos. However, they *were* right. They were charming in a Nordic, overbearing, Neanderthal child kind of way.

Finn and Bo were tall, broad, and classically handsome with strong, square jaws, heavy brows, and big blue eyes that melted women's hearts around the world. They could thank our Norwegian heritage for their good looks. All three of us had light blonde hair and fair skin, though I ended up with light-green eyes as opposed to their blue. Basically, Bo and Finn were Vikings, plundering and pillaging helpless maidens while trailing heartache in their wake.

As I walked to my desk to clean up the spilled coffee, Bo opened my refrigerator and started searching for food. I kept a well-stocked pantry and fridge just for my brothers. They were bottomless pits and it was easier to keep food in the house than it was to listen to them complain about my empty fridge.

Just as I finished picking up the broken glass, I heard the TV mounted over the rock fireplace in my living room turn on.

Instantly alert and slightly alarmed that they appeared to be settling in for a day of binge eating and sports, I turned toward my living room to get them out of my hair. I had too much work to do on my novel and wanted to write in peace. Besides, they had their own homes in which to veg, they didn't need to do it on my new leather sofa. *I* hadn't even vegged out on my new leather sofa yet. If anyone was getting crumbs on the cushions while devouring a bag of chips, it was going to be me.

Rounding the corner, I entered my living room with its kickass view of Swan Lake. Swan Lake wasn't really a lake but a park directly across the street with a large pond that was home to swans.

Ready to insist that Frick and Frack make haste leaving my

home, I stopped suddenly, the TV catching my attention. There was a news report showing police standing in a field on the west bank of the Arkansas River and a body bag being placed on a coroner's gurney. As shocking and sad as that was, it was, however, the man occupying the screen that caught my eye as much as the body bag. He was tall, dark, and dangerous-looking as he scowled at the cameras. He had a policeman's shield clipped to his belt and I could see his weapon holstered at his hip. His hair was dark-brown, maybe even black, and styled in a not-so-standard issue policeman's cut. It was longer than most men wore, but not on purpose. You could tell he just didn't have time, or the inclination, to care if he kept it clipped short. Dressed in jeans, boots, and a black Henley Thermal covered in a black leather jacket, he stood out among the crowd of police officers. He was, in my opinion, the perfect romance novel hero and my writer's mind started taking notes while the woman in me came alive.

"The body of a young woman was discovered overnight in a shallow grave. Police are withholding the name of the victim until family members are notified. This is the third body of a woman found in a shallow grave in the past sixteen months. The first two victims, twenty-five-year-old Lisa Kerns Flanagan of Bixby and twenty-nine-year-old Rosemarie McKenzie of Broken Arrow were both found in shallow graves three months apart in 2014. Police are cautioning women to be aware of their surroundings when entering their cars and homes. The News on Six contacted the Tulsa Police Department, asking them to comment, but they have yet to respond. We'll keep you up-to-date on any further developments concerning the discovery of what appears to be the third victim of whom police have dubbed "The Shallow

Grave Killer," here, on News Channel Six."

"Those poor women."

Intrigued on a creative level, since the story included an honest-to-goodness romance hero, I dashed to grab my notebook from my cluttered desk in order to write down the specifics of the case. I began this habit many years ago when I first started writing. There were pages of news reports, internet folly, and interactions with strangers to help spark my creativity. As I flipped through it, looking for a blank page, I sighed when I saw how full it was. I had a never-ending supply of other people's lives to fuel my stories. Sadly, my own life, or lack thereof, gave me no inspiration. A writer writes what he or she knows, but since I had no real life experiences other than my books and friends, I had to steal snippets from other people's lives to fuel my imagination.

"Meow," Snape said from the comfort of my office chair as I stood there, writing down my impressions of the cop and the terrifying murders of three women.

"Don't mind me, Snape, I'll just stand here and write. I wouldn't want to disturb you while you lick your butt."

When I reached down to tickle his ears before I continued writing, a thought occurred to me and I paused. Maybe the reason I didn't have a life, other than my books, was that the only conversations I'd had in months were with my cats and brothers. Not that you could qualify grunting and chewing as conversation per se (my brothers, not my cats).

I'd been so tied up writing, plotting stories, going to book signings, and researching Scottish history, that I couldn't remember the last time I went out with my friends or on a date.

"How did this happen?" I asked in amazement. "I've turned into a spinster cat lady with no friends. Haven't I, Simi?"

"Meow," Simi agreed from her spot on my windowsill.

"Yeesh, you didn't have to agree so quickly," I argued on a sigh. "That's it. After I finish this book, I'm taking some time off to have a life. I'm gonna get drunk, let my hair down, maybe even get laid by an honest to goodness man. That's if I can find one that—"

"Bo!" Finn shouted from behind me, interrupting my private talk with Simi and Snape, "Nicola's talking to her cats again."

"What's she saying this time?" Bo hollered back.

"Apparently, she thinks she's gonna get drunk and then get laid."

"Excellent, I could use a good workout. I haven't beaten the shit out of a guy in years," he answered.

"Would you guys grow up already? I'm not sixteen anymore," I explained, exasperated as I pushed past Finn.

Finn followed on my heels, laughing, as I went into the kitchen in search of my phone to call Kasey.

"Sixteen or sixty, Nic, it's our job to scare the shit out of your dates."

"Considering every man I've met is as ridiculous as you and Bo, I don't think you need to clean your brass knuckles just yet."

"We polish them nightly, Nicola. As Dad always says, it's better to be prepared than caught off guard."

"Boys in men's clothing, that's what the two of you are," I laughed as I picked up my cell phone and looked up Kasey's number. "I have a book to finish today, so you two children have to leave. I can't concentrate while you're here."

Once I'd found Kasey's number, I hit call and put the phone to my ear as Finn roughed up the top of my head. Shoving his hand away, I grinned, and then turned my back on him while I listened to the call connect.

"Hello?"

"Kasey?"

"May I ask who's calling?"

"You know damn well who this is. My number's programmed under the name Amelia Earhart."

"And just like you, she has gone missing."

"Well, that's about to change, starting today. I realized just now that I talk to my cats more than I talk to humans. As of today, after typing the words "The End" on "Highlander's Pride," I'm taking six months off to do nothing but reconnect with my family and friends."

"Well, I'll notify People Magazine that the hermit Grace Martin is coming out of hiding," she chuckled.

"Fuck you," I laughed.

"Fuck you, too," Kasey giggled. "If you're serious about taking a break, meet me for coffee at Gypsy's, Tuesday at five thirty. Be there or be square."

"Coffee it is. I'll call the rest of the girls."

"No need, we have a standing date for coffee every Tuesday and Thursday. We do Yoga on Thursdays at Om-klahoma before coffee, if you want to come."

"I'm sorry I've been MIA, Kasey. It seems I got lost in fiction. But I swear I'm turning over a new leaf as of today. From now on, I'm going to experience life as much as I write about it."

"Baby steps, Nicola. You've been living in a cave for a while, you might need to adjust to the light first," she laughed. "Just show on Tuesday and all will be forgotten."

"I'll be there, you can count on it. Why, a rugged Highlander couldn't keep me from coming," I vowed.

"Right, we both know that's a lie," she laughed.

Ha, she knew me too well.

"Ok, short of a kilt-wearing Highlander coming forward in

time to throw me over his shoulder, I'll be there.

***

"Vaughn! Get your ass in here."

Detective Dallas Vaughn looked up from his desk and smirked at his partner, Bill Reed.

"Guess he heard," Reed chuckled.

"Guess so," Vaughn answered.

Vaughn rose from his chair, grabbed his gun, and shoved it into his holster as he made his way toward his lieutenant's office. The lieutenant's door was closed, further indicating how pissed off he was, seeing as they had been able to hear him bellowing from behind closed doors. Vaughn knocked and then entered before Lt. Dan Cross had a chance to answer.

"You wanted to see me?"

Lt. Cross was a huge black man with a big bald head that sat on top of a squatty neck. A former linebacker for the University of Tulsa, he kept his bulk while moving up the ranks. He had a degree in criminology and a sharp mind, but he also had a temper.

"Didn't I tell you to keep your fuckin' distance from Hernandez?"

Vaughn leaned against the doorframe and crossed his arms over his wide chest. At six foot three, Vaughn wasn't a small man, but he was leaner than Cross. Lean, like the former wide receiver he had been for the University of Oklahoma. Vaughn also had a degree in criminology. However, unlike his boss, he had no desire to work his way up the ranks. He preferred hunting down the bad guys to administrative duties.

"It was just a coincidence that I happened to be invited to a party at his next-door neighbor's house."

"You don't have any friends, Vaughn. How in the hell did you get invited to the Assistant District Attorney's house?"

"Tickets to next year's Oklahoma—Texas game."

Cross narrowed his eyes at Vaughn, and just when Dallas thought his boss would blow his top, a slow grin pulled across his mouth.

"Are you telling me you bribed the ADA so you could sit in his backyard and watch his scumbag, wife-murdering neighbor?"

Vaughn's lips twitched, but he held his smile. "No, I offered to give him my Oklahoma—Texas tickets because I heard he was serving hamburgers. As for Hernandez," he growled the name, "he's an innocent until proven guilty scumbag, wife-murdering neighbor."

Hernandez, the owner of Hernandez Plastics, was under indictment for the murder of his wife. According to Hernandez, she slipped while holding a knife and it somehow managed to bury itself into her heart. Originally, from Honduras, he was a flight risk and they all knew it. Vaughn had been keeping closer tabs on Hernandez than the law allowed, according to the restraining order Hernandez had filed against Vaughn.

Technically, he stayed far enough away from the man. However, when Hernandez willingly came into Vaughn's space in the ADA's front yard, the restraining order was null and void. That's how Hernandez ended up with a black eye and a busted lip. Vaughn was just defending himself, per the witness statements.

"Were the hamburgers good?" Cross asked.

"Rare, just like I like them," Vaughn replied.

Both men grinned at each other for a moment, but Cross lost his jovial attitude quickly.

"All right, enough about that scumbag. Get your ass out of my office and go find me that goddamned Shallow Grave sonofabitch."

Vaughn's eyes went blank at the mention of the killer. Dallas had had to notify the family of Stacy Lynn White-Cline when the dental records came back as a match this afternoon. He was itching to find that bastard. Dallas could still hear her mother's wailing in his head.

"I'll find him," Dallas vowed, "then I'll send him straight to hell."

"What you'll *do* is find him and hand him over to the DA, am I clear?" Cross bit out, leaning across his desk.

Dallas' jaw tightened, and he nodded once. Turning on his heels, he gritted his teeth, trying not to think about the single mother and the way they'd found her two nights earlier. He knew from experience, after six years in homicide, if you didn't leave that shit at the office you'd burn out quickly. Unfortunately, for him, he never listened and burned a candle at both ends.

Vaughn was a bit of a maverick and did what he had to do to solve a case. If it meant long hours, so be it. All he'd ever wanted to be was a cop. To catch the bad guys and make it safe for law-abiding citizens, no matter the means. He was thirty-four and had a failed marriage under his belt because of his dedication to the job, that, and because Brynne couldn't keep her legs closed to other men. Most days he was tired, frustrated, and needed a vacation. However, he had no reason to go home and the world was getting sicker by the day, so he kept working.

With another body in the morgue, and the only evidence

they had being the fact that the first two women frequented dating sites, according to their families, and traces of crude oil were found on their bodies, the trail was stone cold on the Shallow Grave Killer.

Making his way back to his desk, he searched for Sian Davies, a rookie detective, needing her help. Dallas' mood was as gray as the walls in their office. Every officer in his division was in a bad mood with the discovery of a third victim and wanted in on the case so they could nail that sonofabitch to the wall. Dallas and his partner, Bill Reed, were the lead investigators on the case, but half his division were out running down all possible leads.

Catching Sian at the coffee pot, Dallas called out to her. "Sian, I need you to call over to Missing Persons and ask them for a list of women between the ages of twenty and forty. I don't trust this new computer software, since it has more bugs in it than the Kremlin. Ask them for a hard copy and make several copies when you get it."

Nodding her reply, he watched as she moved to her desk and pick up the phone before he sat down in his chair.

"Let me in on what you're thinking?" Reed asked Vaughn as he sat down.

"All three victims were blonde. Two could be a coincidence, but three feels like an MO. I want to compare any missing women that match the descriptions of our three victims and see if they were visiting online dating sites."

Nodding in agreement, Bill Reed, a twenty-year veteran of the Tulsa Police Department and father of four, powered up his computer and stood with his coffee cup.

"Better refuel. Sounds like it's gonna be a long night," Reed mumbled, motioning to Dallas' empty cup.

"I'm not drinking that shit and you know it. You pull up the files on the Shallow Grave Killer and I'll run over to Gypsy's."

Reed turned back to Vaughn with a smile on his face. He knew that if he mentioned coffee his partner would cringe at the crap they served at the station.

"I want extra cream in my coffee, none of that skimmed crap either. June's got me on a low-fat diet and I'm wasting away as it is."

Dallas' brows shot up at the wasting away comment. Reed was six-foot-one and pushing two hundred and seventy-five pounds. There wasn't anything "wasting away" about the man.

"You'll get your cream, big guy, but if you tell June it's your head, partner. Your wife scares the hell out of me," Dallas chuckled.

"June scares the living shit out of me too, Dallas. She makes the Shallow Grave Killer look like a kitten."

That she did, Dallas thought as he headed for the door. He'd be tempted to put her in a room with the bastard as part of his punishment if he didn't love the woman so much. Then again . . . she might enjoy it.

Two

Gypsy's Coffee House was located in the newly renovated downtown Tulsa arts district. It was an eclectic coffee shop on Cameron Street in the historic Gypsy Oil building. The old three-story, red brick building had been renovated in 2000 to the delight of many who called downtown Tulsa home. Now it served rich, hearty coffee, great teas, delectable desserts, and sandwiches. Brick walls and comfy couches set the décor that was as vibrant as those who hung out there. Open mic nights brought in local talent, and the coffee kept my girls and me coming back year after year. We started hanging out at Gypsy's right after we came home from college. Our new adult lives might have kept us busy, but we always made time for each other and a great coffee at least once a week. That was until I got so engrossed in my novels that I barely had time for my cats.

However, that time was behind me, I'd learned my lesson, and I now sat on one of Gypsy's comfy couches, catching up with my friends. Relaxed for the first time in months, I laughed as Kasey read some of the messages she'd received on a dating site called Plenty of Fish or, as everyone referred to it, POF.

Kasey had created a profile on Plenty of Fish in the past

two weeks and had messaged with a gorgeous man, who claimed to be looking for love. He'd flirted and made plans to meet her for drinks the following week after he returned from a wedding out of town. However, before that could happen, he had amped up the flirting to the point that he was asking her if she wanted to be "his girl." The conversation gradually became more intimate in nature, which prompted Kasey to send him sexy pictures. She was thrilled to have found someone so in tune with her own passions in life, but the conversation always seemed to lead back to him asking for intimate pictures of her. Apparently, she obliged the man and asked him to reciprocate, which he did. The problem for Kasey began when she never received anything other than body shots that didn't include his face. His profile picture showed a gorgeous blonde male with a tantalizing smile, and his Twitter profile matched his POF profile. After three days of flirting, with no new pictures of him being sent, she told him she wanted a current picture of him in the tuxedo he was supposedly wearing at the wedding. That's when he turned from flirty—potential boyfriend material to a man who said he couldn't handle a stage five clinger—all because she'd wanted a current picture of him.

She showed us the messages passed back and forth between the two of them, and we could tell she was crushed that he dropped her so suddenly, but didn't have a clue why he'd reacted the way he did. It had been Janeane who first saw him for what he really was: a catfish who never intended to meet her. All he'd been after the whole time was the personal enjoyment of fooling a woman into believing he was someone he was not, and a few sexy pictures.

"Oh my God, listen to this guy," Angela blurted out. "'Are you on birth control?' he asked her, and then Kasey said 'Yes.'

Then the dickhead replied, 'Good, because I want you to feel my cock pulse inside you.' Jesus, this guy knows exactly what to say. Too bad he was fake 'cause that's kinda hot."

"'Send me one more hot pic of you, I need to cum',' Janeane continued reading over Angela's shoulder.

"Tell me you didn't?" I begged Kasey.

"I did. I know I should have been more careful, but he seemed so real," Kasey defended. "But don't worry, I've learned my lesson. No more sending sexy pics to guys until I've met them first."

I was shocked by this blatant deception, yet intrigued that someone as smart as Kasey could be so easily fooled by this guy. Still, after reading all the messages I could see why she fell for his charming and sexy persona. He was just that good. However, now my writer's brain had come to life and firing on all pistons. I couldn't help it; I started plotting a book.

It's a gift and a curse to be able to take a single conversation with someone and turn it into a book. A curse because I couldn't shut it down. A gift because I made a living doing something I loved.

Excusing myself to the ladies' room, I continued to think about a plot incorporating a dating site like POF and men who went to considerable lengths to create fake accounts just for a few salacious pictures. I was still thinking about how that scenario would play out when I exited the ladies' room, shaking my wet hands because they were out of paper towels.

When I rounded the corner, my head down, looking at my shoes, I collided with a solid body and sent someone's coffee sloshing. My hands went up to stop myself and they landed on a hard chest as my forehead slammed into a solid jaw. A responding grunt made me look up until I saw a pair of gleaming honey-colored eyes. Then I froze and blinked rapidly to make sure I wasn't seeing things.

Nope, it's him, the muse for my next book.

I pushed away quickly as my heart rate picked up. I looked up for a second time to make sure I wasn't dreaming, but I wasn't. It was still Detective Drop Dead Delicious in all his glory, and he was beautiful in that dark and dangerous way bad boys had. His hair was dark-brown, not black, and swept off his face haphazardly as if he'd run his hands through it after his shower and that was it for the coiffing portion of his day. His jaw was chiseled like a granite statue, covered with days-old growth, and it was set in hard contours as he clenched and released it. His eyes were the color of honey and so light, they fairly glowed like the sun. And his mouth . . . Lord, that mouth looked like it could kiss you so thoroughly you'd forget your name, your mother's name, and the boy you lost your virginity to as well. There was a dark arrogance, born of authority, that waved off him and he was wholly masculine to the point of being beautiful. He was tall, he was broad, he was in-your-face spectacular, and he filled the space like one of my Highland warriors exuding predatory power. My knees went weak just thinking about the comparison. No, seriously, even though I wrote this shit and it sounded good in a book, it really happened . . . my knees were like noodles.

I scanned his body and saw large, powerful thighs, shoulders that were incredibly broad and chest and arm muscles that bulged from beneath his white shirt. My eyes shot back to his shirt before I had a chance to finish my inspection and I froze. Thanks to my inattention, it was ruined, and he was looking down at it, scowling.

Hell's bells.

He looked up from his chest, pointed those honey-colored

eyes at me, and glared. I smiled back out of nervous habit and watched in fascination as those golden globes softened in return.

"I . . . I'm so sorry. Let me get a wet paper towel, and I'll buy you another coffee," I rambled as I tried to move around him unable to handle the intense stare he had graced upon me. Unfortunately, he had the same idea and moved at the same time. My hand came up as he turned his body, and I sent his other cup of coffee plummeting to the floor. He jumped back to avoid the disaster as I gasped and threw my hands over my face.

I heard him rumble, "Fuck," as I peeked through my fingers to survey the damage. He had coffee all over his boots and splattered up his jeans. He was, quite literally, a coffee-covered mess. In addition to that, let us not forget the two wet handprints I'd left on the front of his shirt, making it appear that I had groped him.

Humiliated, wishing the floor would open and suck me into a dark hole, I did the only thing I knew to do in this situation. I kept my mouth shut; my arms and legs pinned to my body and waited until he had entered the men's room. Then I ran to the counter, threw a ten at the man, and begged for two replacement coffees for the Detective.

I'd also like to point out that my friends watched this all play out in quiet fascination, with looks of sheer confusion on their faces, when I glanced back at them and grimaced.

I offered to clean up the mess, but the manager shooed me away, so I stood quietly waiting for the detective to return. After five minutes, my muse came strolling out of the men's room, still a coffee-stained mess. When he saw me standing there, he stopped—a good distance away, I might add—and he stared at me. He did a full body scan, mumbled, "Not a drop on you," and then saw the new coffees being offered by the man behind the counter. As he accepted my peace offering, his lips twitched into a sexy half grin. Lifting the coffees in a salutation of forgiveness he then winked at me, which sent my heart fluttering, turned on his heels and he was gone.

I watched his retreating backside while my memory played his wink, his grin, and his tight firm ass over and over. The way he had little flecks of green in his amber eyes, the way his bottom lip was fuller than the top. The way I'd like to bite said lip right before he—.

"What was that?" Angela chuckled from behind me, causing me to jump.

"What was what?" I hedged.

"That coy girl routine you just played with that extremely hot man. Even after the disaster you caused, he still checked you out and you just stood there."

"I wasn't acting coy."

"You didn't rip his clothes off either. What the fuck?" she accused.

"It's complicated," I tried to explain.

"*Un*complicate it for me then," Angela insisted.

Glancing back at the rest of the girls, I groaned as I made my way back to the couch.

Kasey Austin, Janeane Dee, Kristina Kozak, and Angela Shue had been my friends since we figured out that chocolate combated PMS. We'd gone to high school and college together and somehow managed to remain close throughout all of the hormones, men, and bullshit life had thrown our way, including my penchant for disappearing whenever I started writing a new book.

Angela, who was half-Japanese, half-white, but favored

her father's side except for her almond-shaped eyes, managed one of the local chain banks in downtown Tulsa. She was married, but had no children and probably never would. She was as career-driven as her husband of three years was, and they loved to travel. She had short black hair, soulful brown eyes, and a right hook to rival any man, thanks to self-defense classes.

Kasey was divorced with two small boys ages six and three. She had married barely out of college, to a man named Mark who was in the military. His constant deployments put a strain on their young marriage and they'd split up a little over two years ago. Needing to be close to her family and friends, she moved home and opened Om-klahoma Yoga studio next door to Gypsy's six months ago. She had long brown hair, big brown eyes, and legs that went on for miles.

Janeane was single as well and worked as a legal assistant while she went to law school at the University of Tulsa. A second-generation Irish immigrant on her mother's side with strawberry blonde hair, sky blue eyes, and double D cups, she looked like a model, but she had a brain to boot (Highly educated super models are excluded from my stereotypical and unfounded opinion of their IQ, of course).

Kristina was also married, but she and her husband Jake hadn't found the time for children. She was an up-and-coming realtor with goals that didn't allow for children at this time, but was considering freezing her eggs with future children in mind. She had dark-brown hair, a tiny waist, and an ass that rivaled JLo's.

Then there was me. I stood five-foot-four on a good day. My legs weren't long, my boobs weren't big, and my ass wasn't bodacious like my friends. However, I had full pouty lips and long, thick, light-blonde hair with shades of gold threaded throughout and it was bone straight.

The five of us had been friends since high school. They were my soul sisters, my sisters from another mister, the friends who would always be there through thick and thin, and who knew me better than I knew myself. In fact, they knew me so well they only had to look at my face to know that I was in uncharted territory. What they didn't understand was why. How do you explain the unexplainable to someone who isn't a writer?

As a writer, I was constantly running story ideas through my head. If I saw a woman who looked a certain way, I'd build a character around her. If I heard an unusual story on the news, I plotted an outline for a book. If I noticed a devastatingly handsome cop on TV, I'd build a story around him, develop his personality, dream up a heroine for him, and design new sexual positions to fit his personality.

Since I'd seen the detective on the evening news, I'd determined his personality, built his backstory, and imagined myself as the heroine and all that entailed, i.e. steamy sex scenes. What I'd never dreamed, while I built his character and made love to him in my imagination, was that I'd ever meet him.

Normally, writers created characters out of thin air. We developed them, matured them through the arc of the story, and then finally let them go. What we didn't do was ever meet them. Especially since, up until now, my characters had all been medieval and long since dead. Nevertheless, when I watched the news and saw that man, I knew I had to write a story about him. However, he didn't fit into my historical world since he was of this century. So instead of writing another Highlander book I began thinking about a contemporary romance for him. I made him sensitive, gentle, in touch with his feelings—the way men today seemed to be raised. But never in my wildest dreams did I expect we'd meet. Having a fictional character walk into the coffee house while I had just contemplated writing him into a book about Kasey's failed attempt at internet dating, was, discombobulating at the very least.

I was never shy around men since most didn't faze me. I was always outgoing and if I did see a man I was interested in, I stood up and said hi. Yet, when I ran into the detective and saw how he commanded the space like one of my Highlanders, he shook me to my core. Men weren't like that nowadays. They didn't own a room when they walked in. Oh, the gorgeous ones might think they did, but there's a certain arrogance behind their confidence, one that came from knowing they're good-looking.

Not this guy, though: he held himself in a way you just knew he controlled his world and all that was in it. The only time I ever encountered a man like that was in fiction. To have one of my characters walk in and then grin at me before leaving, had left me speechless and unnerved. Not to mention the fact that I'd covered him with coffee, groped his chest, and popped him in the jaw with my head. Seriously, I couldn't have written this scenario any more humiliating if I tried.

"I know him," I started, and looked at each one of my friends as they waited for me to continue. "He's a police officer I saw on TV a few nights ago."

"How does that explain your shrinking violet routine?" Kasey asked.

"I may have cast him in the role of hero in a book I'm thinking about, and it unnerved me to have him standing in front of me."

"He's going to be another one of your Highlanders?" Janeane grinned.

"Actually, I was thinking of trying my hand at a contemporary romance this time around."

"Nic, you promised us. No writing for six months," Kristina replied, sounding frustrated.

Placing my coffee on the table, I nodded in agreement with her. "I did, and I am. That doesn't mean I won't plot a story while I'm relaxing with my friends and family. Writers' minds never sleep, ladies. We can't just turn them off."

"Well, let's hear it then. Tell us your plot starring tall, dark, and dangerous," Kasey asked.

"Actually, I didn't have a specific one in mind for him yet. I'd only built his backstory and personality. But listening to your encounter with the catfish on Plenty of Fish has my imagination running wild right now, Kasey."

"You want to write a romance novel about a catfish?" Angela asked.

"I was thinking more along the lines of a romantic suspense," I explained. "You've seen the news about the Shallow Grave Killer, right? Well, what if I incorporated that type of killings into an online dating story and have the killer be a catfish."

"Oh, and Detective Dark and Dangerous can be the hero who saves me from certain death," Kasey jumped in excitedly.

"Exactly," I agreed.

"Nicola, if you want to do a contemporary romance, you should think about doing it as a BDSM story," Angela threw out. "Those seem to be all the rage right now with that movie coming out."

"I'm not opposed to that, but I don't know anything about

BDSM. Do they have dating websites?"

"You bet they do," Kasey jumped back in, "I was curious myself and signed up on a site called "Sub Seeking Dom.""

"You were looking for a Dom?" I breathed out.

"A little domination can be hot. I'm surprised you never thought about that considering how alpha-dominant your Highlanders are."

"If that's the case," Kristina jumped in, "you'll need to set up a fake account so you can talk to Kasey's catfish, *and* set up an account on one of those Dom sites so you can learn the lingo."

"Speaking of a dominant man, you should probably hunt down that delicious piece of male you dumped coffee on for research as well," Angela threw in. "Don't you need a cop's perspective to understand how their minds work, or how they investigate a killer?"

My eyes widened at her suggestion and I started shaking my head in the negative. I'd plotted love scenes with me in the starring role with the man. I'd never be able to look him in the eyes.

"Oh, yeah, she definitely needs a one-on-one with that hunka hunka burnin' luuuve. Did you see the way he smiled at her?" Janeane laughed.

Knowing full well they wouldn't let this drop, I laughed with them as if the idea of talking with the man didn't make me feel ill. "Of all the coffee joints, in all the towns, in all the world, he walks into mine...," I mumbled to myself.

"What was that?" Janeane laughed.

"Nothing, ignore me. Hey, Kris, you mentioned I needed a fake account to research these guys, and I agree. But won't I need pictures to set up an account?"

"Yeah, you're right. I hadn't thought about that."

"We need someone leggy, curvy, with a great ass and blonde hair," Kasey announced.

"Agreed," we all said in unison.

Leaning back into the couch, I searched my memory for someone who matched the description. Kasey crossed her long slender legs while I scanned my internal photo album, then I looked at Janeane's boobs, Kristina's ass, Angela's eyes and thought about my long flowing hair and pouty lips. If we were to combine the five of us into one woman, she'd be so far beyond a ten most tens would be embarrassed.

"I've got it," I shouted and then lowered my voice when other coffee patrons looked in my direction. "We each have assets that rival any woman. I say we take a picture of those assets and combine them to make one woman."

"How would we combine them to make one woman?" Kristina asked, confused.

"Maybe not combine, per se, but we upload individual pictures like women do on those sites showing off their figures and that should be all it takes."

When they didn't look convinced, I stood up with my purse. "Just trust me and follow me to my house. I'll show you what I mean when we get there."

"Hold up," Janeane said before we could make our way to leave. "Nicola, I want you to make a pact with us before you go any further with this new story."

"What kind of pact?"

"I want you to agree right now that you will only work on this book and messaging men on POF or SSD with us present. It can be a collaboration of sorts. You'll spend time with us, we get to see your creative process at work, and we all get what we want in the end: time with each other. Do you agree?"

"I can only plot this story with all of you?"

"On Tuesdays and Thursdays at Gypsy's after work," she added.

"Um."

"You have to pinky swear," Kristina announced.

Looking at the faces of the women I loved most in this world, I could hardly decline. Besides, it'd be fun to work on this together. Smiling, I stuck out my pinky and the others did as well. We laced our pinkies together, and I repeated the oath we'd used all those years ago in high school.

"I, Nicola Grace Royse, hereby pinky swear that I won't work on this book without the participation of Angela, Kristina, Kasey, or Janeane. I furthermore acknowledge that if I break this oath, I will set into motion events that will mean the destruction of this sisterhood."

I knew they were dire words, but dire words were needed when you were seventeen and more than one of your group liked the same boy. However, we usually only pulled them out in extreme circumstances . . . such as forgetting to tell a friend about a sale on shoes. They seemed silly now that we were grown women, but if it made them feel better, I was happy to give them some reassurance. After all, what could happen while plotting fiction?

Three

It's often been said if you remained friends with someone for seven years, you'd be friends for a lifetime. After fifteen years with these women, I'd say that's true. I could go months without talking to them—I have a unique form writer's block and forget the world around —yet, pick right back up where we left off, never missing a beat. Our connection was forged from love, sweat, and tears. There were no other women in my life, short of my mother, that I trusted more, which is why I'd agreed to let them see my process, to see the inner working of my mind as I plotted my next book.

After leaving Gypsy's, the girls followed me home. I was now lying on my bed, waiting for Kasey to put on my star-spangled bikini. Kristina was mixing amaretto sour in my kitchen while Angela and Janeane laughed about something Angela's husband had said. The sound of laughter and cocktails being shaken, not stirred, made it seem as if time had stood still. Laying around my bedroom just as we did in high school gossiping about one boy or another was a familiar scene. Even Kristina mixing drinks like she did when my parents weren't home hasn't changed.

Lying there watching as the girls laughed and Kristina served drinks I felt the restlessness that seemed to be my constant companion melting away. It hit me then why I'd been out of sorts recently. It was the familiar comfort of laughter and friends that I'd been missing these past few months, and having it back again was like a salve to my soul.

Kasey had to get home to her kids since her parents watched them during the day while she was at work, and later on Tuesdays and Thursdays so she could have nights out with the girls. With this in mind, we wanted to take pictures of her legs first, and then the others would have their turn in front of the camera.

My idea was simple. Each of us would wear the same sexy bikini while our assets were photographed in front of the same background. Boobs, legs, and ass all showing the same outfit would lend to the authenticity of the fake woman. My hair, which was long, thick and light blonde, would be taken from the side so my face would barely show. I decided that not showing a face, only images and a profile of pouty lips gave an air of mystery to the fake woman. Coupled with a picture Angela's sultry, almond-shaped eyes, beckoning them in, it was sure to grab the attention of any available catfish.

Janeane was on her computer setting up both accounts. One on Plenty of Fish and one on the BDSM site called Sub Seeking Dom. She kept throwing out questions we needed to answer for the profile and the five of us answered them all as seductively as we could.

"Oh, are you interested in being a slave?" Janeane chuckled.

"What? What do they mean by slave?" I laughed.

"You know, they tell you what to wear, what to eat, order you around in all aspects of your life, and have access to your body pretty much all the time."

"So it's like a marriage but with more sex?" Kasey laughed.

"I've read in some cases, they actually cage you for hours or even days," Angela replied.

"Like a dog cage?"

"I guess. I haven't seen one."

"I'm not sure I want the book to be that authentic. That's darker than I'm used to writing. I could see hands tied to the bed, maybe some flogging," I explained.

"Google that shit," Kasey told Janeane, so she opened a tab and soon had pictures of naked women in cages. One was built under a bed, and the title said a woman slept there. Others had women in metal cages that looked like dog kennels and my stomach turned a bit. I didn't understand the mindset of people who adhered to the BDSM lifestyle. I didn't fault them for it since sexual preference was as individual as eye color. I just didn't understand why anyone would want to be caged to prove his or her dedication to another person.

"Oh, wow, I could never do that, could you?" I asked.

"The orgasms would have to be off the charts to get me to agree to that," Kristina agreed as she handed me a drink.

Taking a sip of my amaretto sour, I mulled over being that controlled by a man. The idea of being possessed that completely, to be treated as chattel, didn't appeal to me. However, I'd admit that the thought of being tied up with a silk scarf, while a man made your body burn in ecstasy, gave me pause. It occurred to me that maybe this was about a loss of control; maybe these women weren't submissive by nature, but actually so independent that giving up that amount of control in the bedroom was therapeutic for them.

Fascinating, but definitely not for me.

"Ok, let's get these pictures taken so Kasey can get home to the kiddos," I mumbled as I rose from the bed.

"Where do you want me?" Kasey asked.

"I think on the bed, don't you? That way we have the same background in all the pictures."

"Give me two seconds," Janeane called out as she finished typing, then shut her laptop and stood from the bed.

"Are you done with the dating profiles?"

"All but the pictures," she confirmed. "I'll load them once we're finished here."

"Ok, grab my notebook over there and write down the passwords."

"Nope," Kristina answered for Janeane. "We've decided that, since you can't help yourself, the only way you're getting on those websites is with us around. We know you, Nicola: if you have the passwords you'll cheat and you know it."

"But I said the oath," I argued.

"Then you don't need them," Angela explained with a grin.

"You only get to work on this book on Tuesdays and Thursdays starting at five, Nicola. That's the deal. Oh, and don't forget your yoga gear on Thursday. Relaxation, before we pound out this plot, will get your creative juices flowing," Kasey ordered.

"You guys are holding my story hostage, aren't you?"

"Absolutely," they all agreed.

It was clear to me now while looking at their faces, seeing the determination in their eyes, they were blackmailing me to keep me in their lives. They had missed me as much as I had missed them, I guess.

How could I say no?

"Downward dog it is then," I smiled.

While they all smiled at me, Kasey climbed onto the bed. I moved into position for the first shot, but before I could raise my camera to focus on her legs, making sure the bikini was in the frame, Frick and Frack, better known as Bo and Finn, barged into the room.

"Jesus, Nic, where's the love?" Finn demanded. "Triplet code clearly states that any and all photo shoots with sexy friends should be supervised by your brothers."

"Get out," I gritted out between my teeth as I framed my shot. Then I saw Kasey's face through the lens of my camera. She'd had a crush on Finn in high school and now that she was divorced, and if the flirty grin she was throwing his direction was any indicator, it seemed that crush had returned. Her eyes were bright as she grinned at Finn. When I looked over my shoulder and watched him wink at her, matching her grin, I sighed. Oh, boy, here we go again. I only hoped this time around it didn't include midnight phone calls to analyze every look or comment Finn sent her way.

***

It had been two days since we created the fake profiles on POF and SSD, and I was chomping at the bit to see what kind of messages we received. I'd admit now that the lack of control I had over this process was unnerving me to the point that I considered opening my own accounts in secret, but so far I hadn't given in to the impulse. Currently, I was in one of Kasey's yoga classes with the girls on mats, winding down. I was exhaling on a downward facing dog and could feel my muscles relaxing.

Kasey's yoga studio was next door to Gypsy's, and it faced the busy street. She'd hired two instructors and between the three of them offered classes from six a.m. until nine p.m. She catered to those who went to work early and stayed late furthering their careers. Her clientele was mostly high-stress professionals who needed to unwind at the end of the day, or zen out before heading into work.

To attract business, she'd had the bright idea to put her rooms in the front with big windows so women passing by would be drawn in, and men walking past would see women's asses in the air and want to join for the show. It was a brilliant marketing plan and it worked. The number of men who'd joined was actually higher than the women. I couldn't have been prouder of Kasey for making a success out of her business, but at this exact moment, while my ass was in the air, I could have killed her with my bare hands for putting me in this position.

Picture it . . .

Nicola, the fair-haired maiden, was stretching out her Gluteus Maximus when the dark and dangerous hero passed by the window. Imagine if you will how the color rushed further into her face when a familiar pair of boots stopped suddenly in her line of sight. Her eyes looked up between her legs and saw the same gleaming honey-colored eyes with dark, heavy brows staring back at her. Also, imagine, how the sight of those eyes sent her heart racing and her balance waning as she tried to lower said ass to the ground. Unfortunately, the fair-haired maiden was not as graceful as her friends were, you see, evidence to this fact was when she tried to recover. Down she went taking Angela with her as she tried to turn over. Nay, she was unsuccessful in righting her body before the handsome hero seemingly crushed his cup of coffee between his fingers, spilling it yet again down his front.

Get the picture?

"What the hell?" Angela laughed as I tried to climb off of her.

"Sorry, sorry," I replied, embarrassed as I watched Triple D (Drop Dead Delicious) storm down the sidewalk heading back toward Gypsy's.

"Quiet, please," Toni Roseneau, the master yoga instructor, whisper-shouted.

Crawling on my knees and moving back into plank position, I inhaled deeply, then exhaled slowly as I prayed to God Triple D would be gone from Gypsy's by the time we were finished. *Good Lord, I don't know why this guy makes me nervous.* My initial reaction to him made sense, but two days later. I should have shrugged it off and laughed about it by now.

At least this time it wasn't my fault he spilled his coffee.

Shoo!

Paranoid that he'd come back and see my ass in the air again, I kept looking back over my shoulder to check.

"Nicola, you can't focus your mind and relax your body if you keep looking over your shoulder," Toni sighed in aggravation.

"Right, right, sorry," I mumbled.

Angela nudged me on the shoulder and gave me a "what gives?" look. Rolling my eyes I whispered, "Detective Drop Dead Delicious caught me with my ass in the air."

"Sweet, maybe it gave him ideas," she whispered back. "Maybe, right now, he's thinking about that golden pussy you possess and he's waiting for you to finish this class."

"Who has a golden pussy?" Kasey demanded as she leaned in from my other side, whisper shouting as well.

"Nicola does," Angela told her.

"Guys—" I tried to break in as I watched Toni make her way toward us.

"Who's waiting to find out?" Kasey kept going, smiling at

me.

"Detective Triple D," I added as I smiled in apology at Toni, who was now standing in front of me. Then I added since I was already in trouble, "My golden you-know-what is closed for business until it's been buffed and shined. The playground is closed right now so drop it. "

"Triple D?" Kasey asked, ignoring Toni as she glared at us.

"Later," I whispered as I avoided Toni's glare.

Toni could be a little hardcore about her classes. She didn't care that her boss was a part of those interrupting one of her classes; all she cared about was a State of Zen for her pupils. With hands on her hips, Toni raised a brow and shook her head at the three of us.

"Our bodies and our minds have to work together to bring us into harmony. If you can't zip it, then take it outside," she ordered.

The three of us bit our lips to keep from laughing; then, like properly chastised children, we apologized.

"Sorry," we replied in unison as we swan-dived into forward fold while I still kept my eyes on the window.

When class was over, I dragged myself out of the studio with the girls to head to Gypsy's and get down to the business at hand. It had been at least ten minutes since I'd caught the detective staring at my ass, and I hoped he'd left.

As we walked the short distance from the studio to the coffee house, I heard a motorcycle start across the street. As anyone did when you heard the thundering roar of pipes, I glanced behind me and saw the detective on the bike. I stopped suddenly and stared since he seemed to have his eyes directed at me. There was no grin this time, not even a wink. He seemed almost angry as he sat there, perched on his silver beast of a bike, one leg on the ground.

He reminded me of a warlord on a horse, with the western sky at his back, the sun setting with shades of orange and yellow backlighting him like a conquering hero. It was reminiscent of one of my Highlanders as he sat atop his trusty steed surveying his land. He revved the bike again, interrupting my thoughts, then pulled away from the curb and shot past me without another glance.

"Damn, we missed him," Angela cried out as she watched him turn toward the heart of downtown.

"He's just some guy I spilled coffee on. There was no reason for him to wait," I explained, more for me than for her.

Angela and Kasey made eyes at each other when I pulled open the door to Gypsy's. I ignored their looks because I knew if I made more out of it than I already had, they'd keep at me.

The coffee house was quiet, thankfully, commuters going home had stopped in already, but the evening crowd hadn't arrived yet. This worked for me since we were a large group and needed space in order to be comfortable. When our coffees were ready, we found a table big enough for all of us to spread out with the computer in front of us. Janeane pulled up the websites onto two separate tabs, and it began, the process of plotting a story. First were the characters. I had Triple D as the hero, Kasey as the heroine, now I needed a bad guy. A nasty, scary, want to hide under your bed while you read the story bad guy.

"Holy shit," Janeane whispered. "We've got over a hundred messages on POF and fifty-four on SSD."

"Open the first one," Kasey told her.

"Ok, first one is from Fit and Freaky from Edmond. He says, *You're hot, I'm down to drive an hour to meet you if you're DTF*."

"DTF?" I questioned.

"Down to fuck," Janeane replied laughing.

"Seriously?" I questioned as I opened my notebook and wrote down the definition.

"What does he look like?" Kristina asked. "If he's hot, maybe Nicola could use him to break her dry spell."

"I'm not sleeping with some random guy," I huffed, shoving her in the shoulder.

"Beggars can't be choosers," she laughed back.

"See if my catfish messaged her. We put in the same info I had, so Taryn Rivers should have matched with him.

We'd chosen the name Taryn Rivers because we knew a girl in high school who was a real bitch and a fake friend. She'd gone after every boy one of us had dated until we'd caught her in the act. Since our profile was fake, we figured the name was fitting.

"Bingo," Janeane laughed. *"Hey, beautiful, saw you're new on here and thought I'd send you a message. Just got home from a Thunder game, but I'll be up for a while if you want to chat.'"*

"Pfft, he used the same line on me. He said he had season tickets. He even asked me to go to a game with him, the fucker."

I could tell Kasey was getting riled up, so I asked Janeane, "Check the submissive site, and see what we have on there."

Janeane looked at Kasey then back to me and nodded. As she scrolled through the names, she started laughing.

"What?" Kristina asked.

"Well, your choices are a guy dressed as Robin Hood, a guy who should never have posted a penis picture since he's about three inches long and . . . Hey, watch it"

The Robin Hood comment had us all shoving her out of the way so we could see the profile, but the three-inch man was still up on the screen. We all groaned in unison because he was cute and that made his shortcomings even more disappointing.

Angela moved the cursor to Robin Hood, and we inhaled sharply to keep from laughing.

"Is that . . . ?" Angela whispered.

"I think it is," Kristina choked out.

Pictured in a green Robin Hood period costume, leggings and all, was Jared Park, former president of our senior class.

"I knew he was kinky," Janeane grumbled so we turned to look at her. Janeane had gone out with Jared four or five times and had said at the time he was a great kisser, but a little bossy. Now we knew why. He was also president of the Thespian Club in high school, which I guess explained why he was in costume.

"What does his profile say?" I asked.

"Gorean male wants a slave girl slash submissive. Will train the trainable."

"What the hell is a Gorean man? I thought he was Caucasian?" Kasey asked, confused.

Angela opened google and typed in Gorean. Once she found what she was looking for, she began reading.

"People who base their Dominance or Submission on the works of John Norman," she read out loud.

"Ok, but who the hell is John Norman?" Kasey asked.

"Oh, my God, he wrote the Gor books," I whispered. "John Norman is an author of nearly thirty novels about Gor, a primitive, male-dominated planet. The Gor books have men enslaving women, and the suggestion is that female slavery is, in some sense, the natural order of society."

"Ha, I bet the women's libbers hate this guy," Angela chuckled.

"Jesus, you're telling me Jared lives his life according to this man's work? I knew he was a jerk," Janeane seethed.

"Ok, we're getting off-track here. Is there anyone else of interest?" I asked to diffuse Janeane's anger and keep the group focused.

"Yeah, here's one," Janeane announced. "Dark Prince . . . I'm a dominant looking for a submissive slave."

"What does his message say?" I asked.

"'Taryn, your pictures entice me. The hint of the forbidden, a tantalizing taste of what you could offer me, your Master. I require complete submission from my slaves. I will dress you, feed you, and cage you as I see fit. In the easiest possible terms to explain this lifestyle, so there are no misconceptions as I've had with others in the past, I own you. You become my property when you agree to be my slave. I will do with you what I feel is in your best interest and in return for your submission, I will take care of you for the rest of your life—Dark Prince.'"

You could have heard a pin drop when Janeane finished reading and I'd admit that my heart rate increased infinitesimally with the seductive quality of the message.

A slow grin pulled across my lips. I loved it when my characters came into focus early in a project. Before I could give an opinion about Dark Prince, Angela jumped in with a rush of excitement. "I don't know about you guys, and the whole slavery thing aside, but for research purposes this guy is . . . well, he's—"

"Perfect," I finished for Angela.

★★★

Rounding his desk, Dallas Vaughn still had his mind on a

certain heart-shaped ass, and it pissed him off. He should have had better control of his urges at thirty-four, but when he'd seen that ass in the window attached to that girl-next-door face, he'd reacted. His jaw had tightened and his hand had flexed violently when he noticed the pants she wore were practically see-through with the setting sun shining on them. He had sucked in a breath on a half groan at the sight of her rose-colored pussy right before his coffee exploded all over his shirt.

That was twice in one week that woman had been responsible for ruining his shirt and a perfect cup of coffee, and he didn't even know her fucking name. Now, he had images of a firm ass he wanted to spank, and a perfect pussy he wanted to sink into until she shuddered with release, running rampant in his mind.

He'd gone back to Gypsy's and placed his order for a new coffee, glaring at the barista when he asked about his shirt. He'd cleaned up as best he could, grabbed his coffee, and headed back outside to his bike. When Sandra Dee with her big green eyes and long flowing hair exited the yoga studio, he watched her for a moment. Yeah, she's the girl-next-door all right, Dallas had thought, as he scanned her body one last time. Too fuckin' bad he had a caseload a mile high and a serial killer to find. If he didn't, he'd be inclined to find out just how soft that hair was, how firm those breasts were, or how sweet those lips tasted.

"You mind telling me why you've come back twice in one week covered in coffee?" Reed asked his partner, breaking Dallas from his thoughts.

"Nope, just having one of those weeks," Dallas grunted.

"Did this trip to the coffee house include the owner of that perfume you were wearing when you got back last time?"

"Drop it, Reed." Dallas sighed as he pulled the shirt from his body and grabbed a backup he kept in his drawer.

"Waitress?"

"Drop it."

"Barista?"

"No," Dallas grinned since he knew his partner wouldn't quit asking, "Sandra Dee."

Reed whistled low and grinned. It's always the innocent-looking ones the tough guys fall for, Reed thought.

"Are you stayin' late again tonight?"

"Yep, I've got at least twenty more files to go through," Dallas mumbled as he grabbed the top one off the pile. When he saw Reed reach for the next file, he stopped him.

"Why don't you get your ass home before June tears you a new one? This case won't be solved tonight and I can call you if anything comes up."

Reed had eyed him for a moment before he asked, "Are you sure?"

"I'm sure I don't want June to tear you a new one."

Nodding, Reed stood and grabbed his suit jacket from his chair. He watched his partner for a moment, but as he turned to leave, he called out, "See you in the morning, Vaughn. Just so, you know, Sandra Dee may have caught your eye, but it'll take Sandra Bullock to hold your attention. You need someone feisty, willing to talk back to you; not the perfect woman from 1950."

Dallas grinned at his partner and shook his head. For a man, and a cop, Bill Reed had a romantic side. He tried to fix Dallas up on more than one occasion, all of them disasters. Dallas didn't need or want any distractions right now, though. He needed to focus his attention on the Shallow Grave Killer. With that in mind, he opened the file as he watched his partner leave and he began looking for a link to his other victims.

Four

Standing outside the two-story building that housed the detective's division for the Tulsa Police Department, I hesitated. Even though I'd promised the girls I wouldn't work on the book without them, I didn't think speaking with a detective about police procedure qualified. I figured there wasn't any harm in gaining insight into police investigations while they were at work. The reason for my hesitance wasn't that they would be angry, but more about running into a certain detective again.

I'd called ahead and spoken with a Lieutenant Cross. He was a gruff man who'd sounded extremely put out by my request, but finally agreed to let me speak with a detective. I'd specifically asked for a seasoned officer, one who had been on the force more than ten years, hoping to avoid a certain detective for obvious reasons—I was embarrassed he'd seen my ass in the air. I may be extremely attracted to the man, but the last two times we'd come into contact had been disasters. However, attracted or not, since I was using him for my hero it was best if I steered clear of him. Preferably, an ocean's distance between us, but since I couldn't disappear as I always did to write this book, I'd have to settle for precautionary measures such as calling ahead to ask for an older officer to help me. *Dammit, I should have asked for a woman detective. That would have assured me I wouldn't end up with Triple D.*

The Lieutenant had put me on hold, then, after a few minutes, he'd returned and barked out, "I've got someone in-house if you can come within the next hour." I agreed immediately, of course, and he told me to report to the second floor and ask for a Detective Bill Reed. When I asked his age, so there were no surprises, he'd growled, "Old and ugly. You wanna talk to Reed; get down here in an hour." Then he'd hung up as abruptly as he'd spoken.

He was totally going in my book.

So, here I was, entering the elevator of the detective division, on my way up with a notebook, coffee in hand, sunglasses and a baseball cap covering my face and hair . . . just in case.

When the doors opened, I took a deep breath and exited. I walked down the hall until I found the door that read Detectives Division. When I walked in, I found what I expected in a civic building. Gray everything. The walls, the floors, even the desks. The standard and boring city-issued décor was quite honestly kinda cool in a Law and Order kind of way. Since I'd started writing, I'd had to rely on history books and pictures to influence my stories and keep them authentic. Seeing these offices helped to cement in my mind the world my characters would live in daily. It was actually exciting to be able to see firsthand how my fictional world would develop.

After taking in the room, I approached the receptionist. She was an older woman with gray hair and a kind smile, who was dressed smartly in a business casual blue blouse and black slacks. I told her why I was there and she put the phone to her ear and buzzed Detective Reed while she instructed me to take a seat. Five minutes later, a large man with salt and pepper hair, sparkling blue eyes, and a friendly smile came around the corner.

"Are you Miss Royse?" Reed asked me.

"I am. Are you Detective Reed?"

"The one and only. Come on back with me and we can talk at my desk. Most of the detectives are out, so it's quiet."

When he motioned for me to follow him, I stood up and grabbed my notebook and to-go cup of coffee from Gypsy's I purchased on my way to the station.

"I see you like Gypsy's too," Reed replied as he motioned to my cup.

"Too?" I asked as dread seeped in.

"The coffee here is swill, most of the boys grab Gypsy's on their way in," he chuckled as my panic fled.

Reed stopped at a desk that had a twin butted up to the length of it in a mirror image. He had a picture of an older woman on his desk, and you could tell by the mischief in her eyes that she was a ball breaker. The matching desk that I assumed was his partner's, had a picture of a beautiful dark-haired woman with two small children smiling large at the camera sitting on it. It was nice to see that both Reed and his partner were dedicated family men. Seeing their dedication to family, I immediately wanted to put Reed and his partner in my book. I envisioned them as seasoned, yet loving family men, who fought crime and kept the streets safe for everyone else, while they put their lives on the line.

"Miss Royse?" Lost in thought, I jumped at my name and looked toward Reed.

"Yes?"

"You gonna have a seat?" he replied as if he'd already

asked that question.

"Oh, yes, sorry. Writer's block," I explained as I sat down.

"You have writer's block?" he chuckled with confusion written on his face.

"Oh, yes, all the time. I can't go anywhere or meet new people without turning them into characters. My writer's block makes me block out the world and lose myself in my head."

"Sounds like a good place to be if you're a writer, I'd think," he replied.

"Yes, exactly, though my family and friends find it irritating," I laughed.

"Cross said you needed information for a new book you're writing. What can I help you with?" Reed smiled.

He was so nice.

"I need to know basic police investigative steps. I can improvise how they handle the case within the story, say the officer doesn't follow procedure, but I need to know what that procedure is to begin with."

"That would depend on the case and the victim. But, standard procedure would be to take the complaint, investigate any leads, and then make arrests based on the evidence obtained during the investigation. Once an arrest has been made, we would then turn over the evidence and findings to the prosecutor."

"It's all very clinical, isn't it? I don't know why I imagined that each case would be handled based on the evidence, sort of one size *doesn't* fit all scenario. But you're saying that it's pretty much the same no matter the case."

"There's nothing pretty about murder, Miss Royse. If we want the sons of bitches, pardon my French, who commit the crimes to pay then we follow the rules to the T so we can convict them."

Pulling my pen from my binder, I jotted down what Reed had said. While I was writing, it occurred to me that it would be fascinating to see him in action, to see him interview a suspect or witness, even investigate a lead.

"Do you ever permit civilians to ride along? I'd love to see what a day in the life of a homicide detective is like."

"Not as a general rule, but I wouldn't be opposed to taking you," he grinned. "I suppose I could ask my Lieutenant. But I'll warn you now it's boring legwork and you'll likely fall asleep," he chuckled.

"Oh, I wouldn't mind; I'm always looking for new characters for my books and getting out and meeting new people is a great way to fuel my creativity."

"What type of books do you write?"

"Up until now I've always written historical romance novels. However, recently, I've had an idea for a contemporary romantic suspense. My biggest hurdle is that after years of writing about history, I'm finding I haven't got a clue how romance works in this day and age," I explained with a sigh.

"I reckon it's the same now as it was then. Boy meets girl, they fall in love and get married."

I wasn't about to argue with the man since he was doing me a favor, but he was wrong. Boy meets girl, boy ignores the girl for football and leggy blondes with big boobs, and then girl kicks his ass to the curb for all of the above and consumes a carton of ice cream.

With a possible ride-along in my future, I figured I could wait to ask him more questions about a day in the life of a detective. Not wanting to overstay my welcome and push Reed's lieutenant too far, I stood to leave.

"I'll let you get back to work since I'm sure there are bad

guys to catch," I chuckled. "I look forward to working with you, Detective Reed, and I appreciate it more than you know for allowing me to ride with you and see you in action. Do you have a card I could have in case I need to contact you?"

Reed smiled, stood, and pulled out his card and handed it to me as I grabbed my cup of coffee. I had no doubt, looking at his smile and those bright blue eyes, that he'd been a heartbreaker in his day. Broad shoulders and thick hair coupled with those eyes, smile, and handsome face would have melted lots of women's heart.

"I'll ask my Lieutenant about the ride-along after he's had a meal. The only time he's in an agreeable mood is right after he's eaten," Reed laughed.

"Oh, I know all about men who need food to calm their savage beasts. I have to keep my fridge stocked or my—"

"Is that so?" a voice growled from behind me, which, of course, made me jump and turn too quickly. When I turned, my hand, which held my coffee, slammed into a hard chest and erupted down the front of a shirt.

"You've gotta be kiddin' me," Triple D bit out as I looked up at him in shock.

"This is getting ridiculous," I blurted out. "Are you following me?"

"Coffee . . . that shit'll kill ya," Reed chuckled.

"You came to my place of business, darlin', how the hell do you figure I'm following you?"

"I don't know," I argued, "but twice in a few days seems highly unlikely."

"That's three times in four days," he argued as he glared at me.

"No, that's twice in four days. I had nothing to do with your faulty cup yesterday," I also argued as my temper ignited. I had a bad habit of turning to anger as a way to deal with conflict, and, boy, did this fall into that category.

"The hell you didn't," he snapped. "Word of warning, sweetheart; sunlight and spandex don't mix."

"Don't you sweetheart me, you big ape, and what does that even mean, they don't mix?" I asked miffed as he turned to leave.

"It means when a man walks down the street and gets an eyeful of ass, he's gonna react," he barked over his shoulder as he headed out of the room and to what I assumed was the men's room.

"Is she Sandra Dee, Vaughn?" Reed oddly shouted at the retreating man.

"Am I who?"

Reed turned his attention back to me, but didn't answer my question instead, he oddly asked, "What's the name of your perfume? I'm thinkin' my June would like it."

"I don't have any on."

"Not today, you were wearin' it on Tuesday."

"How did you know I was wearing perfume on Tuesday?"

"My partner came back smelling like a beautiful woman after your first encounter."

"He's . . . he's your partner?" I wailed.

"He has been for goin' on six years."

My eyes swung to his desk and the photo of the beautiful brown-haired woman with two smiling kids, and I felt ill.

"I'm sorry, I have to leave," I replied quickly, then bit my lip before I burst into tears over the fact that my dream man was married. God, I felt like an idiot. "How did he even recognize me behind these glasses?" I whined.

"I'm thinkin' it was the spandex."

I looked down at my outfit, which did consist of spandex

running pants in black and another pink, zip type athletic top. Shit, I was practically dressed identical to yesterday.

"I have to go. Thank you again," I rushed out as I turned to leave.

"I'm sure he'll be right back," Reed jumped in as I moved away from him.

"So? He can come back or not come back. What do I care?"

Reed's eyes were gleaming with hilarity, no doubt because I'd mucked up his partner's shirt again.

"You got a card with a number so I can call you about that ride-along?" he asked with a grin.

"I, um," I sputtered, thinking I should avoid Reed since Vaughn was his partner. After thinking about it for a moment, I figured what did it really matter now. I'd been intimidated by Vaughn because I was attracted to him and I'd imagined all sorts of naughty things between the two of us. Since he's married, there was no reason to be intimidated.

"Ok, yeah, I'll leave my card."

I dug one out of my purse, handed it to Reed, and then decided to make a hasty retreat before Vaughn came back. As I made my way toward the exit, for some bizarre reason I had to know Vaughn's full name. It was the final piece of information I needed about the man to build his character. A name said something about the owner, and for that reason, I had to know his. Turning back to Reed, I called out to the detective.

"Detective Reed? I, uh, I wanted to make sure I give credit in my book properly so I'll, um, I'll need your partner's name for my research."

Reed smiled as if he could read my mind, and I was glad I was hiding behind sunglasses. If he could see my eyes, he'd see the misery I felt at knowing the man I'd fantasized about was married.

"Vaughn, Detective Dallas Vaughn," he replied with a knowing smirk.

God, that was a great name.

"Thank you," I answered then hurried out of the office.

Of course, he'd have a beautiful wife, two beautiful kids, and a name that even sounded like a romance novel hero. "Men like that don't exist, mom? They do, they're just taken."

I sighed in despair that Dallas Vaughn wasn't available then I remembered suddenly, he'd winked at me and ogled my ass while he was married. "Shit, mom's right. I'm spinning my wheels, looking for a fictional man that doesn't exist."

***

"Don't say a word," Dallas grumbled when he sat down at his desk.

"Now, why would I say anything?"

Dallas ignored Reed as well as his wet shirt. He hadn't replaced his backup from the last disaster and was stuck wearing the coffee covered mess.

He was still pissed for reacting the way he had when he heard Sandra Dee say she stocked her fridge for her man. In the past four days, his mind had kept drifting to the girl-next-door when he should have been working, and when he walked in and saw her standing there, he took it as a sign to proceed. He figured, fuck it, he didn't have time for a relationship, but he wasn't gonna ignore the fact that everywhere he turned, there she was. If he couldn't get her out of his mind, couldn't stop thinking about her cupid lips and big green eyes, there was a reason. Except now, there wasn't a damn thing he could do about it because he didn't mess with another man's woman.

"What the hell was she doing here?" Dallas finally asked out of curiosity.

"It's the damnedest thing," Reed chuckled. "Seems your Sandra Dee, who I'd like to point out is more of a Sandra Bullock, is one of them romance authors. She came in to discuss police procedure for a book she's writing."

"Jesus . . . Please tell me you don't agree to help her," Dallas asked with a sigh. The last thing he needed was a constant reminder of what he couldn't have.

"Oh, I agreed all right. I'm gonna take her out with me once I get the okay from Cross. A man my age doesn't often get the chance to spend a day conversing with an angel."

"The hell you are," Dallas bit out fiercely. "We don't exactly interview law-abiding citizens. She'll end up hurt or worse."

Reed thought Vaughn's outburst was telling, which made him even more determined to get the okay from Cross. "I'm not stupid, Vaughn," Reed egged Dallas on. "I've got a few interviews with an eyewitness to that drive-by shooting over at Shady Park that should interest her, I think."

Shady Park apartments were a safe haven for criminals. Officers who went there during the course of an investigation did it with eyes in the back of their heads and their hand on their gun. Vaughn knew this, of course. Reed watched as Dallas' eyes became intense and his jaw ticked at the mention of Shady Park in his Sandra Dee's future. Reed chuckled at Vaughn's obvious display of irritation and decided to let him know he was joking. "Rein in your temper, for Christ sake, I'm only kidding."

Dallas stared his partner down, then broke eye contact as he picked up his phone. "What's her name?" Dallas asked as he punched in the code to retrieve his messages. When a business card landed on his desk, he picked it up. The card was light pink with the name Nicola Grace Royse printed across the front in fancy script. It didn't escape his attention the card was as feminine as the owner was.

Tossing the card back to his partner, Dallas pushed images of Nicola Royse and her firm ass, full lips, and silky hair that he wanted to bury his hands in out of his mind and listened to his messages. When he got to the third, his eyes shot to his partners.

"They found a foreign hair on Stacy White-Cline's body," Dallas told his partner. "It's dark-brown and our victim was blonde. They're sending it off for DNA analysis."

"About fuckin' time we got a break in this case," Reed responded.

"It'll take months for the DNA to come back. But it's something," Dallas agreed.

"This guy covers his tracks like a pro; we need all the help we can get. If dating websites are where he stalks his victims, then there's no trace of him. It's as if he's able to delete all traces from the sites and their lives."

"That's because whoever we're dealing with is a computer expert," a tall man, dressed in a black suit that couldn't have spelled out FBI any clearer than if he'd had the words tattooed on his forehead, replied.

"Who are you?" Dallas bit out as he stood from his desk.

"Agent Dane Parker, FBI," the man answered, pulling out his badge.

"Is there a reason you're showing up unannounced and uninvited?"

"I'm on a special task force investigating The Harvest Killer. Your Shallow Grave murders pinged on our radar. I'm here to take over the investigation until we can ascertain whether we're dealing with the same man or not."

"The Harvest Killer hangs women on poles like a scarecrow. How the hell do you figure it's the same killer?" Reed asked in anger.

"Serial killers are known to change their MO," the agent replied. "Your Shallow Grave Killer leaves them in fields just like the Harvest Killer. It's possible this is his home base and when he's not traveling the highways, killing at harvest time, he's quenching his thirst for the kill at home."

"So I'm supposed to do what exactly? Hand over our investigation and play nice while you're in town? Is that what you're tellin' me?" Vaughn seethed.

"It became our jurisdiction the minute it tied to our case," Parker informed Vaughn. "I've already met with your lieutenant and he knows the score. He assures me you'll cooperate fully with our investigation."

"Right," Vaughn growled, looking back at Cross' office. "Tell me, Parker, the minute you figure out this case isn't connected to yours, are you gonna hightail it out of here?"

Parker grinned at Vaughn because he knew the man already had ideas of running him out of town. "My priority is the Harvest Killer, so yeah, Vaughn, I'll get out of your hair when I'm done. Though, we'll assist in an advisory capacity once we've determined the cases aren't connected. Until then, the investigation is ours."

Reaching across his desk, Dallas grabbed the Shallow Grave file and shoved it into Parker's hands.

"Have at it, hotshot," Dallas grumbled as he headed for his lieutenant's office.

"Hey, Vaughn," Parker called out as he watched the detective leave. When Dallas turned around, his jaw ticking as he tried reigning in his temper, Parker replied, "You've got something on your shirt."

Dallas didn't knock on his lieutenant's door: he barged in unannounced and found the man on his phone. Cross looked up and narrowed his eyes at Dallas before he bit out, "I'll have to call you back, baby. Apparently, Vaughn has a death wish."

Dallas crossed his arms over his chest and waited for Cross to hang up. As soon as he ended the call, Dallas thundered, "You brought in the fuckin Feds?"

"I don't answer to you; you'd be wise to remember that, Vaughn," Cross barked out. "The captain and I want this bastard caught. We sent what we had two months ago and they showed up unannounced this morning, spouting off this was now their case, and that it's tied to the fuckin' Harvest Killer."

"How the hell do they figure it ties into their case? Agent Parker's explanation reeks of manipulation of the facts."

"Captain Daley said hand it over, Vaughn, so I handed it over. That's how it works. If our government says it ties in, then it fuckin' ties in," Cross growled.

"Bullshit," Dallas snapped back. "Captain Daley hates government interference more than you do."

"That may be, but he isn't balking this time, so play nice with the feds, Vaughn, or look for another job," Cross advised.

"Right," Dallas seethed and then turned on his heels and headed for the exit. He might back off since his hands were tied, but he'd keep a close eye on Parker. Something wasn't jiving with their bullshit explanation and Dallas hated unanswered questions.

Dark Prince opened his browser and read the last email Taryn Rivers had sent him for the third time. She was perfect. Long legs that could wrap around his hips as he pounded into her, lush, full breasts he could clamp to bring her more pleasure, more pain. An ass that could handle any strap or crop he owned. But his favorite part was her hair. It was the perfect shade of blonde. Not so light that is was like snow, but it had glimmering shades of gold throughout that made it perfect. Staring at her picture, he felt his cock lengthen when he thought about putting Taryn in a cage, about strapping her to a St. Andrews cross as he broke her in. His blood heated to a boiling point as he thought about his hands wrapped around her neck, squeezing until she lost consciousness. It was time to find her and bring her home.

He opened the detailed information on her email and copied the IP address, dropping it into a program he designed. He'd written this program specifically for his own needs so he could find his slaves easily without waiting for them to correspond. He liked to watch them from afar while he messaged with them, to make sure they fit his needs. However, he didn't need to watch Taryn to know he'd finally found the perfect slave. She'd responded to his orders quicker than any slave had before. She'd wanted to please him, didn't question his commands, just answered him quickly, seemingly truthful, and had no hesitation taking a picture for him.

When his program finished searching and came back with a business address instead of a residence, he frowned. He'd given specific instructions for her to follow, one was to take a picture of herself and send it back to him within ten minutes. A picture that required her to be shirtless with the words "Master's Good Girl" written on her chest in lipstick and she'd done it with a minute to spare. How had she done this at a coffee shop? Was she piggybacking off their wireless system?

Dark Prince opened each and every email she'd sent the night before and noted that the IP address was the same. Hitting reply to her last email, his jaw ticked, and his breathing increased as he typed his instructions. He needed her at home, not out at some fucking coffee house where there were witnesses. He'd been careful, put safeguards in place to remain undetected, and he wasn't about to risk being seen with his future slave by approaching her in public. He needed her at home so he could claim her for his own.

Hitting send, he opened the program that allowed him access to Plenty of Fish and Sub Seeking Dom incognito. Opening Taryn's profile on both sites, he routed all her messages to his computer as well so he could keep an eye on who she was interacting with. If anyone got too close before he had a chance to secure her, he'd just have to take care of that problem as well.

***

Women have been disappointed by men since the dawning of time. Sure, there's been a good one every thousand years or so—ok, maybe not that long, but it feels that way. However, for the most part, they have left women wanting.

My brothers were a perfect example. Bo and Finn were handsome, funny, immature, and left women crying in their wake. Then there was Dallas Vaughn, with his bulging biceps and honey-colored eyes, who didn't wear a wedding ring so women knew he was taken. And I knew why. He's a man.

Period.

End of story.

Say no more.

I'm sure you all decided after reading that that I'm bitter, that I'd had my head in the clouds for far too long. Well rest assured I've been converted.

Anyhow, now you know what I was thinking after I left the detectives behind while I headed to Kasey's yoga studio for a little bestie pick-me-up. Yeah, the word bestie made me cringe, too, but that didn't make it any less true: it's our BFF's that got us through life's disappointments—that and a half-gallon of rocky road.

"Men are pigs," I announced when I walked in.

"What have Finn and Bo done now?" Kasey asked without looking up from her desk.

"Nothing today, thank God, but there's still daylight left so I'm sure they will. I'm talking about Dallas Vaughn, not my wayward brothers," I exclaimed.

Kasey still didn't look up, but her mouth pulled into a grin. "Ok, I'll bite. Who's Dallas Vaughn?"

"A certain detective who is *married*," I informed her.

Kasey finally looked up from whatever report she was working on and gave me her full attention.

"How do you know that?"

"I made an appointment to interview a detective about police procedure and ended up talking with his partner."

"And he told you he was married?"

"No, I saw a picture on his desk of his wife and two kids. Kasey, *two*—count them: one, two—and he ogled my ass, the pig," I whined. "I'm glad I poured coffee down the front of his shirt today."

"Hold on, you poured coffee on him again?" she laughed.

"Yep, and he deserved it. God, to think I was attracted to

him *and* writing a book about him, and he's just like all the rest. Do you know he blamed me for his coffee mishap yesterday, can you believe that? The arrogant schmuck!"

"Let me guess, it was your fault he looked?" she chuckled as she rose from her desk.

"Exactly! He said something about spandex and the sun don't mix, whatever that means."

"Oh, shit," Kasey gasped as she threw a hand to her mouth.

"Oh, shit, what?" I squeaked out thinking I wasn't about to like what *"Oh, shit"* meant

"Do you wear underwear with your yoga pants?"

"No, I don't like panty lines," I muttered, feeling the punch line coming.

"Then he probably got a good look at your cherry pie."

One eye started ticking as I envisioned Vaughn walking down the street, minding his own business, until I shoved my ass in the air and gave him a shot of my Twatus Maximus. Well, hell, I guess you couldn't blame a guy for that. I'd probably look, too, whether I was married or not.

"Ok, so that explains him ogling my ass," I replied as I fell into a chair. "But he still winked at me and flashed the sexiest grin I've ever received, and I'm pretty sure a married man shouldn't wink and grin at another woman, so he's still a pig."

"Does this revelation mean he isn't gonna rescue me in your book?"

"No, I'll keep him as the hero, since I've built the story around him. But I won't enjoy writing the sex scenes."

"Oh, man, can I help you write them?" she asked excitedly. "I haven't had sex for over a year and could use some visuals for my dates with B.O.B.

Horrified at the thought of imagining Kasey in all her naked glory, I shook my head vehemently and I cried out, "I can't write sex scenes with you as the heroine. I always put myself in that role so I can feel what they are feeling. If I didn't, they'd be wham-bam-thank-you-ma'am. No freakin' way do I wanna envision your ass or any other body part in my head, Kasey."

Kasey sighed dramatically and was about to argue my point when my cell phone rang. Pulling it from my purse, I noted the call was from Janeane and answered.

"Hey, what's up?"

"We gotta meet. Dark Prince just sent an email, and there's another list of instructions that we have to complete by eight tonight, or we aren't "trainable," he says."

"Oh, for the love of . . . have you had lunch?" I asked her, looking at my watch.

"Nope, what are you thinking?"

"I'm with Kasey right now. We can meet you for lunch if you can get away and answer his questions."

"Nic, I'm not writing on my boobs again for this guy. I still have lipstick stains on my chest from last night."

Boy, we had to think fast to get that order accomplished in the time frame allowed. It had to be Janeane's boobs so we'd hauled her into the bathroom, stripped her down to her underwear, and wrote "Master's Good Girl" on her chest. Luckily, the walls in the bathroom at Gypsy's were stained wood, and it looked like a room in a home. If he'd asked for a specific location like a bed, we would have been screwed.

"We'll figure it out. Can you meet us at Gypsy's? I'll order you a sandwich so you don't waste time waiting."

"That'll work, see you in ten."

Five

True love doesn't happen in a moment of our choosing. It sneaks up on us accidentally in a single heartbeat, a single flutter, an inexplicable moment that changes our world and keeps us off balance until the day we die. Love cares nothing for reason or logic. It only cares that it consumes you to a point that all of your thoughts encompass one person. You're helpless to stop it and even if you could, you wouldn't. Love, quite simply, is the act of handing over your soul to someone and trusting them to protect it with their life.

"What are you writing?" Kasey asked over my shoulder as we waited for Janeane to arrive.

Since my encounter with Dallas Vaughn, I'd been thinking long and hard about what it would be like to fall in love with someone and to trust him with your heart. I knew the couple in my new book would evolve into a passionate relationship filled with a soul encompassing love, so I was trying to put into words how Taryn would feel once she fell for the hero.

"Just some ideas I have for the book."

"Interesting. So, speaking of your brothers," Kasey segued oddly, "Is Finn seeing anyone?"

"Um, we weren't speaking of them, but if we must, then no, not that I know of. But you should stay away from Finn since we *are* talking about my brothers now," I told her.

"What's wrong with Finn?"

"Nothing if you're his sister. Well, that too, but definitely not if you're a newly divorced female with two kids. You don't need three on your hands, Kasey."

"How bad can he be at this point in his life?" she questioned.

Hell's bells, that's a loaded question.

"Other than a few more laugh lines . . . he hasn't changed at all since high school. Neither of them has. Oh, they work hard, which is the only grown up thing about them, but where women are concerned? They love them and leave them. Trust me, Kasey; you don't want to go there."

"You know, Finn kissed me once," she blurted out, surprising me.

"What? Why didn't you tell me?" I gasped as my brows shot up in surprise. I was stunned. All those late night phone calls I used to get during high school that centered on Finn and not once had she ever mentioned this to me.

"It was junior year when we were at Hilary Burk's party. We'd all been drinking, as you know, and I was alone in the kitchen refilling my beer when all of a sudden he cornered me and then kissed me out of the blue. The next time I saw him he acted as if it didn't happen, so I never said anything. I figured he was too drunk to remember."

"That's probably a safe bet since I remember my parents grounding all three of us for drinking that night."

"Your parents grounded you for drinking on a regular basis. I'm surprised you remember any specific weekend," Kasey laughed.

She wasn't wrong. Another disadvantage of being a triplet was they insisted on being wherever I was to keep an eye on me. Fun and games always seemed to follow the twins wherever they went, and since I was with them, well, I got sucked in. Thinking back on high school, it's a wonder any of us came out of it unscathed, what with all the alcohol that flowed freely every weekend.

"Do you remember that road trip up to Stillwater?" Kasey laughed.

"How could I forget? We were grounded for two months after that."

Bo and Finn were invited to a frat party up at Oklahoma State University our senior year by some friends of theirs, who had graduated the year before. I begged to go and bring the girls, so we lied to the parentals and said we were at each other's house after school and would be home by curfew. We all headed up on a Friday thinking that we could hang with the older kids for a few hours and then drive home to make our curfew. Yeah, we were wrong. One beer led to another, and soon it was midnight. We couldn't drive back because we were drunk, so we had to call home and let them know we lied and wouldn't be home until the morning. That road trip got us two months of punishment, but it was worth it since I got to make out with Freddy Hart. That is, until Bo and Finn found out. It's a wonder I ever lost my virginity, considering the way they guarded me.

Kasey and I were laughing over the memory when Janeane walked in followed by Kristina and Angela. Kristina and Angela placed orders for sandwiches before they all came over and sat down.

"Did you call Angela and Kris?" I asked.

"Yeah, Angela swung by and picked me up, and then we grabbed Kris."

That's the great thing about living in a city the size of Tulsa.

The downtown area was small enough that you could drive from one end to the other in about five minutes tops, depending on the traffic. All four women worked downtown, so it made it convenient for them to have lunch together several times a week.

"Ok, let's hear what Romeo has to say," Kristina urged as she ate.

Janeane nodded, then opened the email he'd sent on her phone and began reading the missive.

"*Taryn, as your Master you will obey my every command, or I will determine you are untrainable and end our association. Do I make myself clear? You showed great promise last night and obeyed me without question. Let's see if you can do it again today, with the same enthusiasm. By eight tonight, I must have in my possession a picture of you masturbating with a penis shaped vibrator. Also by eight, you must delete your account on SSD to prove you belong to me and only me. From now on, we will only communicate via Kik app so I may reach you immediately. Once you have downloaded the app, send me an email with your picture and Kik ID to prove you have completed my instructions. Then, and only then, will I know you are trainable. Don't disappoint me, Taryn. Dark Prince.*"

"Holy shit," Kasey blurted.

"Um, question," Angela broke in, "Do we really need this guy for the book? I mean, this is getting out of hand just for research. A picture of boobs was pushing my limits, but masturbating for some creep?"

"I agree," Janeane replied. "This guy is way over the top just for background information on the lifestyle."

"Is it just me or does he sound angry for some reason?" I asked.

While Janeane had been reading the email, a sense of dread enveloped me. He seemed angry, as if we'd done something to piss him off, almost as if he knew we were lying to him.

"Sorry, but I'm not masturbating for anyone but myself," Kasey mumbled.

"Oh, I agree with you. No way are we going that far for a story. We'll just look for another guy on SSD and ignore any more correspondence we receive from the creep. Janeane, send him a reply saying you've come to the conclusion that being a slave isn't what you're looking for and wish him well."

Janeane nodded and began typing on her phone as I sat back and breathed a sigh of relief. I didn't know until we began talking with Dark Prince how intense the dominant world was.

"If I didn't need the research I'd pull off that site," I mumbled.

"You could always read BDSM romances for your research. It's not like you're writing a BDSM book—it's just the world the killer lives in, right?"

"Good point. Maybe I should focus on the catfish aspect of the book and see how they draw women in and fool them into believing they are someone they aren't."

"Wow, he responded back already," Janeane interrupted, scowling at her phone.

"Why are you frowning?"

"He said a slave doesn't tell a Master what he can or can't do with his property. He expects us to complete the orders by eight p.m. tonight, or the punishment will fit the crime, whatever that means. It was sent from his iPhone so he must be in his car or something."

"Don't respond to him again. Just change the email account associated with the profile, so his messages bounce back to him," I ordered.

"I'll have to do that when I get back to the office."

"The sooner, the better. This guy's giving me the heavy jeevies," Kasey shuddered.

"Hey, Melissa," Angela hollered toward a blonde woman with short hair, a killer figure, and black spiked pumps I'd kill to own. Dressed in business attire, she wore a black pencil skirt with a bright red silk blouse that looked great with her fair complexion. She finished the look off with bright red lips, and I immediately cast her in the role of prosecuting attorneys in . . . in . . . "Yes . . . I've got it," I shouted.

"You've got what?" Kristina asked.

"The title of our book," I explained. "I've been racking my brain trying to come up with a title that fit, and it just hit me. Dark Prince kept calling us his property, right? It made me think of those T-shirts athletes wear that say, "Property Of" such and such school. I say we title the book "Property Of."

I looked around the table and saw four smiling faces all nodding approval. BFF's had a binding contract and within that contract, it clearly stated that all bullshit would be left at the door. Only the truth was allowed when in each other's presence, so when I looked around the table and saw four smiling faces I knew they liked the name.

"Booyah," Kristina exclaimed as she leaned forward for a high five that started a chain reaction.

"Property Of" who? The killer or the hero?" Janeane questioned.

"I'd say both. The Killer deems her his personal property, and the hero makes her his property when he falls in love with her."

"Nicola, you need to remember that in present day, not like in your historical romances, women aren't property," Kristina scorned in reply.

"Yeah, right," Kasey complained. "All men think you're their personal property, whether society has changed or not. Especially alpha males like my ex. They're a breed all their own, and it takes a special woman to put up with their shit."

"Is that what happened between you and Mark? You couldn't handle his possessiveness?"

"Part of it. That and he was never around. We grew apart, basically, and had nothing in common but the boys. I need a man who likes to have fun, not grunt orders at me."

"No wonder you're interested in Finn," I chuckled. "You couldn't find a less serious man if you tried."

As we chatted about possessive men and ridiculous brothers, Angela's friend walked up to us, smiling at everyone.

"Were you celebrating something when I walked in?"

"Melissa Webster, meet Nicola, Kristina, Kasey, and Janeane. Girls, meet Melissa, a loan officer at my branch. We're celebrating a book that Nicola is going to write and we're helping her with."

"Is this your first book?" Melissa asked me as she sat down at our table.

"No, but it's my first contemporary novel, and the girls are helping me with research," I explained.

"I don't read," she told me with a shrug. I held back, with effort, the cringe that was my automatic reaction to hearing someone didn't read. "But I'll read this one when you're done with it since Angela's involved. What's it about?"

Angela explained to Melissa in detail about Kasey's catfish and how the story evolved, leaving nothing out, including, to my utter horror, the part about Dallas Vaughn. Tulsa was a small city, and you couldn't go anywhere without meeting someone only to find out that you knew some of the same people. The last thing I needed was to find out that she knew Dallas. Which, of course, would prompt her to tell his wife about the pitiful writer who had a crush on her husband. Just thinking about the humiliation made me shudder.

Fortunately, Angela didn't know his name or that he was married, since I hadn't told her. But, unfortunately for me, she went on and on about the grin, the wink, and his ogling of my ass as I slumped further into the couch.

"He sounds hot. What's his name?"

"No idea," I blurted out giving Kasey a "zip it" look.

"It's fascinating how you merge bits and pieces of real people together to form a story. I can see why you would use the detective as the hero. And that Dark Prince guy sounds sadistic. He's clearly a nut case, which makes him perfect for the part of the villain. God, there are so many creeps out there lurking in the shadows just waiting to take advantage of women. You guys were smart to end the association," Melissa replied with a nod.

Twenty minutes later, after a long discussion about internet dating and how it would influence my book, Finn walked into Gypsy's unexpected and sauntered over to our group.

"Well, well, well, if it isn't Nicola and the Coffee Clutch Gang."

"Hilarious. What are you doing downtown?" I asked.

"Royse Construction is handling the renovations of one of the rooms at the Mayo Hotel. We're shorthanded so I'm lending a hand."

"Shocking, you mean you left the comfort of your office and nonstop ESPN to work?" I joked.

Finn rolled his eyes before leaning down to mess up my hair. As he did this, he noticed Kasey and a slow grin pulled across his lips. "Kasey," he mumbled in greeting. "Gotta run, Nic, I've got people to hire and places to go. You ladies have a good day," Finn stated before kissing the top of my head and moving to the counter to order a coffee.

All the women at my table watched Finn walk to the counter to place his order. I heard sighs of lust around me and I rolled my eyes in disgust. When I looked back at my friends, they all had a look that said Finn had a starring role in their fantasies.

"Seriously, guys? Ewww."

"Hey, I can't help it. Your brother's hot," Angela, laughed.

"Uh, could you *not* drool over him when I'm in the room at least?"

"Nope," Janeane laughed as she looked at her watch and announced, "Shit, I gotta run."

Everyone stood, except for Melissa, who was pecking away at her phone.

"Are you heading back to the bank?" Angela asked her.

"No, I'm heading to Texas this weekend and I need to get home and pack. I'm gonna hang here and finish my coffee," she smiled as her eyes drifted back to her phone

Nodding, Angela replied, "See you on Monday then," as the rest of the girls and I threw out, "Nice to meet you," and waved goodbye.

"Any chance we can meet here for coffee every day next week?" I asked before we went our separate ways for the weekend. Having to wait to work on the book until Tuesday and Thursday, when I was used to eight hours a day, seven days a week, was going to kill me. I'd already broken my promise to the girls about not working on the book without them last night and was hoping to redeem myself. If I could get more time with them, then maybe I wouldn't need the secret accounts I'd created last night on POF and SSD. They all stopped dead in their tracks and looked back at me smiling. Ha, I'd totally gotten them hooked on the process of writing a book.

"Works for me," Angela smiled.

"Ditto here," Janeane greed.

"Hell, I'm free on Sunday," Kristina answered.

"Just tell me where and when is my motto," Kasey laughed.

"We're gonna have to buy stock in Gypsy's if we spend all our time here," I chuckled as we headed for the door.

"This is true, but there is something so Emily Dickinson or T.S. Elliot about writing a book in a coffee house, don't you think?" Angela laughed.

I hugged the girl's goodbye then jumped into my light blue convertible Beetle to head home. I pulled left onto Cincinnati to head toward Highway 51, but was stopped at a red light at the corner of Cincinnati and 6th Street when a silver motorcycle came thundering up 6th Street, turning right onto Cincinnati with Dallas Vaughn on the back. I clenched my jaw at the sight of him because he was so friggin' everything I could barely stand it. The way he rode his bike kind of hunched over in the back, casual, as if he didn't have the weight of protecting the world on his shoulders was even more disarming. He looked like a White Knight or a current day Highlander on that bike. All he needed was a sword at his side as he rode his trusty steed and he'd be perfect. Then I remembered he was married.

"He grins sexily and winks at women while he's married. He may look like a hero, but he's a wolf in sheep's clothing," I muttered to myself.

Continuing to Cincinnati, Dallas jumped onto the same highway, so I stayed two car lengths behind him as we navigated the turn. When he took the Utica exit, the same one I had to take to get home, I held my breath. Half a mile from my home, he turned left off of Utica into a housing addition with cute gingerbread houses and I was tempted to follow him just to see where he lived. "Why are the hot ones always a disappointment?" I whispered as my eyes followed him down the street. Distracted by all that was Dallas Vaughn, I forgot what I was doing so when I turned my attention back to the road I had to slam on my brakes to avoid rear-ending a car.

"Jesus, Nicola, you're an idiot," I mumbled to myself as my hands shook and adrenaline pumped through my body. "Don't get yourself killed for a book."

***

His rage was palpable as he struck the fatal blow, one that fed the monster that lies within him. Her blood sprayed the wall like macabre crimson art as he covered her mouth to muffle her screams. His cock throbbed in exquisite pain as her legs gave out; his movements swift as he lowered her, his emotions on autopilot as his fury guided his actions. Air seeped from a pierced lung and blood mixed with her raspy gasps as she tried to fill her lungs. But, try as she might, breath still eluded her.

Blood masked his blank expression. The terrifying facade of calmness he wore disguised his rapid heartbeat, the lust he always felt for the kill . . . the shock that he always wanted more. As her blood dripped like teardrops from his chin, he watched her eyes grow wide with the knowledge that death was coming quickly.

Death doesn't care if you're young or old, rich or poor; it takes your gift gladly with little fanfare, he thought. One minute you're a living, breathing soul with your whole life ahead of you. The next you're lying on the floor in a pool of your own blood, listening to your heart gallop, adrenaline feeding its fight to survive. And then bit, by agonizing bit, it slows to a slight thump, thump . . . thump, thump . . . thump . . .

Dark Prince rose from the floor and looked at his glove-covered hands. Blood dripped from his fingers as he turned them over and inspected the thick, red liquid coating the surface. He'd never killed with a knife before; he preferred his bare hands as his instruments of punishment. However, standing there now, feeling the very essence of her being coating the skin of his face, he smiled.

Six

"Meow."

"Quiet, Snape," I mumbled as I tried to ignore the guilt I felt about the Plenty of Fish and Sub Seeking Dom accounts I created on Thursday night. I thought I could resist the temptation of working on the book until Monday when the girls and I met at Gypsy's, but I found out something quite unsettling about myself. I had no self-control.

After dealing with Dark Prince on Thursday, I knew I needed more control than I had over my creative process or I'd go nuts. But I also knew if I broke my word to the girls and worked on the story without them, they'd be pissed. I weighed my options and came up with the only conclusion I could.

My mental health won out.

Therefore, I decided to create accounts in my pen name and was now on POF and SSD as Grace Martin using my real photo, and my profile clearly stated that I was doing research for a book. But I still felt guilty, with good reason. I was breaking my oath.

Even though the girls had promised to meet me for coffee after work five days a week until we mapped out the story, the weekend stretched out in front of me and I gave into temptation by Saturday night.

So here I sat, trying to convince myself that there was no harm in looking at the messages in my in-box. That I was only doing what needed to be done for the book, yet, I hesitated.

On Thursday, I'd been determined to message with as many men as possible in order to get a feel for the type of guys who frequent these dating sites. I wanted to see the vast differences between the catfish Kasey encountered and honest men just looking for love. In addition, if truth were told, I was tired of sitting at home, so *if* in the course of research I stumbled across someone I was interested in, mores the better.

It had been two days since I'd posted both profiles and I was shocked to find them so full. Either there were a lot of desperate men in Tulsa or there weren't a lot of women to choose from in this area. It wasn't as if I was a knockout. I'm more of the kid sister type. More cherub faced than an exotic beauty like Angela, pint sized in comparison to Kasey's long slender frame. My boobs were just average next to Janeane's double D's and my ass was put to shame by Kristina's Voluptuous Maximus. Basically, I didn't stand out in a crowd, but wasn't exactly plain either. My best feature was my hair, but the rest of me wasn't bad either in a short, blonde, big-eyed, firm legged, glowing skin kind of way.

I scanned through the messages while I fought with my guilt, but I figured what's the harm in just looking. I opened the first message and I laughed instantly when I read, "*I'll sum up internet dating in two words for your book. Hopeful and emasculating.*"

I continued to scan through the messages, which ranged

from insulting to downright rude. There was *"Hey, baby, you'll be starring in my wet dreams tonight"* to *"If I agree to an interview, I accept all forms of payment. But fucking is my preferred form."*

Disappointed by the selection, and not seeing a catfish in the bunch, I scrolled back up to the first message and checked out the man's profile picture. Thomas Sheldon was extremely good-looking, with light brown hair and green eyes. He reminded me a bit of Dallas, though he didn't have that dark hero look to him. It was rugged yet more refined, more GQ if you will, than the jeans wearing detective.

"Married and a jerk, Nicola, so move on," I reminded myself.

With nothing but a night of reading ahead of me, I figured I'd come this far already in breaking my oath to the girls, I might as well correspond with the man.

One hour later, after exceptional discourse, I hesitantly agreed to meet him Monday at seven for a drink to discuss my book further.

Picking up my Kindle after signing off my computer, I'd at least listened to Kristina's advice about reading a BDSM novel in place of corresponding with a man like Dark Prince. Powering up my kindle, I opened Katherine Rhodes' *Consensual* and picked up where I left off before logging on to POF.

"A good Dom will help their sub learn what they need to know so both of them can derive pleasure from the act. As I said, it can be as simple as some sensory play or it can get as deep as master-slave play. It could be a blindfold and hot lingerie or it could be forced chastity and cock and ball torture."

Nathaniel's eyes grew wide. "Cock and ball torture?"

"Those in the lifestyle would ask you not to judge, Mister Walsh," she

76

said, a bright smile shining in her eyes. "There is a tenet in the lifestyle which everyone should adopt in life: always safe, always sane. Always be in possession of all of your faculties when you engage in play. Do not start a paddling session if you are angry. It changes from sex to revenge, then, and the pleasure is tainted forever. It will always be in the back of both of your minds—pleasure or true pain. And as such, if you are both safe and sane, there is almost nothing off limits."

"What the fuck is cock and ball torture?" Bo shouted in outrage from behind the couch, causing me to jump out of my skin. Finn appeared in front of me and grabbed my Kindle, ruining what had been a quiet evening with a cup of coffee and a book.

"Hey, give me that back, you miscreant," I shouted. Snape went flying to the floor when I stood up and glared at Finn.

"Miscreant? Jesus, Nic, you need to get out more. Repeat after me: asshole, douche bag, or rat bastard are acceptable terms in the twenty-first century," Finn chuckled.

"Finn, I mean this with all the love a sister can have for a brother when I say: please give me my Kindle, then get out and don't come back for a year."

Of course, he ignored me and started reading my book instead.

"Why are you here?" I asked Bo as Finn chuckled.

"*We've* come to the conclusion you're a hermit and need a night out on the town with us."

"I'm not a hermit, Bo, and my idea of fun is not hanging around strip clubs while you attempt to make it "rain" when you can only afford to "drizzle.""

"Jesus, Nic, we were kids when we took you there."

"Bo, that was last year," I pointed out.

"And your point is?" he grinned.

"Out," I shouted, grabbing my Kindle from Finn. "I was

having a lovely evening with my book."

Finn looked at Bo and shook his head in brotherly "Nicola's nuts," fashion before he leaned down, put his shoulder to my waist, and pitched me up and over. I was used to this maneuver so I didn't fuss. Whenever they wanted me some place else they hauled me with them against my will. It was futile to throw a fit; they would only laugh and ignore me.

"Promise me no strip clubs . . . unless it's male strippers," I decreed. I wouldn't be opposed to bare-chested men, but the look of "in your dreams" Bo gave me as he walked behind Finn said it was a no-go.

"We have something better in mind. All you can eat pizza and bumper cars."

"Incredible Pizza?" I blurted out in excitement.

Finn put me down and grinned at my excitement. I loved Incredible Pizza. It's the only place in town you could overdose on pizza, and then play laser tag, bumper cars, and putt-putt golf.

"You know it's sad, Nic, that a kiddy arcade makes you this happy," Bo exclaimed with a sigh as we headed out my door.

"You only say that because I kicked your ass at putt-putt on the last trip. Do you want a chance to redeem yourself or are you a chicken?" I goaded him with a chicken dance as he stared blank-faced at me.

"Double or nothing," he growled as we climbed into Finn's truck.

He was so going down.

"Like taking candy from a baby," I bragged as we pulled out for a night of family fun.

Too bad, it was short-lived.

***

Incredible Pizza was really just a Chuck E. Cheese on steroids. It was geared toward older kids, but they took into consideration that parents would be hauled along for the ride, therefore they had bumper cars, a racetrack, bowling alley, and laser tag to keep everyone entertained.

The place was hopping with folks of all ages since it was Saturday night and a favorite place for families to spend time or have a birthday party for their kids in one of their private rooms. These private rooms were where my night went from family fun to all-out war with my brothers and a certain detective.

You see, there's a shortcut of sorts that runs along the wall of the private rooms from the theater area to the food court. That's where I'd cut through to get more pizza for my bottomless pit brothers. When I rounded a corner, once again with my head down, my mind on putt-putt and laser tag, I slammed into, yet again, a certain married detective.

It had to be said that the fates weren't on my side. This made four—count them, four times—that I'd been responsible for covering the man with liquid. However, this time around there was a healthy dose of pizza and salad mixed in. And to make matters worse, Bo and his big mouth came up the rear after the collision laughing before I could apologize.

"You've gotta be fuckin' kiddin' me," Dallas Vaughn growled as pepperoni fell from his shirt.

"Oh, God, I'm so sorry I—"

"Hey, you wanna watch your fuckin' mouth?" Bo barked out in brotherly defense.

Oh, brother, here we go.

For some reason neither of my brothers thought I could take care of myself.

"Bo, telling someone to watch their mouth while swearing doesn't give the desired effect," I pointed out.

"Nicola, who gives a—"

I threw my hand over his mouth to stop his remark, and he glared at me, but held his tongue, thank God. I turned back to Detective Vaughn, hoping to smooth things over, and found the same brown-haired beauty from the picture standing next to him, smiling as she picked cheese from his shirt.

I'll admit now it was a bit of a punch to the gut to see them together after almost a week of fantasizing about the man. Then I remembered he was a pig who winked and felt sorry for his wife.

"I'm so sorry I made a mess for you again," I blurted out to his wife. She turned toward me smiling then did a double take. "You're Grace Martin," she blurted out.

"She's Nicola Royse," Dallas bit out, "and a walking, talking disaster," he continued as he pushed past us and headed toward (for the fourth time this week) the men's room.

"Dallas," she scolded sharply as he glared back at me.

"I am *so* not a walking, talking disaster," I grumbled at his retreating backside.

"You kinda are," Bo laughed.

"I thought your name was Grace Martin?" his wife continued.

"Technically, I'm Nicola Royse. But I'll answer to Grace Martin since that's my pen name."

"Well, either way it's nice to meet you; I've read all your books. And please ignore my brother; he's a little hotheaded at times."

"Your brother?" I choked out, feeling my cheeks heat

instantly with embarrassment. *Hell's bells, I'm an idiot.* I just ruined four of his shirts *and* any chance I may have had with the man.

"Unfortunately, but I claim him most days," she smiled.

I nodded, since I understood her sentiment, but I was mostly stunned. I'd thought the worst about the man and decided he'd deserved all the coffee I'd spilled on him. But he wasn't married to her, she was his sister . . . unless.

"He's not married?" I blurted out, determined to know for sure.

"Who, Dallas?"

"Um, yeah, your brother," I asked, looking back over my shoulder.

"No, probably for good reason too, I'm not sure any woman can handle him. He's kind of a caveman and grunts a lot. He's the kind of man only a sister can love, you know what I mean?" she laughed.

"Uh, yeah, I understand that feeling more than you know," I chuckled, "Bo here is one-half of my twin brothers and they drive me to the brink most days, while eating me out of house and home."

"How do you know my brother?" she asked.

"I don't, well, not really. I've run into him a few times this week with, uh, my coffee to be accurate," I grimaced.

"That was you?" she laughed.

"Guilty."

We both giggled in female camaraderie as Finn walked up laughing.

"What's so funny?" I questioned.

"You've been busy," he answered oddly.

"Busy doing what?"

"Pissing off cops."

"What? How did you—"

"Get this, bro," Finn chuckled as he turned to Bo. "I walked into the men's room and there was this pissed off guy trying to clean off his shirt. When I chuckled to myself at the mess, he looked up and glared at me. Then he said he had arrested murderers who were less trouble than my 'woman'. Jesus, Nic," he grinned at me, "you're gone, what, five minutes tops, and you piss off the only cop in the place. That's gotta be some kind of record."

"I am *not* a walking, talking disaster," I grumbled again as I rolled my eyes.

"You kinda are," Finn laughed.

"Whatever," I snapped then turned to Dallas' sister, "It was very nice to meet you, but it's time for putt-putt and ass whooping.

"I'm Erin Johnson, by the way, and it was a pleasure to meet you, too. I need to get back to my son's birthday party as well, but a word of advice before I leave, if you don't mind. His bark is worse than his bite if you're interested," she told me with the identical wink as Dallas.

Not about to admit I was more than interested, but knew without a doubt that ship had sailed, I waited until she left before I headed toward the arcade instead of the food area. I was in emotional upheaval right now and needed to hit something. I couldn't believe I'd spilled food and drink all over Dallas Vaughn again. Not to mention, I was still reeling from finding out he wasn't married. It figures that I'd send the first guy I'm attracted to in years running and screaming for the hills.

"I'm tired of waiting, Bo, let's get this grudge match over with," I threw over my shoulder as both twins followed me, still laughing at my expense.

Thirty minutes later and another victory in hand, we exited the putt-putt arena and headed toward the bumper cars. In line about ten people ahead of us was Dallas and whom I assumed now were his nephew and niece. He watched us walk up with a somewhat confused expression, looking back and forth between the three of us. Then Bo mumbled, "I think the light bulb just went off."

"What light bulb? What are you talking about?" I asked.

"The cop. He just figured out we're your brothers, not your boyfriend."

"Yep, two plus two just made Nicola single. Too bad for him we don't like him," Finn joined in.

"Why don't you like him?" I blurted out as I watched Dallas turn from rigid to relaxed in the course of a heartbeat.

"He's got a look," Bo grumbled.

"Oh, for God's sake, what kind of look?" I demanded as Dallas started to grin.

"That look."

"What look?" I fairly shouted.

"A look that says I'll be coming by your house without calling first for a sneak attack," Bo explained.

"He doesn't."

"He does."

"He hates me."

"He wants you."

"I spilled coffee on him."

"He wants—"

"Three times, well, technically two, but my ass in the air caused the third, and if you count the pizza and pop, that makes four times in five days," I rushed out.

Bo and Finn looked at each other with their brows raised in disbelief. Then, in some silent twin communication, they nodded, grinned slowly, and then replied in unison, "Tag team."

"Oh, dear Lord . . ."

Picture it . . .

Round one went to the young knights as they cornered their prey with the bumper cars. It wasn't really a fair fight since they boxed him in and slammed him into the wall any time he tried to move. The handsome warlord said nothing during this. He just clenched his jaw and narrowed his eyes at the fair-haired maiden, of all people. Then the knights took their battle to the newly installed "Rock and Joust," an inflatable gladiator ring with a free-floating, rocking pedestal where opponents attempted to knock each other off. It was ugly—for the knights, that is—for the dark and dangerous warlord was a trained professional in the art of all things brawny, and barely flinched when each knight tried to dethrone him. Down one would go, and then the warlord would turn toward the other and motion him forward with the crook of his finger. While all this was happening, the fair-haired maiden watched in silent appreciation all of the dark and dangerous heroes' manly skills . . . and tight ass.

Once the knights had been defeated in the jousting competition, they threw down another gauntlet in the form of laser tag. Aye, that's right, the stupid knights wanted to test their aim in a dark space against a man who carried a gun for a living. The warlord grinned at their foolishness and shook his head at this challenge. For he knew too well the arrogance of the young knights and that their abilities in the course of battle would pale in comparison to his own.

The fair-haired maiden was dragged kicking and screaming into this fight, then strapped into a harness with glowing lights as a laser gun was shoved into her hands. The knights instructed her to, "Aim to kill," and then off they all jogged into the black lights of a laser tag maze. Then the massacre commenced. There was grunting and shoving, and the occasional, "The guy's like a ghost," as the warlord's points kept adding up. When the smoke had cleared on the knight's challenge, and the scores were tallied, it was clear that the warlord had killed the young knights ten times over.

Get the embarrassing picture?

"Are we done playing "intimidate the cop"? I want to go home and forget this night," I fumed at the two idiots.

Dallas and his nephew, along with other kids from the birthday party, were standing on the opposite side of the room peeling off their laser tag vests as I chewed on my childish brothers. Bo and Finn were smiling at me as I ranted because, clearly, they had a death wish.

"I'm changing my locks tomorrow," I informed them. "You are officially off my invited guest list."

"How are we supposed to build that bookshelf you want if you lock us out?" Bo laughed.

Oy, he had a point, and they owed me big time for this.

"Ok, after you build the bookshelf you are officially *off* my invited guest list."

"What about the other list of things you need repaired in the house?"

"I'll hire someone," I threatened.

They inhaled sharply and it felt as if the air had been sucked from the room. I knew better than to threaten them with a competitor, 'cause idiot brothers or not, they were the best in town. But I was pissed and had to make a point. I had to deal with Dallas (wishful thinking) because of his partner and I didn't need the hassle he was sure to give me for their childish behavior.

"No one touches that house but us, and you know it. We didn't spend a year remodeling it to have some amateur fuck something up," Bo growled as we made our way out of the laser tag room.

"It's not your problem anymore," I explained in anger. I had to stick to my guns with these two or they'd walk all over me.

"Jesus, Nicola, we were only testing the guy to see if he was worthy of you, you don't have to go off half-cocked."

"Worthy of . . . worthy of me!" I shouted. "I have to deal with that man for my book and now you've put me in an embarrassing position. He wasn't giving me a "look" other than one of hatred, for God's sake."

Bo was grinning at a point over my shoulder, which irritated me to no end that he wasn't listening to me, so I turned around to see what he was looking at and saw Dallas marching toward us with a phone pressed to his ear.

He barked out, "Keep everyone out until forensics are on the scene, I'll be there in twenty." He swiped his phone off as he stopped in front of us and I forgot to breathe. He glared at my brothers for a moment while I stepped back and out of the way of the fireworks I figured were coming. Instead of fireworks, he stunned me beyond comprehension.

"This shit you just pulled all evening, I get it. But just so you know, if I wanted her, you wouldn't have stopped me. Are we clear?"

The twins had been grinning at Dallas as he started to speak and when he was done, they were full-on smiling. When he was through with my brothers, Dallas turned, ignoring them both, and walked right up to me. I held my breath for what came next and he didn't make me wait long. He leaned in, pinned me with those honey-colored eyes, and growled, "You aren't goin' on a ride-along with anyone but me do you hear me?" Before I could answer, he reached up, grabbed my neck, and jerked me forward, slamming his mouth over mine. The kiss was hard, brief, but had the desired effect—it left me speechless.

When he pulled back, he added with a gentle voice, "And just so *you* know, you won't be able to stop me either." Then he winked, grinned, and tugged my ponytail before he turned on his heels and left me standing in a state of shock.

"That's the look," Finn chuckled as he walked up next to me and threw an arm around my shoulders.

***

Death had a smell beyond that of rotting flesh. You could smell the victims' fear right before they took their last breath. That was running through Dallas Vaughn's mind as he stared at the mutilated body of Melissa Webster. She lay on the floor of her living room, dressed as if she'd just returned home from work when she was attacked. Her eyes were still open, staring lifelessly at the ceiling, and even though her face had softened with her untimely death, Dallas could still see the terror in her eyes.

Dallas had arrived on the scene before his partner and surveyed the body with rookie Sian Davis. Davis had been assigned to his department three weeks earlier and was wet behind the ears when it came to dealing with the sights and smells of a brutal murder.

"There's so much blood," she whispered to no one particular.

"If you're gonna get sick, take it outside so you don't contaminate the crime scene," Dallas relayed gently.

Shaking her head, but not taking her eyes off the victim,

Davis sucked in a deep breath to ward off the nausea.

The crime scene had been photographed and forensics was dusting for fingerprints. Dallas turned when he heard Reed enter the two-bedroom house that belonged to the victim and waited for him to approach.

"Jesus, Joseph, and Mary," Reed mumbled as he looked at the victim while making the sign of the cross.

It would take an autopsy to determine the cause of death, or, more to the point, which knife wound caused her death. From the amount of stab wounds in her abdomen, Dallas figured close to twenty; his guess was exsanguination

"She was a looker, that one," Reed observed.

"And blonde," Dallas pointed out the obvious.

"Not the same MO, Vaughn, he doesn't rip them apart with a knife; he asphyxiates them."

"He could be escalating or maybe he couldn't get away with her so he stabbed her to keep her quiet."

"That's all conjecture at this point and you know it. Let forensics clear the scene, then we'll see what we've got. Not every blonde in the city who's murdered is a victim of The Shallow Grave Killer," Reed advised.

Reed knew his partner had a hard on for the sonofabitch, but he needed him to focus on the evidence before jumping to conclusions. Not to mention that even if this was a Shallow Grave murder, they'd be handing it over to the FBI to investigate. That is, until they realized they were barking up the wrong tree, Reed thought with pent-up anger. It was just like the feds to stroll in and take charge. If they decided the Shallow Grave murders were the same sick fuck, then he and Dallas would be lucky if they were invited to sit on the task force. After Vaughn's pissing match the day before he doubted Agent Parker would let him fetch his coffee, let alone sit in on their investigation.

As the partners talked, Davis suddenly threw her hand over her mouth before she turned and ran outside to empty her stomach.

"Do you remember your first bloody crime scene?" Reed asked motioning toward the door Davis had ducked out.

"I remember them all," Dallas bit out, his eyes on the front door as well.

"She'll get her sea legs," Reed mumbled and moved on. "They find the weapon yet?"

"Yep, on the floor next to the body."

Reed turned from the body and took in his partner, ready to ask him if they'd found any other evidence, when he noted the front of his shirt covered in what looked like food.

"Jesus, Vaughn, did you have a food fight with those kids of your sisters?"

"Nope, I ran into Sandra Dee," he grinned.

"Did ya now? You know, if you ignore all the signs, it's bad luck, my sweet mama always used to say."

"What signs would those be, that she's a danger to my wardrobe?" Dallas chuckled.

"Fate, Vaughn, fate. There aren't many women is this world who look like that and are as sweet as a newborn baby. You need to get in there before someone beats you to the punch."

"Jesus, you're a romantic," Dallas smiled.

"You gotta make time for what matters most in life, son. You think we bust our asses hunting these sons a bitches' so we can go home to an empty bed?"

"You forget I tried that once and it didn't work out," Dallas reminded him, not about to tell him he'd already put Nicola on notice. He'd never hear the end of it either way, but figured, until he'd had time to explain how it was gonna be with

Nicola, he'd keep his partner in the dark.

"You chose the wrong woman, Dallas. You take my June, for example. Sure, she's hell on wheels, but she keeps me in line and makes life exciting. Makes it worth gettin' up each day to fight the good fight and when she thinks no one is lookin' she's as sweet as a kitten. That, my friend, makes what we're standin' here viewing tolerable. I know when I leave here I've got warm and sweet waitin' for me when I walk through the door."

"You do know if June caught you callin' her sweet she'd castrate you."

"It's the only thing that keeps me from callin' her my sweet June to her face," Reed chuckled. "Are you gonna listen to me and take Ms. Romance Novelist out for a drink?"

Dallas stared back at his partner and grinned.

"Nope, I'm gonna take her on a ride-along."

"Christ, I gotta teach you about the art of—"

"Detectives?" a uniformed officer called from the hallway.

Reed turned, and Dallas followed suit, heading toward the officer.

"Did you find something?" Reed asked.

"In the bathroom on the mirror," he responded.

Dallas brushed past the officer and pushed open the door to the small bathroom sandwiched in between the two bedrooms. The house wasn't more than twelve hundred square feet like many of the homes in the small neighborhood that were built after World War II. Dallas scanned the room and noted it was in disarray unlike the rest of the tidy house. Dallas looked at the mirror, but didn't see anything at first glance.

"Move to the other side of the room and look back toward the mirror at an angle," Officer Rodriguez instructed.

Dallas moved across the small space, then turned around and looked at the mirror. It was faint, but you could see a word on the mirror, as if it had been written when the mirror was steamed over.

"Does that say master?"

"That's what I was thinking as well," Rodriguez agreed.

Dallas motioned Reed in and moved out of the way so his partner could get a look. Reed moved his head back and forth to catch the light coming in from the window and then paused.

"Sonofabitch," Reed mumbled. "What the hell does he mean by that?"

"Hell if I know, but we'll figure it out," Dallas vowed before he turned to the officer and ordered, "Tell Jenkins with the crime lab about this. He needs to dust the mirror for prints and to pull the drain for hair and blood. If that bastard washed his hands to get rid of evidence, I want it."

When Rodriguez nodded and turned to leave, Dallas halted him. "Rodriguez, nice catch. If you ever wanna make a move from patrol to homicide, let me know. I'll put in a good word for you after you've taken your exam." Rodriguez gave Vaughn a nod in acknowledgment before he turned to find Jenkins.

Dallas felt a headache forming as he turned back to Reed. All he had wanted was one day off from the ugliness of his job, a day to enjoy being with his family. He'd gotten neither.

"We need to canvas the neighborhood and contact her family," Dallas reminded Reed as he rubbed his neck with the flat of his hand, exhausted at the thought. "Christ, the family. Whose turn is it to break someone's heart?"

"It's mine," Reed answered. "Go home, Vaughn, I'll handle this one. This shit'll be waiting for us on Monday either way."

"Home? To do what, exactly, pace the floor while I work the case in my mind?"

"Have a drink, hell, have a bottle. But get some fuckin' sleep for once. Dream about blonde hair and green eyes, for Christ's sake. It's not that hard: you lay down on a bed and close your eyes."

Dallas sighed at his partner's dramatics then grabbed him by the shoulder, giving him a shove. "Jesus, enough henpecking already. You're like an old woman when you get like this."

Reed shrugged at his outburst and then answered with a grin. "I learned from the best."

Seven

Best friends are the people you turn to when your life is going down the toilet, when you need a shoulder to cry on, and who support you unconditionally. They don't judge you, they hold your hair up when you've had too much to drink, and they always make a pitcher of margaritas when they show up at your house to listen to you bitch about men on a Saturday afternoon. One call was all it took and the girls came running. I'd called them first thing when I woke up after Dallas Vaughn had rocked my world the night before with his arrogant belief he could snap his fingers, and I'd come running.

Sure, I was attracted to him, and I'd imagined several love scenes with him for "Property Of," starring me in the leading role. However, imagining it is one thing, being told I couldn't resist him if he were so inclined to grace my world with his tight ass and firm muscles, was a completely different story. So mind-bogglingly different, it took ten minutes after he kissed me to come up with a retort; such was my astonishment that he was that arrogant. Though, I'm quite certain if I'd uttered, "When pigs fly," he'd have laughed at me.

The whole thing reminded me of high school when the star quarterback deigned to talk to a girl who wasn't in the "in" crowd. Then he'd ask her out like, "Friday, you and me, babe.

I'll pick you up at seven." As if the notion she would say no never occurred to him even though he knew she had twin brothers that would beat the shit out of him for some much as looking at her. Only this time, her twin brothers had high-fived themselves after the quarterback insulted their sister.

I'd come home and told Snape and Simi all about it, and they'd agreed wholeheartedly with me that Mr. Dallas Vaughn had some nerve thinking he could woo me so easily. I'm not some naive girl who can't say no for Christ's sake. I can control my hormones long enough to keep him at arm's length if I was so inclined. And after his arrogant belief he was *so* irresistible I couldn't stop him, I *was* so inclined.

Now I was sitting in my living room surrounded by my best friends explaining the whole sordid night.

"Let me get this straight . . . Bo and Finn tested him all night to see if he'd what? Back down?" Kasey asked.

"Apparently it was some kind of bro code. You know, see if they could intimidate him and if they couldn't, then he was worthy of wooing me. Can you believe that shit? As if I'm some prize and the spoils would go to the victor," I explained. "It was ridiculous and embarrassing."

"And he knew what they were doing and he played their game?" Kristina inquired as she filled my margarita to the brim.

Sucking down a healthy dose of frozen delight, I nodded, then explained with a sigh, "He got right in their faces and all but pounded his chest and said, 'This shit you pulled all evening, I get it. But, just so you know, if I wanted her, you wouldn't have stopped me.'"

"And then he told you the same thing?"

"Yep, right after he grabbed my neck and kissed me."

"Was it a hard kiss or a soft kiss?" Janeane asked.

"I don't know. What does it matter?"

"Oh, it matters. Was it soft and sweet, meant to make you tremble, or was it hard and fast like a branding?" Janeane continued.

I thought about it, but all I could remember was that I'd tingled all over. "Um, hard and fast, like he was trying to shut me up," I explained.

"Branding," the girls replied in unison.

"What difference does it make?" I asked the room full of smiling women.

"Well," Angela, started, "if he had given you a soft peck with a touch of tongue, it would have meant he was testing the waters to see if there was a spark, a connection. If he devoured your mouth, then he would have been telling you "hey baby, lets fuck." However, a hard and fast kiss is more of a branding. Sorta like a dog lifting his leg around his yard to mark his territory. He was branding you, saying this belongs to me."

"You made that up," I chuckled, yet something I couldn't put a name to shot fast and hard through me at the idea that he had claimed me.

"How is it that you write romance novels and know nothing about men?" Kristina laughed.

"I write about Highlanders. They don't court their women; they marry because of alliances with other clans. Most of them don't fall in love with their wives until they've been married a few months."

"Well, let me explain how it works in modern-day America. When a man is interested, a real man that is, you can't stop them, nor should you try. Because sister, they have the determination of a dog with a bone, a bird after a worm, a hooker after a John," Kristina, in all her infinite married wisdom explained.

"Are you saying my only choices in today's single scene are men like my brothers who love you then leave you? Or men like Dallas who are so full of their own appeal that they think women will fall at their feet?"

"No, that's not what I'm saying, what I'm saying is that when a *real* man sees something he wants, he goes after it and doesn't stop until he's obtained it."

My heartbeat picked up its pace thinking about being pursued by a man like Dallas Vaughn. Then I remembered he said *if* he wanted me, as if he didn't, but was letting me know *if* he did, I couldn't stop him. Sorry, but that just seemed arrogant and insulting to me. In fact, the more I thought about the man I decided his eyes were too golden and his body entirely too muscled. Moreover, his hair was too thick and dark and his lips way too full, all of which told me, he was used to getting his way. Probably just by crooking his finger at any woman who looked his way.

The girls kept going on and on about real men and how they act while wooing a woman while I continued to think about Dallas and his actions last night. I was so engrossed in all of Dallas' shortcomings (I was lying to myself, obviously) that I didn't hear my front door open. When Finn boomed, "Real men like us," as he and Bo walked into the living room, followed by one of their crew, I jumped out of my skin. Eye rolls commenced (except for Kasey) as my brothers set down their tool belts and grinned at the room. I hadn't met the man who'd accompanied them, so I gave him a cursory look. He was very tall, very big, and very hot with black hair and blue eyes that seemed a little too focused on Janeane's breasts.

Typical man!

Once he was done inspecting Janeane's double D's, he

scanned the room and smiled. There was a collective sigh from all five of us as his perfect white teeth, surrounded by a sexy goatee, flashed across his face.

"Excellent! We came just in time, bro," Finn joked as he grabbed my glass and took a drink, breaking me from my hot guy induced spell.

"Did you bring a new lock?" I asked with a hint of anger to remind them I was still pissed about last night.

"Funny, Nic. We're here as a peace offering, okay. We know we pissed you off last night, so to make it up to you we're gonna fix the shit on your to-do list and take measurements for the bookshelf."

I couldn't help but grin when I heard that, Bo and Finn had to be sweating bullets, if they were spending their Sunday afternoon fixing my broken tile and leaking faucet. I hated letting them off the hook because they had gone too far last night, but I couldn't hold a grudge where they were concerned. Standing up, I grabbed my drink back from Finn and glared one last time at my most beloved idiot brothers. Then I kissed them both on the cheek to let them know all was forgiven. When it was all said and done, what they'd done last night was more about how they felt toward me, than embarrassing me, so how could I stay mad.

"Why don't we take this out back since it's a nice day and let these idiots work in peace," I prompted the girls then turned back to Bo and Finn. "I was planning on grilling burgers. Since you're here, you might as well eat."

"Make mine a double," Finn shouted, as I made my way to the deck.

The previous owners had built a huge covered deck off the kitchen that was perfect for entertaining, and this would be my first official barbecue with my friends since buying the house last year. Angela and Kristina's husbands were off golfing together, and Kasey's ex-husband had her boys for the weekend since he was being deployed next week. Therefore, we had the whole day to kick back and relax.

The house came with a sound system that fed into the back yard, so I plugged in my iPod and found my country favorites list. Blake Shelton started singing, "Just South of Heaven" as I pulled off the cover to my gas grill and the girls brought out our drinks. As the girls were making their way outside, one of my living room windows was suddenly shoved open, and I heard Bo shout, "Turn it up." So, I cranked it up.

After lighting my grill, I grabbed the grill brush and began scraping off the remnants of my last cookout as the girls grabbed a chair around my square, tile covered patio table. My backyard wasn't huge, but it was landscaped as if a master gardener lived there. Billowing gardens of wildflowers of every color were bursting through, now that spring had arrived, and soon much of the yard would be an English garden paradise. I loved the haphazardly placed beds of fragrant flowers, both short and tall, mixed with the large oak trees and wispy grasses. It reminded me of a cottage garden you'd find in England, where hundreds of feet of a yard were dedicated to a variety of flowers and shrubs, that at times seemed to have no rules of organization. I knew when I spied the backyard I had to have the house.

"Hey, Nicola," Kasey shouted from my kitchen. "You know how you said when you took this break you were gonna get drunk and maybe get laid?" I turned around and watched as Kasey came out of my kitchen holding up a bottle of Tequila. "I can help you with the drunk part, but you're on your own with the getting laid part."

"I heard that," Bo laughed from inside.

Rolling my eyes because I had said that, I eyed the bottle then thought about my schedule for the next day and knew I could indulge in a few rounds of shots. Smiling, I grabbed the bottle and unscrewed the lid as the girls started chanting, "Drink, drink, drink," in unison. Heat burned my throat as warmth ran through my veins, and that's pretty much the last sober thing I remembered, the rest of the day was an alcohol induced blur.

***

Sundays for Dallas meant forgetting about work for a few short hours while being fed by Bill's wife, June. He had a standing invitation to eat dinner with his family on Sunday afternoon and he didn't miss many. Dallas was an honorary member of their family. When he divorced Brynne two years ago, June had insisted he join them for dinner at least once a week so she knew he was eating.

June was an opinionated woman who ran Bill's home like a well-oiled machine. She kept their kids on schedule, their house a home you could kick back and relax in, and she adored her husband even though she only pretended to put up with him.

Their home was in midtown Tulsa in one of the older neighborhoods, not far from Dallas. A two-story colonial, painted white with black shutters, it sat on a large corner lot with plenty of room for their four daughters. Their house was never quiet, always hormonal, and entertaining as hell as only four girls between the ages of twelve and nineteen could be.

Today was no different.

"Not in a million years are you leavin' this house in that

99

getup. Upstairs and change or you can forget about goin' out with your friends."

"Mom! Daddy's being a stick in the mud," Trisha Reed whined as Dallas entered the Reed residence.

"Daddy's just trying to save some poor boy's life, angel. If you walk out of this house wearin' that short skirt and tight top, I'll have to shoot someone."

Stomping her foot, Trish turned to Dallas and attempted, per usual, to get him on her side. "Uncle Dallas, is this skirt too short?" Trish cried out as Dallas stood there enjoying the banter.

Trisha Reed was a precocious fifteen-year-old with long legs, long brown hair, and a body that should belong to a twenty-year-old not a kid. So yeah, it was too damn short, too damn everything for a girl he loved like a younger sister.

"Not only yeah, but, hell yeah. I'll ground you myself if you walk out of this house in that getup," Dallas bit out then braced for the fallout.

About now was when the bottom lip usually started trembling. Right before the tears streamed and the wailing started as she sprinted up the stairs to her room.

Three, two, one, Dallas thought.

She didn't disappoint.

"I'm never speaking to you again," she screamed as she ran up the stairs and slammed the door to her room, no doubt throwing herself on her bed at the injustice of the world.

Grinning, per usual, when he'd won an argument with his daughters, Bill turned to Dallas and clapped him on the shoulder, his fifteen-year-old all but forgotten. Both men headed toward the kitchen where June was cooking a pot roast for dinner. Upon entering, she turned around and smiled at Dallas, but frowned at her husband.

"What did you do this time?" June accused.

"Jesus, woman, I didn't do anything. She was tryin' to sneak out of the house in a strippers outfit."

"The black skirt and red top with the skulls?" she asked.

"That's the one. Why in the hell does she own that shit in the first place?"

"Do *you* wanna go to the mall with her when she has birthday money from your mother and supervise?"

"I catch murderers for a livin', ain't that punishment enough?"

"Oh, please. I'd take your murderers any day over four daughters with PMS," June argued. "You couldn't just give me sons who would take care of their mama when she is old and gray. No, you gave me four daughters, all built like supermodels, and then leave me to fend for myself while you have all the fun shooting people," she groused in outrage, then narrowed her eyes and announced, "*I* want to shoot people."

Bill was smiling by the time she finished so he grabbed June around the waist and hauled her to him, nuzzling her neck as he whispered, "Do you wanna go to the gun range tomorrow, and shoot somethin'?"

"Only if it's with bottles of pop and large caliber ammo. You know I prefer it when the targets explode," June told him as she wrapped her arms around his neck.

"Deal," Bill chuckled before kissing June's neck.

Once Bill let his wife go, she rounded on Dallas and pointed her finger at him, which made him smile. He knew this would be good because the woman wasn't happy unless she was lecturing or ordering someone around. Dallas figured it was a conditioned response from having raised four girls.

"Ask the woman out."

"Sorry?" Dallas chuckled, at a loss for what she meant.

"The coffee girl, the writer, Bill told me *all* about her. He said she was as cute as a button and sweet as apple pie." Dallas' eyes shot to Bill, narrowing them on his partner. The last thing he needed was June on his case about dating. The woman locked her jaws on a topic like a Rottweiler when she smelled blood. And Dallas finding a woman was about as big of a bone of contention with June as there was. "And don't give me any of that 'you don't have time for a relationship' crap, either, Dallas. A man can't live by bread alone. You need someone waiting at home for you at the end of the day."

"I'll take that under advisement," Dallas replied with a smile, not about to tell her he'd already made that decision. He'd never get any peace if she knew he was headed to Nicola's house after dinner.

"The hell you will! You'll bury yourself in your work like you've done the past two years, is what you'll do."

"June," Dallas tried to interrupt, but she stopped him and demanded, "Jesus, Dallas, make time for love before you're old and gray. If you don't, you'll have no kids to look after you while you relive your glory days."

Dallas knew better than to argue with the woman so he walked over, put his hand to her head, leaned in, and kissed her forehead. "I'll see what I can do about not bein' alone in my golden years."

June shoved Dallas back and pointed at him one last time before turning to the stove to finish making dinner. All while grumbling that he was more stubborn than her Bill.

"Make yourself useful boys and set the table. You'll only get in my way in here."

Dallas turned to the cupboard that held the dishes, and

asked, "How many for dinner," as he started pulling down plates. June's answer was interrupted by Bill's cell going off, so she waited for him to answer, and then told Dallas, "Only five," would be adding to the noise level of their home.

When Bill laughed then replied, "Sorry, Nicola, you'll have to slow down," Dallas turned to his partner, his brows raised in question as to why she was calling him.

"No, darlin', you can't claim self-defense if you actively plot someone's murder. Who do you want to kill?" Bill asked, holding the phone away from his ear while smiling at Dallas. His forehead soon pulled into a frown though as he listened to her explain further.

"Can I claim self-defense for bludgeoning someone for grabbing my breasts?" Nicola shouted into the phone. Dallas could hear what sounded like other women screaming in the background and then a deep voice growled what sounded like, "You fuckin' cunt."

Bill had put the call on speakerphone about the time "Fuckin' cunt" was shouted and Dallas saw red. He barked out, "Where the hell are you?" but didn't get a reply as the women erupted in outrage.

"You can't call me a cunt," Nicola shouted from the other end, *"You're the miscreant who felt me up."*

Grabbing Bill's phone off the counter, he demanded again, "Nicola, where are you, and who the fuck grabbed you?" Before he got an answer, however, the call ended right as he heard shouting from what sounded like her brothers.

"I gotta go," Dallas barked out as he pulled his phone from his pocket and dialed dispatch. Dallas had pulled up her house address before leaving for Bill's and he hoped like hell that that was where she was. Two minutes later, he had a patrol car on the way and his legs hugging his Harley as he blazed down the street toward her home.

When he arrived, he knew he'd been right on the money. Chaos had ensued on her front lawn and he watched her brothers pound a man repeatedly. In addition, to that, Nicola was in the mix shouting at her brothers, "Stop, before you kill him."

Dallas jumped off his bike, rushed to huddle, and pulled one of the twins from the man ordering, "Back off." He pulled the other brother off the man, who was down on the ground covering his head, as blood dripped from his nose.

"Someone needs to explain what the fuck is goin' on," he roared.

Nicola, who seemed to be in shock that Dallas had arrived out of the blue, and was hauling her brothers off the asshole, gained her composure quickly. "The girls and I were drinking and Kasey let slip I wanted to get laid in the near future. This idiot thought I meant by the next available man," she shouted incensed. "I was in my bathroom washing my hands and he came in and pinned me to the counter. Then he copped a feel even though I told him to stop. The girls heard me shout and came busting in, so I grabbed a tool off the counter and whacked him in the nose." When she was done, Nicola bent at the waist and shouted at the prone man, "And just so you know, I'd do it again. No, means no, you big jerk!"

"Not only are you fired, Shockley, but you'd better watch your back," one of the twins threatened, pushing against Dallas' hand at his chest.

Turning to face the man who'd assaulted Nicola, it was all Dallas could do to keep from letting her brother go and dealing with the man himself. Thankfully, years of training kicked in. Dallas pulled out a pair of cuffs, rolled him onto his stomach, and put a knee to his back applying more pressure than was needed. Then he cuffed the man's hands behind his back as he reined in his control.

"You have the right to remain silent," Dallas bit out.

"Jail won't save you from me," a twin growled.

Jerking his head around, Dallas had had enough. He knew he needed her brothers out of the equation before he lost control of the situation. Looking up at Nicola, he demanded, "Get your brothers inside before I arrest them as well."

Still in shock that Dallas was at her home, Nicola ignored his request and asked, "How did you know to come?"

"I was at Bill's when you called. Now get your brothers in the house."

"You came running when you heard I was in trouble?" she gasped.

Dallas didn't have time to play twenty questions, so he softened his voice and asked instead of ordered, hoping to get her cooperation. "Babe, please take your brothers inside and let me deal with this asshole before this escalates, all right?"

He watched her eyes widen in surprise at his request. Thankfully, she listened this time and told her brothers, "Righty-ho, you heard the man. Get inside, he's got this covered."

Surprisingly, the twins listened to their sister, and headed toward the house while glaring at the man on the ground. When she reached her front door, he saw her friends peering out from the inside staring at him with wide eyes. Nicola turned when she reached the door and looked back at Dallas. He watched as a small grin pulled across her mouth. Something he could only describe as calm filtered through his body when she pushed a strand of silky hair behind her ear, grinning shyly at him before she closed the door. When she was inside, he kept his eyes on the door for a moment, wondering what it would be like to come home to that every day. Peaceful he figured. Looking down at the man in his custody, his jaw clenched in anger when he thought about how his hands had touched Nicola. Leaning down, so only he could hear, Dallas mumbled quietly before reading him his Miranda Rights.

"You fucked with the wrong woman, asshole. Now you're headed to jail and I'm gonna have a real close look at your record. I promise you, if you so much as breathe in her direction again, I'll bury you, do you understand?"

Once Dallas had interviewed everyone inside the house, and secured one Micah Shockley in the back of a squad car, he headed back toward the front door of Nicola's Craftsman home. He hadn't taken in the house when he first arrived, but now, as he approached, he was impressed by the masculine lines of the exposed rafters and beams. Her house wasn't painted as many older homes were, but stained a rich brown, giving it a rustic feel that appealed to him. As he took the steps of her wide front porch the over-sized front door, that looked as if it had been fashioned out of 12x12 timber planks and stained to match the house, flew open. Nicola stood there staring at Dallas in her bare feet, a pair of cut off denim shorts, and an Eskimo Joe's T-shirt. She'd pulled her hair up into a high ponytail since going inside and now looked about sixteen, instead of the woman that she was. Christ, she was Sandra Dee in a nutshell, and it set his back teeth aching at how damn much he wanted to rip that ponytail out of her hair, and then wrap it around his hand as he devoured those full lips.

When he reached the front door, Dallas stopped and looked down at Nicola. He watched the way the sunlight highlighted the different shades of gold mixed in with the lighter blonde of her hair. He noted that not only were her eyes green, but the color of light jade. They reminded him of a tropical ocean with white sandy beaches and warm summer breezes. She was tiny; the top of her head barely reached his shoulders. She had small round breasts, a slim, yet womanly figure, shapely legs, and a heart shaped ass, if his memory served correctly. She was an all-American girl all right, born and raised in a state where baseball and apple pie still meant something. Her Sunday afternoon barbecue shouldn't have been interrupted by filth. By a man who thought cornering a woman half his size, and putting his dirty hands on her, because she had a few drinks, was his right.

Taking in the house, the yard with its flowers, the best friends who had her back, and brothers who'd kill for her, Dallas decided he was done waiting. He wasn't gonna go slow, he wasn't gonna see how it went, he was going in fast and hard because a woman like Nicola was one in a million, and he wasn't about to let her slip through his fingers.

With this in mind, he put his hand to her stomach and moved her back into her home. When he'd closed the door, she was looking up at him confused, so he decided to enlighten her.

Dallas moved toward Nicola until she retreated and he had her pinned to the wall. He put his hands on the wall, near both sides of her head, and then leaned in close to her ear.

"Meet me at the station tomorrow at ten a.m. and I'll show you the ropes," he whispered, then ran his nose along her ear, grinning when she shuddered.

"Okay, I can do ten," she whispered back on a shaky breath laced with desire.

Hearing the longing in her voice, Dallas moved in closer,

pressing his body into hers to make his point. He took hold of her neck, both thumbs caressing her jaw as he lowered his head and looked into her eyes. Nicola's own grew wide as his head descended; positioning his lips a hairbreadth away from hers. Then finally, when he felt her pulse pounding rapidly under his hands, saw her eyes hooded with desire at his closeness, and felt her breath coming in gasps, he ordered, "The next time you feel the need to get drunk with thoughts of getting laid, you call me, and no one else, understand?" When her breath hitched at his boldness, he leaned in, nipped her bottom lip, and then touched it with his tongue to ease the sting. He then released her and watched with satisfaction as she shivered from head to toe from his touch. When he heard one of her brothers clear his throat, he grinned slowly, seductively at Nicola, then winked, tugged her ponytail, turned, and walked out the door, smiling when he heard her whisper, "Hell's Bells."

Eight

My breath caught as I eyed the Highland warlord on his great beast. Perched on an emerald hilltop with mist floating low on the horizon, he looked almost mythical. His Herculean size showed no softening around the middle, nay; he was fit from daily training for a warlord would die on a field of battle if he didn't keep his best weapon, his body, honed and ready. His long dark hair was tied at the nape of his neck, his body covered in his clan's green and gold plaid. God's truth, he looked like Zeus surveying the land from atop Mount Olympus. When his head turned slowly toward me, he looked like Lucifer himself as he began to undress me with his honey-colored eyes. His slow grin told me my maiden's sensibilities were in danger so I picked up the hem of my skirts and started running back down the hill. Aye, I ran all right, but the brute's mighty beast roared to life and he flew down the hill cutting me off as he came to a screeching halt in front of me.

"The next time you feel the need to get drunk with thoughts of getting laid, you call me, and no one else, understand?" the honey-eyed archangel whispered as he reached out his large calloused hand . . .

Waking with a start, I listened as a motorcycle roared down

the street mixing with my fantasy. I could still see warlord Dallas from my dream reaching out to me, so I closed my eyes again to soak in the memory.

It was Monday morning and in a few short hours, I was supposed to meet Dallas for a ride-along to see firsthand how detectives conducted interviews. I was still in shock that he'd shown up like some kind of White Knight saving my brothers from possible prosecution. And when he'd pressed me against the wall and made my head spin with his warm breath and hard body as he made it clear where he stood about wanting me, I couldn't speak. The whole day was like a crazy mixed-up dream starting when that asshole had cornered me in the bathroom.

He'd come up behind me as I washed my hands, rubbing his crotch on my ass while grabbing hold of my boobs. I'd been pissed, not scared, because I knew the girls were in the house with me. I'd also thought I could handle the dickhead. Sadly, I'd been mistaken. He was stronger and more determined than I thought he'd be when I elbowed him in the gut. He'd only grinned at me disdainfully as if my saying "let go" meant nothing. His callous behavior told me I needed help, so I'd screamed bloody murder to bring the girls running since my brothers had left the house.

Luckily, the door hadn't locked when he shut it (another item to add to my growing to-do list for the house) and the girls came busting in about the time I was reaching for a crescent wrench. When they burst in, they'd distracted him long enough for me to whack him across the nose so he'd let go. Cursing had ensued as he grabbed a towel to staunch the flow of blood running down his face, but that didn't stop the girls from attacking. While he was busy warding off the attack of the BFF's, I grabbed my phone and the card Bill

Reed had handed me because I was sure a homicide was about to be committed by one of the girls, but most assuredly one of my brothers when they got back from Lowes.

Why Detective Reed? Well, I'd had just enough alcohol in my system that I wasn't thinking clearly. Therefore, calling Reed instead of 911 made complete sense to me at the time. He was, after all, an expert in all things murder. Of course, unbeknownst to me, Dallas was at his house when I called. While I was talking to Reed, Finn and Bo had arrived home and of course, the ass kicking had commenced. Dallas had shown up ten minutes later gunning his bike as he sprinted up the street, jumping off agilely as he took in the scene.

Lord, it was like watching Sir Lancelot meets Jax Teller the way he rode in on that silver Harley. Then he'd taken control, calmed my brothers, and called me "Babe" forcing every idea I'd had about him being arrogant, and not worth my time, to fly right out the window. In fact, it flew so far out the window it detoured south and was taking an extended vacation in the South of France because I hear the summers there are quite mild.

After taking control, he arrested the creep, marched up my steps, and then pinned me against a wall while I'd tried to remain standing on noodle legs.

All my life I'd waited for a man like him, a man who was strong, protective, and above all a man's man. One who acted like a man not a watered-down version of what the male's species should be like. I knew some women thought it makes our gender weak to rely on a man for anything, that as women we should strive to stand on our own two feet, to live our lives with or without a man. However, I'm of the opinion that it's in our genetic makeup to rely on men, that as women we seek out the strongest, most virile men for a reason. Take for instance my books. My heroes are the biggest bunch of macho men that has ever graced the pages of a book, and my readers beg for bigger, bolder Neanderthals every time I complete one. As women, we're attracted to men that we know will protect us because our DNA is programmed that way. Who among us wants to be the one who gets up when there is a bump in the night? Equal pay and equal rights is one thing, but when it comes to choosing someone who will protect you and your children, do you want Peewee Herman or Conan the Barbarian?

Please, the Barbarian would win by a landslide.

"Oh, my God, what should I wear?" I asked the wall as I contemplated my upcoming day and close quarters with Dallas. I glanced at my clock and knew I had to decide quickly, and then jump in the shower. With no time to spare, I grabbed my cell off my nightstand and called the Fashionista of our sisterhood—Angela.

"Comfy jeans, a tight tee, and leave your hair down so he wants to touch it," she answered like a woman who'd known me half my life and lived inside my head.

"You don't think I should dress professionally?"

"Do you, or do you not, wear sweats when you write and forget to shower for a few days?"

"Well, yeah, I get on a roll—"

"Then *your* professional attire will not give him ideas about the two of you, they'll send him running for the hills," she broke in, then mumbled, "Shit, gotta go. See you at Gypsy's after work. I can't wait to dissect your day."

Okay, rude, but she had a point. Jeans it is then.

One hour later I was scrubbed, buffed, landscaped (precautionary), and ready to drive downtown to the police station. I fed Snape and Simi, who were eyeing me as if they could tell I was strung tight with anticipation, grabbed my notebook, jumped into my beetle and left.

The whole drive I told myself to act naturally, be professional, you're there to watch and learn, not rip his clothes off. Today, he's doing you a favor and nothing more. You're two professionals spending a day together mano a mano or mano a womano. Just play it cool, Nicola, don't read too much into the lip bite, or the wall press.

Yeah, right!

Twenty minutes later, I walked around the corner to the offices led by the receptionist to find Dallas talking on the phone, dressed in tight jeans, a black tee, and his black boots. Upon seeing all that was Dallas, my mouth dried up, my heart started pounding, and all thoughts flew from my brain. When he looked up and saw me walking toward him, he winked, causing me to stop dead in my tracks and gape.

Clearly, his winks were some sort of superpower, because I swear that if he asked me to jump from the roof of a tall building and then winked, I'd jump.

Okay, enough is enough, time to pull on my big girl panties and be a professional. He cannot make me melt like butter if I don't allow it.

So, with a deep breath, I pushed my shoulders back and off I went to walk the remaining ten feet separating us. He watched me cross the distance and the closer I got, the twitchier his mouth became. By the time I was standing in front of him, he was biting his lower lip in an attempt to keep from grinning. I said attempt, once I was standing in front of him, he let go of that lush bottom lip and it pulled into a sexy grin.

Right, apparently I wasn't as successful as I thought showing I was unaffected.

I ducked my head quickly before my eyes glazed over, and became fascinated with the notes I'd taken from my earlier conversation with Bill. Thinking I needed to look serious, I pulled out a pen and underlined words in an attempt to look as if I wasn't affected by the man. While attempting this ridiculous charade, a sheet of paper was pushed into my line of sight and wiggled to capture my attention. I grabbed the sheet without looking up and saw it was an "Exempt from Liability" form. Scribbling my signature, I handed it back just as Dallas hung up his phone.

There was a moment of silence between us as if he was waiting for me to say something, so I raised my eyes to his and that's when the grin pulled into a full-blown smile.

Man, he had a great smile.

My own lips were twitching as I tried to hold back a stupid grin when he finally said, "Hey."

"Hey, yourself," I replied back, but it came out breathy like an asthmatic.

"You ready to get out of here?" he kinda rumbled low in his throat.

"Ready, willing, and able," I answered in return before I realized what I was saying. Which, of course, earned me an even bigger smile and a chuckled to boot.

Hell's bells kill me now!

Still grinning, Dallas opened his desk drawer and pulled out his weapon, shoving it into his shoulder holster. He looked around the room when he was finished and his eyes stopped on a woman with a badge on her hip.

"I'm heading out with Ms. Royse. Tell Reed I'll be back in this afternoon," he called out.

Without warning, he then reached down, grabbed my hand, and started heading for the door.

114

My breath caught when he grabbed my hand, but I acted as if he held it every day. He let go of my hand before entering the elevator and we rode down to the parking garage in silence since there were other people in it with us. Once in the underground garage, he took my hand again and walked us to a standard police issue, black Crown Victoria. I stood back as he opened the door, but when he turned around to let me in the car, he stopped in front of me and looked down.

"Before we leave, I wanna make it clear you're to follow my instructions to the letter today," he dictated. "You're to observe only and if I tell you to stay in the car I expect you to do it, are we clear?"

"I'm not stupid, Dallas. I don't plan on getting in your way. But I'll warn you now, when I conduct research for a book I tend to ask a lot of questions."

"I'll answer your questions if you'll answer mine."

"What kind of questions?"

"We'll get to those questions later; right now I need to get to an interview." Nodding, I got in the car and watched as Dallas rounded the back and climbed in. He ordered, "Buckle up," and watched while I did, then explained where we were going. "Our first stop is in connection with the murder of a young woman. I have to go to her place of employment and interview her boss and coworkers. I'm allowing you to sit in on the interviews under freedom of the press, but everything you see and hear is off the record, understand?"

"I understand. Just so you know, I'm not looking for plot material, just an understanding of how interviews are conducted, you needn't worry I'll repeat anything."

"Needn't worry?" he chuckled.

"What?"

"That's kind of an outdated word."

"I write historical romance for a living," I shrugged, "it slips out. Sometimes antiquated words work better."

Smiling, Dallas turned toward me and his right arm came up and lay across the back of my seat. He seemed to be studying me for some reason. His eyes suddenly softened as he oddly said, "Jesus, you really are Sandra Dee."

"What?"

"You're apple pie and baseball."

"Um, are you saying I'm the-girl-next-door?" I blurted out.

"Sweetheart, if you were any more the-girl-next-door you'd be married with two point five kids. Lucky for me, most men like tits, ass, and attitude."

Looking down at my chest, I supposed it wasn't the first thing men saw when they looked at me, but I asked him to clarify anyway. "Did you just say I don't have tits and ass?"

"No," Dallas grinned, leaning in closer, "I said, lucky me."

"Oh," was my highly intelligent reply as he leaned in further, close enough that if I had a mind to, I could have lean forward and capture his lips with mine. I don't know if he was testing my resolve, but he didn't close the distance as I expected and, if I was truthful, wanted more than my next breath. He just held my eyes as a slow sexy grin pulled across his mouth. As if he read my mind about kissing me, he mumbled, "Jesus, I don't wanna know what you're thinking or we'll never leave this spot." I rolled my lips between my teeth to keep from telling him exactly what I had been thinking (I'd moved from kissing to foreplay) as he leaned back and started the car.

We drove in silence while I got my hormones under control. I didn't trust myself not to open my mouth and ask him to take me home and ravage me until we both were spent. Looking out the window so he couldn't interpret my wicked thoughts, I noticed he'd driven further into downtown instead of away. I expected him to take one of the roads that led to the interstate, but instead, he turned right into the bank parking lot where Angela worked. He parked, but I didn't move when he got out since I wasn't sure if I was supposed to follow. When he rounded the car to open my door, I grabbed my bag, stepping out of the car.

Angela's office faced the parking lot, so she must have seen us get out, because she was waiting in the lobby grinning from ear to ear. Dallas had interviewed all my friends the day before, so he recognized Angela immediately.

"You work here?" he asked.

"I'm the manager. Is there something I can help you with or has she driven you nuts already and you're dropping her off?"

"Not yet," Dallas mumbled with a grin, "but it's early so I'll let you know. Actually, I need to talk to you in private about a case if you have a minute?"

"Oh, intrigue on a Monday morning, sweet. Do either of you want some coffee; I can grab some from—"

"No," Dallas jumped in looking back at me, "no coffee. I'd like to get through one day without wearing it."

Rolling our eyes in unison, Angela chuckled while motioning us down a long hall toward the back of the bank. She entered a boardroom with a large mahogany table set with pens, a pitcher of water, and matching glasses. I could have used a drink of water, but figured Dallas would object so I ignored it and pulled out my notebook. I sat a few chairs away to give them space so wouldn't intrude. I was curious as to what Dallas would say, but I certainly wasn't prepared and neither was Angela for the news, because we both reacted with a gasp.

"I'm sorry to inform you of this, but Melissa Webster was murdered Friday evening."

"What? Are . . . are you serious? Oh, my God," Angela responded as her hands flew to her mouth.

"Friday? After we had lunch with her?" I blurted out.

"You know the victim?" Dallas asked surprised.

"No, I mean, yes, kind of. I met her on Friday. We all ate lunch together at Gypsy's."

"What time did she leave?"

"I don't know it was after I spilled coffee on you and the girls and I had to discuss the book, I'd say we left close to one. But she didn't leave with us, she stayed behind."

"Did she come back from lunch?" Dallas asked Angela.

Shaking her head no, Angela explained about her trip.

"She was going out of town. She took the rest of the day off to pack."

"Did she ever mention having a boyfriend or a man who might be angry with her, someone who'd have an axe to grind?"

"No, no, she wasn't, she wasn't seeing anyone. Her last boyfriend moved to California, but they remained friends. She was a nice person, Dallas. Nobody hated her. I can't believe this," she whispered as her eyes glistened with unshed tears.

Reaching out his hand, Dallas covered hers to give comfort and then in a soft voice he said, "I need you to round up everyone who worked closely with Melissa or anyone you think might know anything about her personal life and send them in one at a time. Can you do that for me?"

Angela was quiet for a moment, nodding in answer to his request. She took a deep breath, looked at me, then stood, and headed out of the room as I sat in utter disbelief. I'd never known someone personally who'd been murdered. It was an odd feeling knowing that we may have been the last people to see her alive.

"I didn't hear anything about this on the news," I muttered, still thinking about the vibrant blonde and her red silk blouse. "When I met her I immediately wanted her in my book. She was going to be the prosecuting attorney, I mean she will be."

"Is that how you come up with characters?" he asked, obviously trying to distract me.

Before I could answer, however, Angela walked back into the room with an older woman, both of them with red eyes. I stood when the woman sat down and headed toward Angela, determined to do something that would help when she left the room without looking back.

"You okay?" Dallas asked me with concern in his voice before I left the room.

"No," I answered truthfully, "can I get a rain check? Angela needs me right now." When he nodded, I went in search of my friend.

I found Angela in her office sitting at her desk with her hands to her forehead. I closed the door, sat down across from her, and waited.

"She was so smart and loved to laugh," Angela finally said when she looked up at me.

I didn't know what to say to her so I just listened.

"She wanted a family, a big one. She said if she could only find the right man she would get pregnant immediately and have a house full of kids."

"Are you sure she wasn't seeing anyone?"

"Yes," Angela replied, "she was still looking."

"Dallas will find who did this, I'm sure of it," I told her, realizing I meant what I'd said and they weren't just words to comfort my friend. I may not know him very well, but something told me he was dedicated to justice and would stop at nothing to find Melissa's killer.

We settled in to wait while Dallas finished interviewing those who worked with Melissa. After an hour of crying that left us both with a headache, he emerged from the closing room and knocked on her door.

"Are you ready to go?" he asked me, but didn't take his eyes off of Angela. Probably using his cop instincts to assess her state of mind.

I turned to Angela to see if she still needed me, but she nodded that she was fine and then reminded me, "Gypsy's after work."

Dallas took my hand and led me back to his car without saying a word. We drove in silence again, but when he headed away from downtown and pulled onto Eleventh Street, I looked at him in confusion. He told me, "Lunch first, then I'll take you back to the station."

A few minutes later, he pulled into El Rancho Grande, a Tex-Mex restaurant owned by an old school friend of mine and I smiled. They had the best margaritas in town and I loved their chicken fajita salad. In the same location since the 1950, the old red brick building still had the original neon sign out front beckoning in its customers.

Since we arrived before the lunch crowd, we were instantly shown to a table near the windows. We ordered quickly then were left alone to stare at each other. For once in my life, I didn't know what to say. I racked my brain, but the only thoughts in my head at that moment I couldn't ask because it was case related. So, of course, I went with the most embarrassing thing imaginable.

"Why did you pin me against the wall yesterday and kiss me on Friday?"

Dallas was chewing on crispy chips they'd placed on the table when I asked, but that didn't stop him from smiling.

Reaching out, he grabbed his water and took a drink, then placed it back on the table. Well out of my reach, I might add.

"To prove a point," he chuckled.

"What point would that be?"

"That when I see something I want, I go after it."

"And you assumed you were so irresistible that I'd swoon on the spot?" I responded, miffed again at his arrogance.

"Sweetheart, I'm a cop. I don't take anything at face value, nor do I assume. I'd been thinkin' about the taste of your lips since the first time you spilled coffee on me. Since an opportunity presented itself, I took it," he answered with a shrug. "As for yesterday, I decided I was done thinkin' about the taste of your lips and was putting you on notice."

I didn't know what to do with all that, but something he said caught my attention more than his thinking he could put me on notice—whatever that meant. And since I clearly liked to embarrass myself, and he was willing to answer, I decided to go for the gusto. Drawing in a deep breath for courage, I leaned forward and asked, "Um, how exactly did I taste?"

I *really* needed to know the answer to this. I've written this scene a hundred times, the one where the hero talks about a woman tasting sweet like honey, and I had to know if it was true.

Dallas' eyes seemed to turn from a rich honey to a darker amber color, and the air around us hummed with energy as he stared back at me. My heart started beating rapidly when he leaned forward, so only I could hear, and whispered, "Like apple pie and sex."

"Really?" I whispered back as my gaze moved to his lips, wondering if he would ever kiss me again.

"Nicola."

"Yeah?" I answered as I thought about nipping his lower

lip, then sucking it into my mouth.

"If you don't stop starin' at my lips I'm gonna haul you out of that chair and kiss you until your legs give out. Then I'll carry you to my car and everyone in this place will know exactly what we're doin'."

"Does that really happen?" I breathed out as my eyes shot to his.

Clearly, something about this guy brought out my inner hussy since the thought of sex in his car wasn't exactly the deterrent he thought it was. I was honestly considering testing the truthfulness of his statement.

"Does what really happen?"

"Being kissed so thoroughly your legs go weak."

"Babe," was his only reply, as if I'd insulted his ability to kiss me senseless.

"Oh, wow." I sighed.

His response . . . "You better fuckin' believe it!"

Nine

Have you ever watched a movie or a TV show where the bad guy got away by running down a crowded street, and the people just watched him run past and they did nothing? In addition, the whole time you thought, "I would so stick my foot out" which would trip the criminal and he'd crash to the ground, giving the cop enough time to nab the bad guy . . .

I used a door.

Picture it . . .

After a delicious lunch, the golden-eyed warlord guided the fair-haired maiden to his car. But not by hand this time. Nay, he'd thrown his arm around her shoulder after her old friend, and owner of the restaurant, came forward for a hello hug. She introduced the warlord to her most handsome friend, who, by the way, was married, and hid a smile when he seemed to grow taller and wider as he shook the man's hand. She'd bit her lip to keep from smiling when a possessive arm was slung across her shoulders, and felt a thrill of excitement at the thought of his jealousy. After the introductions, he guided her to his car, never once removing his arm. It was then she was sure he would kiss her and she was right. He backed her into the door, placing both hands on the roof, boxing her in. She then watched as his eyes grew heavy as he gazed upon her countenance, and mentally shouted at the warlord to kiss her already. Finally, his tongue swept across his lips as he lowered his head, bit, by agonizing bit. Just as his lips brushed gently across her own, and a pleasant warmth rushed to her loins, the crackle of his police radio broke the magical spell. You see, a murder suspect had just been spotted, one that the warlord had been hunting for his dastardly deed. So, they jumped into his car to catch the man.

He lectured the fair-haired maiden the whole way about how she was to remain in the car until help arrived. She, of course, listened, for she wasn't a stupid bubbleheaded Miss. That is until an evil looking man came running down the street with his eyes bugged out like he was running from a ghost. He, of course, was being chased by the warlord who was at least a half a block behind him. So, she reacted. The evil doer was headed straight for her, and naturally, after watching so many criminals get away without intervention on TV, she grabbed the handle of her door and used it to stop him in his tracks. Down he went when his face collided with the window and out she jumped shouting, "You have the right to be a douche bag. Anything you say, can, and will be used against you, 'cause you're a douche bag." This is when the warlord arrived, hauled the stunned bad guy off the ground, cuffed him, and then turned to the fair-haired maiden and breathed fire like the devil himself.

"I told you to stay in the fuckin' car," Dallas roared as he threw the bad guy on the hood of his car.

"He was gonna get away," I defended.

"He was on foot and I was in pursuit. He had nowhere to go and backup was one minute out," he growled.

"Oh . . . Well, carry on then," I replied.

Normally, I don't take kindly to being yelled at, but he was beyond pissed at that moment so I let it go. He was also amused. I could tell that as well. His brow was furrowed in concentration, but every so often, his lips would twitch when he scowled at me. That being said, and considering he was wrestling with a criminal who was kicking out with his legs, trying to break free, I decided to give him one less thing to worry about and got my ass in the car until the cavalry arrived.

Three patrol cars came to a screeching halt with sirens blaring, as if the suspect hadn't already been apprehended by, well, me. I watched Dallas shove him into the back of one, then turn to the three officers smiling. There was a discussion of sorts and several grinned, looking my direction. Eventually, Dallas was surrounded by five more policemen, and I could hear laughing. Not long after, the officer who was driving the suspect downtown turned and saluted me right before he got into his car. I smiled, and waved back, but when I looked toward Dallas, he shook his head and scowled.

Guess he wasn't done being pissed.

Five minutes later, he climbed in the car and off we went back to the station. Dallas drove with his head braced in his left hand that was supported by the door. He kept rubbing his forehead, deep in thought it seemed, then he'd look at me and glared.

I liked him, a lot, but he'd better learn quickly I'm a doer not a watcher. I get involved when something goes wrong and I won't apologize for it. Therefore, instead of apologizing, which I'm sure he was waiting for me to do, I just smiled.

"I don't know whether to kiss you or put you over my knee," he finally replied with a sigh.

Pfft, I knew which one I'd choose.

"I plead the Fifth."

"You can't plead the Fifth Amendment to get out of admitting you should have stayed in the car and not put yourself at risk," Dallas argued.

"You don't know me well enough to know this, but I can't sit idly by and watch stuff happen. It's a flaw in my personality, I like to help."

"That's not a flaw, disobeying an order is a flaw for Christ sake."

Disobeying an order? What am I, a solider?

"Dallas . . . by the way, who named you Dallas, it's an unusual name," I asked in an attempt to change the subject. I didn't want to get off on the wrong foot before we'd even started, but his thinking that he could order me around was making my eye twitch.

"My mother, she's from Dallas," he answered, but his raised eyebrows, and the glint in his eyes, told me he knew what I was doing.

"Is your sister your only sibling?"

Dallas rolled his lips between his teeth to keep from yelling, or laughing, which one, I wasn't sure. He then closed his eyes for a moment and shook his head slowly, as if he were dealing with an errant child. When he opened them, I could tell he was expending effort to keep from yelling by the color of his face (a pale shade of rage).

"Erin is my only sibling," he answered abruptly.

"Are your parents here in town, are you close to them?"

"You know avoiding the topic won't make it go away, Nicola."

"I'm not avoiding it. I admit I didn't listen to your suggestion to stay in the car and took a risk. But what's done is done, Dallas, and I won't apologize for doing what I thought at the time was helping. So let's move on and you can tell me about

126

yourself," I urged.

"All right," Dallas agreed surprisingly, "since you seem to want the long and short of it, here it is. My Mom and Dad retired to Florida about two years ago. Erin and I are close. I went to OU on a football scholarship, but didn't get much game time. I've been on the police force since I was twenty-two. I worked my way up to homicide by the time I was twenty-seven. I was married for three years, but it ended two years ago because I worked too damn much for her liking and she became involved with another man. I don't have any kids, though I'd like two or three, and if you *ever*," his voice became growly at this point and his brows pulled together as his honey-colored eyes burned into mine, "take a risk like that again, I'll put you over my knee. Are we clear?"

I was too stuck on the fact he'd been married to be outraged over the threat of being spanked. I wasn't sure if I was scared or just jealous he had an ex-wife. Therefore, I rushed out in a slightly louder tone, "You were married?" before I could stop myself.

Dallas must have heard the surprise in my voice because he didn't answer immediately. Instead, his body seemed to tighten infinitesimally as the hand that held the steering wheel gripped it tighter, turning his knuckles white.

"Is that a problem for you?" he asked cautiously, keeping his eyes on the road.

"No, why would that be a problem?" I outright lied. I had visions of some supermodel ex-wife, one I could never live up to, dancing around in my head. Why would he think that was a problem? Men can be so dense sometimes.

Dallas turned and looked at me as we sat at a red light, studying my face for a moment. I guess I pulled off the air of "Your ex-wife is no big deal" I'd been attempting to convey because he loosened his hold on the wheel, relaxed back into the seat, then called me on my lie.

"You blurted that out like it pissed you off."

Ok, so maybe *he* wasn't dense.

"What? Why, why would I be pissed off?" I answered truthfully, as I schooled my face. I wasn't pissed; he'd misinterpreted my emotions by a mile, I was scared of being inferior. Not measuring up to what he lost to another man.

"All right, if you aren't pissed then is it a deal breaker?"

It may have been a few years since my last relationship, which ended badly because he couldn't handle that I wrote explicit sex scenes and spent way too many hours trying to recreate them. However, even though I was a novice at relationships, I knew we'd been moving toward this moment all day. What with all the talk about why he'd kissed me and then the almost kiss at El Rancho Grande. Nevertheless, I still wasn't sure if Dallas had been flirting, was interested in a possible relationship, or just wanted a wham-bam-thank-you-ma'am. Therefore, I wanted to know what kind of deal he was talking about before answering.

"A deal breaker for what, exactly?"

"A deal breaker that says six months or a year down the road you decide you don't want to be with a man who has an ex-wife. An ex-wife that I never talk to because she remarried over a year ago, thank Christ. An ex-wife that I was too young at the time to see was selfish when I married her or I'd never have put my ring on her finger. An ex-wife, I didn't miss all the fuckin' much when she left."

He'd pulled into the underground parking lot while he explained more than thoroughly that his ex-wife had no hold over him, and we were now sitting next to my Beetle as he finished. "An ex-wife that pales in comparison to the woman who spilled coffee on me, shoved her ass in my face, and took out a criminal because she wanted to help rather than worryin' about breakin' her fuckin' nails. I have no doubt you've got friends that deal with exes fuckin' up their lives, but that's not the case with me. She left, I let her, and we don't talk. Ever."

Well, then . . .

"First off, I didn't shove my ass in your face, and secondly, I don't judge a person for having been married. I was just surprised and admittedly a tad jealous that you'd been in love once, not to mention the whole "she's probably a supermodel that I can't live up to" insecurity rolling around in my head. That being said, even if you did have to deal with her daily I think after growing up with the twins I'd be up for the challenge. If, like you said, in six months or a year we're still seeing each other, of course." Then I added, "You should probably know that I've never been married, and what few relationships I've had have been short-lived. Not because I'm afraid of commitment, it's because the men weren't men, they were . . . Well, I don't know what they were, eunuchs I'm guessing."

Dallas was smiling at this point which I thought was a good sign, then he made me flat out swoon when he said, "I already knew you hadn't been married since there's no way a real man would let someone like you go."

Oh, man. Is it too early to say I love you? Yes? How about shagging him in the car?

"Would it be alright if I ripped off your clothes?" I breathed out, obviously not thinking about what I was saying or caring in the least.

"Cameras," was all he replied.

"What?"

"There are cameras in the garage," he explained in a deep, hoarse voice.

I looked up and saw the big black glob pointed right at us and I sighed. Good Lord, two seconds longer and I would have been on YouTube under the heading, "Author does research in a parking garage."

"Nicola, I need you to get out of the car," Dallas growled. When I looked back at him, I noted his eyes were glowing with intensity, the honey color was a deeper shade of amber, and he was breathing deeply through his nose. Seeing that intensity told me I better get out of the car like he had asked or my ass *would* end up on YouTube. So out I got. Quickly, I might add.

Fumbling with my purse to keep from looking at Dallas, I moved to the driver's side door of my car and unlocked it. Before I could open it, however, I was swung around and backed into the door. I had about a millisecond to recover before a warm mouth was on mine, and the gasp I'd let out in surprise allowed his tongue to invade my mouth without hindrance.

I was finally receiving the kiss I'd imagined all day . . . and then some.

This kiss wasn't a branding kiss, it was somewhere between, "Yes, I'll bear all your children" and "Are you happy to see me or is there something in your pocket."

When his arm wound around my back, hauling me firmer into his body, I dropped my purse, hooked his neck with my arms, and flattened myself against his chest as he leaned me back against my car. After more than a yearlong drought with no men in my life, and considering he wasn't just a man, but an honest to goodness man's man, I lit up like a tree in a forest fire.

There's something magical about a first kiss. The way the air seemed to buzz around you like Jacob's ladder electrifying your atoms. The rhythms of your mouths as you drink in their taste. The feel of their lips gently moving across yours, teasing at first, and then deepening as your bodies react to the pheromones you each put off. The push and pull, the groping and moaning as you discover each other and learn what they like or dislike. Dallas liked control, which was apparent in the way he kissed, the way he held me, and the way he wanted my mouth to submit to his.

I was a romantic at heart, but I was also my own woman, one who'd put words on a page one summer and never looked back, determined to be a writer. I took care of myself, managed most of my business myself, and didn't rely on anyone for anything. I guess you could say I liked control too. But there was something so completely satisfying about giving control over to someone else, to allow them to take the lead, and in this situation, I was more than willing to bend to his wishes and let him lead me where he wanted. And where Dallas wanted me, was trapped against my car.

All thoughts about cameras flew from my mind as I moaned deep in my throat when his hand rode up my side, stopping just below the curve of my breast. His thumb swiped not once, but three times against my nipple, igniting me further, until I couldn't help but rub myself against his leg I was now straddling. His hand moved from my breast to my ass when he felt me move against his leg, pulling me further into his body, grinding me slightly against his thigh. When I whimpered, because it felt so damn good, he ripped his mouth from mine on a growl of frustration as I panted like a prized racehorse after the Kentucky Derby.

"Jesus, if you kiss like that with your clothes on, I'm gonna retire now and keep you in bed for the rest of my life," Dallas groaned as he pressed his forehead to mine, catching his own breath. He moved to my neck next and placed tongue touches precisely where I'd feel them most as I tried to calm down, his hands still moving over my body.

"Does that mean you'll call me sometime for dinner or was that a "see you around" kiss?" I replied with a gasp when he nipped my ear.

"I see you have a sense of humor to go with your brains," he whispered in my ear.

"You have to with brothers like Bo and Finn."

Dallas chuckled since he'd met my brothers, then he pulled his head from my neck and kissed me sweetly one last time. When he was done, he moved back, pulled me away from my car, and opened the door for me. I climbed in on weak legs as he bent down and handed me my purse. When I looked up at him, he chuckled and tugged my hair.

"You'd better straighten your hair and clothes before you go anywhere."

I looked in the mirror after that remark and saw to my horror that my hair looked precisely like someone had buried their hands in it while making love to my mouth, as if I'd been well and truly kissed.

"Guess I won't be stopping to speak with Father O'Callaghan," I laughed as I tried to smooth down my hair.

"Probably not a good idea," Dallas agreed as he leaned into my car and kissed me one last time for good measure. Complete with a lip nip and tongue touch.

It was the best goodbye kiss I'd ever had.

Dallas watched as I started my car and pulled out. He raised his chin in the unofficial man's man acknowledgement as I waved goodbye. I watched Dallas from my rearview mirror as I drove through the parking garage. He stood there a moment watching me leave then turned on his heels and headed for the elevator. All I could think as I watched his muscular frame walk away was that I had to revise my character's personality for my hero in "Property Of." I was way off. Instead of sensitive and caring, he needed to be dark and brooding with a bossy side. Oh, and he had to smell sinful like soap, musk, and sex.

***

The girls all arrived at Gypsy's within ten minutes of one another, and we'd all gathered in a quiet corner to discuss Melissa's death, and give our support to Angela.

Shock was the prevailing emotion in our group as we thought about the vibrant woman with the red silk blouse. For Melissa's life to end that way, made the loss even harder for Angela. Death had a way of silencing you like nothing else can. It leaves you morose, stealing the joy from your life, and replacing it with dark thoughts of "What if."

What if she had worked the whole day, would that have stopped someone from breaking into her house and killing her? Or, was she targeted by some unknown maniac, who wouldn't have stopped until he'd ended her life? One could drive themselves crazy thinking about the "What ifs." However, as with all experiences in life, it too served a purpose. To help you process the loss.

"I've never known someone who was murdered," Angela told no one in particular.

"Did Dallas say how she died?" Kasey asked.

Shaking my head no, I explained. "He can't discuss the specifics of the case, only what is public information."

As if on cue, the TV that sat up front on the counter broke into our thoughts as the anchor recounted the top stories of the day. "*Tulsa police don't suspect at this time that the brutal death of a Tulsa woman is connected to the string of murders that have been dubbed "The Shallow Grave Murders." Melissa Webster was found Saturday evening when she failed to arrive for a weekend with friend's out–of–state. Police reported that Webster was repeatedly stabbed in her home sometime Friday afternoon after leaving work. This is the seventh homicide this year in Tulsa, which is down from the same time last year. At this time, Tulsa police have no motive or suspects and are asking anyone with information to call the crime stoppers tip line.*"

No one said a word after hearing the gruesome details. Kasey and I, who were sitting closer to Angela, grabbed her hands and held on as she took deep, shuddering breaths to gain control.

"Jesus," she whispered, blinking back tears.

Kristina looked lost as to what to say, so she went with humor to break the tension in the room.

"So, Nicola, did you play tonsil hockey with triple D, or what?"

Angela burst out laughing, seemingly grateful for something to focus on besides her friend's murder, and threatened, "I'll divorce her if she didn't."

"I did, you'd have been impressed," I joked, going with the change of topic for my friend. "I even rubbed myself on him like a common hussy. Are you proud?"

"Aww, Nicola's all grown up," she laughed while wiping tears from her face.

"Well, don't leave us hanging for God's sake, tell us what happened, and leave nothing out," Janeane ordered.

Leaving nothing out, as Janeane put it, I told them about the rest of the afternoon. They'd hooted about the criminal I took down and sighed when I told them Dallas had called himself lucky. They were impressed with my make out session in the garage, but couldn't agree when it came to how to handle Dallas as the relationship progressed. Angela urged me to jump him, Kasey said to take it slow, Janeane asked me why I had to tie myself down to one man, and Kristina tried to explain that if I showed too much enthusiasm he'd back off and keep me guessing.

"Listen to me," Kristina continued, "men are like that. If they know you're hot for them they'll take their time calling just to make you sweat."

"Kristina, he doesn't seem like the type to play games though," I argued.

"Does he like control?" she asked.

"He's a man that goes without saying" Kasey scoffed.

"Hold on a minute. How would you know, Kris? You've been married for eight years," I reminded her. "Dallas isn't some college boy with overactive hormones."

"That's how Dave hooked me in," she explained. "I told him, "Call, don't call, what do I care?" So he left me hanging because he could see right through the lie. By the time he did call, I pounced on him, so his plan worked."

"Wait, if you told him, "call, don't call," then how did he know you were interested?"

"Um, it may have been the text messages I sent him," she laughed.

"So you're saying he didn't call you, because you were too busy texting him, he didn't need too?"

"Exactly, see how they work?"

Oh, I got it. I got it so much I decided just to smile and do my own thing. Dallas seemed to like that I was honest about what I felt, and he didn't run screaming from the car when I told him I might have been a tad jealous of his ex-wife. I was positive he wouldn't play games, which, by the way, is a trait of a real man.

While the girls continued to argue about what not to do were Dallas was concerned, the alarm on my phone went off and I pulled it out. I'd set an event reminder for this evening and gasped when I looked at it. With everything that had happened since Saturday, I'd completely forgotten that I agreed to meet Tom Sheldon, the man I'd chatted with Saturday night on POF, for a drink at Rusty Crane; a bar and grill that was only three blocks up from Gypsy's.

Hell's bells.

"Why are you frowning?" Angela asked.

"I, um."

"What's on your phone?" Kasey inquired.

Oh, lord. How do I explain this without pissing them off?

"I, uh, I made a date for tonight at Rusty Crane and my phone is reminding me."

"Why didn't you tell us? Here we are advising you on how to play it cool until Dallas calls and you already have a date?" Kristina replied.

"It's with someone else," I explained, then watched as four eyes widened and then narrowed because they couldn't believe I hadn't confided in them before now.

Lord, I was in a mess of my own making!

"Ok, here's the deal—"I got out, but Toni Roseneau, Kasey's yoga master, interrupted when she walked up and sat down.

"So this is where the infamous book plotting takes place, huh?" Toni replied. "I want to hear all the gory details about this Dark Prince freak Kasey mentioned this morning."

Saved by the nosey yoga instructor!

"I'll let the girls tell you all about it, Toni, I have to run. Talk to you later, ladies," I threw out as I jumped up and got the hell out of dodge.

I couldn't cancel this late with Tom and I knew it, so when Toni walked up, I saw my opportunity to make a run for it and took it. I was still lying by omission, but I didn't have time to explain, apologize profusely, and make it on time. I had ten minutes to make it to Rusty Crane, of which I need three, and if I walked slowly, I could kill five of them. Being early was more appealing than having my lifelong friends hang, drawn, and quarter me. I'd just have to tell them the truth tomorrow when we meet back at Gypsy's, and hope they would forgive me.

Shouts of "Hey, Nic, what gives?" echoed in my head as I walked slowly toward Rusty Crane. Lord, not only am I the world's worst friend by ignoring my oath, but a part of me felt like I was cheating on Dallas for showing up for this date. Not that we were dating officially, but I'd be a simple minded fool not to believe that wasn't exactly where it was headed based on what he'd said, did, and how he kissed me today.

"Tangled web, Nicola," I repeated my mother's age-old saying as I rounded the corner heading for The Rusty Crane. "And, oh so true, mother," I agreed.

Ten

Dallas finished filling out the report on Jerome Warner the man Nicola had captured single-handedly. On the run from authorities for the past six months, desperation had led him to a pawnshop. He'd acquired several aliases over the years and was stupid enough to use one when pawning a gun. To Dallas' way of thinking, most criminals were stupid as hell, so this hadn't surprised him. Most law-abiding citizens knew a gun dealer had to get your information in case the gun being pawned was reported stolen or used when committing a crime. When the owner had entered his alias information into the system, which they'd tagged, and bingo, they had him.

The kid had gotten lucky he'd taken a chance that Dallas wouldn't shoot an unarmed man when he'd entered the pawnshop with his gun drawn. He'd rushed Dallas and they'd struggled, but the kid had gotten free when a customer came in. Dallas had let go to make sure he wasn't being attacked from behind and that's when Warner made a break for it. He'd then made the mistake of running past Dallas' unmarked car with Nicola inside, and in a move worthy of a Hollywood comedy; she'd taken him out with the car door. Every time he thought about how she'd opened that door and jumped out calling him a "douche bag" he wanted to roar with laughter.

The only thing that kept him from laughing through the whole arrest was the need to get it through her head that brave or not, she was nuts for attempting it.

Jesus, that woman could piss him off and turn him on quicker than any other woman he'd met. The sounds of her moans as he ground her crotch on his thigh were still tumbling through his brain as he filed Warner's arrest report.

History told him to go slow with this woman, but hell if he could get on board with that. He wanted her, planned to have her, and wasn't gonna dance around it either. Once he made up his mind that he wanted something that was it. Be it criminal or woman, he always got his man or in this case woman.

Reaching for the Shallow Grave file so he could comb through it as he'd done for the past sixteen months, he scowled when he realized it wasn't his case anymore. Leaning back in his chair to see if Agent Parker was still in the office he'd sequestered, he watched as the agent left. Dallas was tempted to march into his office and see if he could find out what was really going on. Something about Parker's explanation didn't hold water. About to rise and take a chance on being caught, probably breaking all kinds of federal laws that would land him in jail in the process, his attention was diverted when a book landed on his desk. When he looked up, he found his partner smiling.

"What?"

"Your Ms. Royse has a dirty mind."

Dallas' brows shot up his forehead in surprise. "You wanna explain?"

"My sweet June gave me that last night," Reed told him as he pointed to the book on Dallas' desk. "Your Ms. Royse writes about Scottish Highlanders. June went out yesterday and bought that book. She said it's so good she wants me to speak with a Scottish accent and wear a kilt for fuck's sake. I ain't got the knees for a kilt, or the gut now that I think about it. Though the idea of the boys hanging free has an appeal I'll admit."

Nothing that came out of his partner's mouth *ever* surprised Dallas, and this time was no exception. Chuckling, Dallas picked up the book and read the back description. Thumbing through the pages, he found several dog-eared. While he read the marked passages, Dallas felt his dick twitch. "Jesus, that leaves nothing to the imagination."

"Turn to page two forty-five."

Out of sheer curiosity, Dallas turned the pages until he found what Reed had marked. His dick didn't twitch this time he was at half-staff after two lines so he shut the book. Christ, he hadn't had a reaction like that since he was a kid looking through his friend's playboy magazines. It was all he could do to keep from standing up and heading for his bike, destination, Swan Lake Drive and a certain Craftsman home.

Dallas wondered how long she'd been writing these sorts of books. How long she'd buried these desires while she waited for someone to unlock them. Grabbing his mouse, he logged on to the internet and typed in Grace Martin, author. A list of websites for her books pulled up, along with a Wikipedia page showing her age, education, and publisher. Then his eyes caught sight of a familiar website in the search engine. A link for a Grace Martin on Plenty of Fish stared back at him so he clicked it and froze when Nicola's face filled his screen. After the kiss, they shared, and the way she'd lit up for him, the thought that other men were contacting her caused his jaw to tick, and his trigger finger to itch.

From the time they had been investigating the Shallow

Grave Killer, they'd only had limited access to the online dating websites. They could view profiles and see how long a person had been a member, but they couldn't get into their messages without a court order

At least not legally.

Dallas followed the law when it came to evidence. Though sometimes to get ahead of the criminals, he employed people to find information that otherwise couldn't be obtained. This information never saw the light of day, of course, but if a secret message passed between lovers pointed him in the right direction, he slept at night knowing he skirted the law just a hair.

Picking up his cell, Dallas punched in a number he knew by heart. He'd come to an agreement with a local computer hacker to dig for information in places he couldn't legally go. His hacker, Greg Powers, worked free of charge in exchange for Dallas' expertise in law enforcement, a swapping of skills if you will.

When Powers answered, he was direct and to the point. "I need to know if a Grace Martin on Plenty of Fish, occupation, writer, who lives in Tulsa, is messaging with anyone. Her account says she created it on Thursday, March nineteenth."

Dallas waited for a reply, then answered, "Right, when you get the information fax me what you pull up," and then he hung up.

"Oh, Jesus, she's on the dating sites?" Reed asked. He was aware of Dallas' hacker and kept a close eye on Dallas to make sure any information he garnered didn't compromise any case they were working. He knew Dallas had a tendency toward winning at any cost and most of the time turned a blind eye to his activities.

"Not for long," Dallas answered as he stared at his fax and

waited. He didn't care if his actions were intrusive. He wanted to know who, if anyone, he was up against.

***

Murphy's Law clearly states that, "Anything that can go wrong, will." Truer words were never quoted. You know how you think you've gotten away with something even though you really ought to have known better?

Picture it . . . oh, screw it; it was too humiliatingly infuriating with a huge dose of "I suck as a friend" to break down into a romantic fairy tale.

So here's the long and short of it. I trudged around the corner and up the street to Rusty Crane, a fun little bar and grill that specialized in outdoor dining. Thomas Sheldon, I found out, was *not* Thomas Sheldon at all, but a sexy FBI agent by the name of Dane Parker. Color me surprised when he pulled out his badge and began explaining that he was on a special task force hunting the notorious Harvest Killer and they wanted my help. Now, I've explained before that I'm a doer not a watcher, so that being said, I was all ears and ready to do my part after he explained.

Agent Parker informed me that the Harvest Killer was some sort of computer expert and that our own Shallow Grave Killer, who they suspected might be one and the same, was most assuredly stalking his victims on a dating sites. When you considered the fact, I was about to write a book on the exact same subject, you can image my writer's brain stood up and took notice.

Agent Parker, who had gorgeous green eyes and light brown hair and who appeared to be older than I was by a few years, continued to explain that they'd had great success in the past tripping up predators who stalked victims online. Unfortunately, they were never successful with hackers because they knew they were being hunted. They were suspicious of anyone online and because of their skills knew how to ferret out the truth. This was where I came into play.

I was a real person, someone the hacker slash killer could verify. My pictures were out there on my book covers so there was no reason for the Shallow Grave Killer slash possibly the Harvest Killer to suspect me of working for the police. Agent Parker explained that they wanted, with my permission, to tweak my profiles on POF and SSD to attract the killer, and then they would monitor my conversations to see if he took the bait. They had a psychologist on staff who would analyze the men's responses to my FBI issued questions, then determine if any of them fit their profile.

Coupled with the eerily coincidental fact, I was going to write a book about an online killer, and my almost obsessive need to help when I could, I hadn't hesitated to answer, "Yes, of course, I'll help."

"You know when our computer expert happened upon your profiles almost immediately after you signed up on both sites, I had a feeling it was providence," Agent Parker smiled.

"I have to tell you something though. I was online looking for research for a book I'm writing, as you well know, but what you don't know is that the book is about a serial killer who finds his victims online."

"Life imitates art," Parker replied, "but you understand you won't be able to use any of the information gained during this investigation in your book. Any information that passes between you and those who respond, once you agree, will be considered evidence obtained during a criminal investigation. You'll have to sign a waiver to that effect before we continue."

"I'll agree to that if you'll allow me to write my book loosely based on what happens during the course of the investigation. The names would be changed and the location would be different and any conversations I may see, of course, would be altered so they aren't the same."

"So we're talking about fiction, not non-fiction?"

"Exactly, I wouldn't compromise your investigation, I'd just use creative license with the facts. I'd even agree to let your own legal department read the book before it's published."

Agent Parker sat back in his chair and grinned. I, of course, had noticed what a good-looking man he was but when he smiled like that, he was downright sexy. He wasn't as dark and brooding as Dallas was, though it may be the standard issue black suit he was wearing that made him seem more civilized. Either way he was eye candy, and I made a mental note to create a character for him in my book.

"I'm curious about something," I asked as I sized up Special Agent Parker. "Why didn't you just confiscate my profile and have one of your own agents message the men?"

"That's easy enough to answer. In the past, when we've used agents to draw out an UNSUB, they've been tripped up answering personal questions, such as "What's it like to be a writer. The predators aren't idiots and know when the answers don't ring true. They disappear before we can get a lock on them. By using *you* to answer their personal questions it assures us the best possible chance of catching this guy."

Leaning forward so our conversation wouldn't be overheard, Parker leaned forward as well, until we were only a few scant inches apart. When I opened my mouth to ask him exactly how this would work, I heard a motorcycle pull up at the curb out front of Rusty Crane. Rusty Crane's patio area ran the length of the building and wrapped around the side. We were sitting on the side and could see the street. Glancing to my right, I watched dumbstruck as Dallas got off of his bike and leaned back against it as if he was waiting for someone. When I uttered, "Shit," Agent Parker turned his head and froze.

"Is he a friend of yours?"

"Um, you could say that."

We were far enough away that he might not recognize me, if he wasn't looking for me. However, I had a sneaking suspicion that he was. *Damn, he must have run into one of the girls.*

Agent Parker muttered, "Fuck," then stood suddenly and took my hand drawing me from my seat. *Right you are Agent Parker. Let's go inside the restaurant where I can hide.*

However, he had other ideas.

This is where Murphy's Law came into effect.

See, what I didn't know was that he knew Dallas and they'd already gone head to head in some kind of macho man pissing contest (the rules known only by macho men and baboons). That being said, Parker decided not only to drag me down to the street where Dallas stood, but he wouldn't let go of my hand while he did it. Which confused me to no end until they spoke.

Dallas was leaning against his bike, arms crossed on his chest, legs crossed at the ankles, giving off the appearance of someone who was laid back, relaxed. However, he was anything but if the jaw muscle he was working was an indicator. He stood from the bike when we got within five feet of him and thankfully, Parker let go of my hand. As soon as I got within touching distance, Dallas' right hand shot out and

145

grabbed me at the elbow, drawing me away from Parker and to his side. Parker watched this maneuver with a grin, then replied, "I see we have the same taste in women, Vaughn."

Um, What?

"You've got one minute to explain," Dallas fumed as he curled me into his side, which was all-kinds of nice, but I was too busy thinking 'what the hell' to enjoy it.

I looked back and forth between the two and saw one angry badass Detective and one grinning FBI agent who seemed to be enjoying himself.

What on earth was going on?

"Just setting a trap with the help of Ms. Grace, is that a problem?"

"Say that again?" Dallas bit out as he tensed and the arm around my shoulders grew tighter.

"The FBI has asked Ms. Grace to help catch the Harvest Killer," Parker explained.

I looked up at Dallas when I heard a swift intake of breath right before he fumed, "Are you nuts? No way in hell will I let you set her up as a target for some psychopath."

Whoa, whoa, whoa, hold the damn phone.

"Now wait just a damn minute," I jumped in, stepping away from him, "you can't tell me what I can or can't do. I've already given my word I'll help."

"Babe, I'm not about to let you set yourself up as bait just so I can dig you out of a fuckin' grave," he growled.

"That won't happen 'cause I'll never meet the guy."

"We don't have a fuckin' clue how this guy is gettin' at his victims. If you tweak his interest, and I promise, someone like you will tweak his interest pretty fuckin' fast, he won't stop until he has you."

"Dallas this guy needs to be stopped I'm sure the FBI can

protect me."

Dallas' face flushed a scary shade of rage this time and I took a step back since he seemed ready to explode. Enraged or not, I was going to stand my ground. I wasn't about to let him intimidate me when we hadn't even been on one date (which every girl knows has to happen before a man can claim any type right to tell her what to do, and vice a versa). Suddenly, I heard the girls call out from across the street, so I turned and moved toward them, more than happy to distance myself from the anger rolling off Dallas in waves. As I approached my friends I heard Dallas seethe, "You don't use civilians to catch a killer. What the fuck are you thinkin?" to which Parker responded, "The FBI has in the past with great success, I might add. We need Ms. Grace—"

"Her name is Nicola Royse," Dallas interrupted on a hiss, "and no fuckin' way is this happening. You got control of my case, but you aren't putting my woman at risk."

His woman?

"What's going on?" Angela asked. Her eyes were as wide as mine were when Dallas got in Parker's face.

"That's Agent Parker with the FBI, my date. Apparently he and Dallas know each other and from the sounds of it, the FBI has taken over one of his cases."

All four women's eyes glazed over when Parker got in Dallas' face and replied, "The FBI isn't in the habit of putting civilians in harm's way. Nicola's my responsibility now as agent in charge, and there is no way I'm gonna let anything happen to her. I'll be with her the whole time."

Five sets of lungs sucked in a breath when he finished. I looked between the two men wondering what in the hell was going on. Parker wasn't flirting with me when we spoke earlier, and now it seemed like he was insinuating an interest

147

in me just to push Dallas' buttons.

"Are you telling me you kissed Dallas this afternoon and this evening you were out on a date with that government issued hotness?" Kristina breathed out on a sigh.

"Um, yeah, but it's not like you think."

Hearing that, Angela grabbed me around the neck, hugged me to her bosom, and smothered me for a moment. When she released me, she exclaimed, "I couldn't be prouder if you were my own daughter."

She shoved a Gypsy's to-go cup in my hand then and pointed at the two macho men, and said, "Here, choose your favorite and then throw coffee on him to announce the victor."

"I'm not throwing coffee on either one of them," I griped. "Dallas just told Agent Parker he wouldn't "allow" me to help with the investigation. He's acting like he's my father and I'm some sixteen-year-old kid who can't think for herself. Then he called me his "woman" for God's sake, can you believe that? Like I was a piece of property! If that's his idea of a relationship, dictating instead of coming to a mutual agreement, then I'm not interested."

"He sounds like a typical alpha male to me. It's their way you know, they beat their chest, call you their woman, and then drag you off by your hair," Kristina explained.

"Wait a minute. How the hell did you get mixed-up with the FBI?" Angela asked as she looked between the two men.

Hell's bells.

"Nicola?"

"So you think I should pick Dallas right? I mean Agent Parker is hot and all but he's no dark hero slash warlord slash—"

"Oh, my God . . . This has something to do with the book, doesn't it?" Kristina jumped in. "You worked on the book without us, didn't you?"

Hanging my head in shame for a moment, I looked up at their faces and cringed. All four of them were scowling at me.

"I can explain," I rushed out as they all glared at me.

"You promised," Angela snapped. "After all this time, we were finally being included in your life and you couldn't go a week without leaving us behind."

"Angela—"

"Save it Nicola, your word means nothing," Janeane retorted. Janeane had the worst temper of our group and could hold a nasty grudge, if you pushed her too far. It was obvious I'd done that when she turned on her heels and started walking down the street.

My eyes grew wide as I watched each of them turn and follow her, none of them looking back at me once they'd left. I was only now realizing what it meant to them that I'd broken my oath. *God, I'm an idiot.* Once again, I'd let my thirst for writing overshadow my better judgment. My only thoughts had been that I get what I needed for my book and damn the consequences.

I stood there and watched until they had rounded the corner heading back to their cars parked at Gypsy's. When I turned back around, Dallas was watching me. Agent Parker seemed to be watching the two of us, analyzing our interaction for some reason, but I blocked him out while I took in Dallas. I studied him for a moment and saw the man I'd been waiting for all my life. Now that he seemed within my grasp, I hesitated. When I took a step away from him, he came at me, wrapped his hand around my neck, his arm around my waist, and pulled me in swiftly for a kiss. I pushed against his shoulders for a moment then melted into him. I realized it was another claiming kiss, but gentler this time, meant to weaken my defenses. When he was done, he ripped his mouth from mine and stated boldly, "I told you Saturday that you won't be able to stop me. This is happening so get over your snit. I'm not gonna apologize for caring that you're being used as bait for a killer."

I was too upset about what I had done to the girls to deal with his arrogant, bossy attitude. Needing time to think, I stepped back, looked at Parker for a moment, then turned and kept right on going until I'd also rounded the corner to Gypsy's and my car. I didn't know how I was going to make it up to the girls, but I would die trying if I had too. I'm the one who broke this and I had to fix it somehow.

So, boys and girls, the moral of this tale is quite simple. You're only as good as your word, don't lie to those you love or anyone, for that matter, and once you've picked yourself up off the ground, after realizing you're a subhuman devoid of any redeemable qualities, learn to grovel.

***

I knew better than to approach the girls before the morning so I sent a group text that simply read, "I'm so sorry." I'll admit I kept checking my phone most of the night to see if one would respond but I knew they wouldn't. As for Dallas, I didn't have a clue what to do about him. I was attracted to him more than any man I'd ever met, but I wasn't sure I could handle his overbearing personality. Since I couldn't talk to the girls about it, I sat at home with Snape and Simi and had a big glass of wine while I berated myself for my stupidity.

Bo called during the evening and I'd cried on the phone when I explained what I'd done to the girls and how Dallas seemed to want to order me around (leaving out that the FBI wanted my help since I wasn't stupid). He, of course, was no substitute for my friends because his response was, "Women," and "Do you want me to kick his ass?" I obviously didn't want him to do that, nor did I remind him that Dallas would probably wipe the floor with him, so I distracted him with what happened with the criminal and how I took him down.

Before we hung up, my ape of a brother pointed out something that I'd seen myself about Dallas, but I was amazed that he picked up on it.

"You know I'm surprised you have a problem with Dallas, Nic. Ever since you were a little girl you've wanted the type of man who would act just like one of your heroes. Dallas is just being a normal man when he orders you around. That's how we are, we're programmed to lead. It doesn't mean we think women are inferior, we just instinctively want to protect you that's all."

"So you're saying you order women around because you must?"

"Exactly, and women should listen to us because they must."

"God, give me strength to keep from murdering my brother . . ."

"God won't help, Nic, he's a man. He knows I'm right," he laughed.

Do you see what I have to put up with?

After we hung up, I checked my phone one last time for return texts from any of the girls. There were none so I climbed into bed and cried my miserable, selfish self to sleep. Now it was six a.m. and the still dark sky fit my mood. I'd spent most of the night tossing and turning so, I was wide-awake stewing about how I could set things to rights.

Kasey would be the easiest to reach and since her job was running the yoga studio, she would have more time to talk in between morning sessions. Ready to grovel, I fell out of bed and started my day. I'd take a class with Kasey and when she was done, I'd explain what an idiot I'd been and beg her to accept my apology. After that, I'd head to the bank and talk to Angela and so on 'until I'd at least apologized in person to all of them.

Then there was Dallas.

Considering the way I'd walked away from him the night before, it was possible that I'd already severed any budding feelings the man may have had. I figured I could buy him a coffee and try to explain that I just wasn't the type of woman he could order around and hope he understood and would agree to curb his bossiness. As for Agent Parker and his obvious attempt to goad Dallas into a fight, I had a few questions for him as well before I agreed to let the FBI use my account.

Hopeful that I could pull all this off I changed into a yoga outfit, fed Snape and Simi, then headed out to find Kasey. I arrived twenty minutes before her first class started and was happy to see a light was on. I didn't see her car, but she parked in the back at times, I got out and tried the door. It was unlocked, so I entered the lobby calling out her name. When she didn't answer, I walked around the corner, knocked on her office door, and waited.

Nothing.

It occurred to me she might have earbuds in, listening to music; I grabbed the handle and turned the knob. Kasey's door opened in and in order to see her desk you had to walk through the door and then close it. So I pushed open the door, walked through it, opened my mouth to shout at her,

152

but my voice caught on 'Kasey' and I screamed.

Eleven

Screaming was one of the last things I remembered before passing out. That, and crimson streaks across every surface, lifeless eyes staring back at me, and the sight of internal organs that should never see the light of day. It was too much at once and my mind shut down in terror at the scene in front of me. I gulped air, trying to catch my breath as the room spun. I fell to my knees in a puddle of blood, my legs unable to bear my weight. Lifting my hands, I saw they were dripping with blood; I wiped them on my shirt trying to get it off. I tried to crawl toward the foyer for help just before the lights went out, but I never made it. I laid face down in a pool of blood when Kasey found me.

***

Consciousness came back bit by bit when I heard a familiar voice shriek my name. My eyes fluttered open slowly as the same voice, one I'd known for half my life, screamed, "Send an ambulance, I need an ambulance at Om-Klahoma Yoga studio at 303 North Martin Luther King Jr. Boulevard. One of my employees is dead and my friend, Nicola Royse, has been stabbed. Oh God, I think she's dead, just like Toni," Kasey

154

cried out, her breathing irregular as she panted for air. "Oh, Jesus, Nicola please don't die . . . Oh God, I think, I think I'm gonna, I think I'm gonna pass out, there's so much—"

My muddled brain registered Kasey's body landing with a thud, but I continued to lay there trying to regain my bearings. I heard the sound of sirens in the distance and told myself that was good, help was coming, Dallas would be here soon, and he'd know what to do.

The sound of screeching tires told me help had arrived. I rolled over and tried to sit up. When a firm but soothing voice ordered, "Don't move, ma'am, help is on the way," I shook my head to explain I wasn't hurt. "Please get my friend and me out of this room."

"We have to wait for the ambulance, you have to be checked out," he argued.

"I'm not hurt," I wailed. I could feel Toni's blood seeping into my clothes and I started to shake.

Then I heard him, Dallas had arrived. He barked out "Where the fuck is she?" and my tears fell harder. One minute a nice officer with concern in his eyes was hovering over me and the next Dallas was in my face, panic etched in his honey-colored eyes.

"Nicola? . . . Where the fuck is the ambulance?" he roared as he scanned my blood-covered body.

"I'm not hurt, it's, it's not my blood," I cried out, "Please, help me up I don't want to be in here."

Dallas scanned my body once more, then nodded; convinced I was telling the truth. Without concern for his own clothes, he picked me up from the floor, held me close in his arms as I buried my head in his neck, and bawled for all I was worth.

He mumbled, "I've got you, baby, you're safe," before

ordering someone to help Kasey to her feet and get her out of the crime scene. Dallas felt like safety, protection from the world at large. I tightened my hold around his neck and drank in his scent as I tried to block out what I'd seen.

I heard the sound of a door swinging open and looked up to see he'd taken me into the ladies locker room. When he sat down on a bench and tightened his arms around me, I finally took a deep breath.

"Jesus, Nicola, I thought you were dead. When I heard the call over the police ban—" he paused mid-sentence; his control seemed to slip now that we were alone.

"There was so much blood," I whispered.

"Don't think about it."

"I was coming here to apologize for being an awful friend. I thought Kasey was in her office. I, I just walked in and—" my voice broke and the hiccups finally came while I tried to push the sight of Toni out of my head.

"Did you see anyone?" he asked as his arms tighten around me.

"No."

"Was the door unlocked?" he continued.

"Yeah, that's why I thought it was Kasey. She opens and Toni closes."

"That means she was killed last night after her class before she could leave. Do you know what time they close?"

"Um, nine, I believe. Toni usually stays behind and wipes down the mats after everyone leaves."

"Nicola, this is the second stabbing victim you and your friends have known. I don't have a good feeling about this. Can you think of anyone that you and your friends have come into contact with that may hold a grudge?"

Until that moment, I hadn't remembered Melissa's murder,

and Toni's body lying on the floor covered with blood came rushing back in, only it was Melissa's face I saw.

"Did Melissa die like that," I whispered as my body began to shudder.

"Are you cold?" he asked in a concerned voice when the shuddering turned to full-blow shaking and my teeth rattled together.

"No," I replied, feeling light-headed.

"Nicola, you're going into shock," Dallas stated in a no-nonsense voice looking around the room.

I nodded my agreement because I was indeed in shock. I figured he was looking for a blanket and when he didn't find one he came up with a better idea to warm me up. Without a word, he grabbed my neck, pulled me to his lips, and kissed me. The shaking subsided and moved into tiny tremors of lust as his tongue swept the recesses of my mouth. Plunging in and chasing mine, then retreating as I chased his back, moaning at the unbelievable feeling he was evoking. One arm wrapped around my lower back and the other braced my neck as he bent me slightly taking his fill. When the door banged open and Kasey barged in, we pulled apart and looked toward her. Tears were running down her face, so I broke out of Dallas' arms and ran to her. We collided, burst into tears, and I wailed, "I'm so sorry Toni is dead, but I'm so fucking glad that wasn't you."

"I thought you were dead too," she wailed back.

The sound of women screaming caught our attention. We pulled apart and I looked back at the door. "The girls have arrived," Kasey sniffled.

"How'd they know so soon?"

"When I woke up from my nap, I saw you were gone and thought you'd been taken away in an ambulance. I panicked and called Angela who called Janeane and Kristina. The girls were already in downtown heading for work so they headed straight here. It wasn't until after I'd hung up and was waiting at the door for them to arrive that an officer informed me you weren't hurt, but in the bathroom." Kasey explained through her own hiccups.

Dallas walk up behind us and I was about to ask him if we could see the girls to reassure them we were all right when an officer poked his head in and replied, "Uh, detective, we have a problem out front."

Dallas' reply was swift, "I bet you do."

***

The next few hours were a blur. Dallas allowed me to shower before we headed downtown to the station. I had on a pair of Kasey sweats, which were too long for me; I had to roll them up at the cuffs and sleeves. I looked like a kid playing dress up in my mother's clothes.

Statements had to be given and questions had to be asked of us, including Angela, Janeane, and Kristina. They'd put each of us in a different interrogation rooms, given us coffee, and then probed our memories for what seemed like hours. Of course, none of us could think of anyone we knew, who had a connection to Melissa and Toni. We were acquaintances, they were employees, and neither the girls nor I had hung out with either one of them except at work, therefore the notion that any of us might know the killer seemed far-fetched.

At one point, Agent Parker made an appearance, but after I'd seen what had happened to Toni, all thoughts of working with the FBI were gone. I liked to do my part, but the reality of what someone with a sick mind could do had shaken some much-needed sense into me. Even remembering how I opened the car door to stop a criminal made me shake my head at my stupidity. Everything that had happened in the last twenty-four hours came rushing to me like a speeding train and one thing had become abundantly clear. I'd ignored Dallas' warning, pooh-poohed him off as an arrogant man, who liked control when, in fact, he wasn't being arrogant (well he was but not in this case), but was concerned for my safety and had no problem voicing that concern in no uncertain terms. He was, in fact, right to be concerned. I was wrong about my opinion of him, wrong that I wasn't putting myself in danger working for the FBI, just plain wrong about everything. Between hurting my friends and turning my back on Dallas, thinking I knew better than he did, I felt like a worm. No, a slug, one who leaves a slimy trail wherever it goes, letting everyone know they've been there but making them cringe at their sliminess.

That was what I was thinking when Dallas walked back into the interrogation room, carrying paperwork for me to sign. I wondered, as he approached the table, if he was done with me. He'd kissed me in the ladies' locker room and I was hoping that meant he hadn't lost interest. Then again, he'd kissed me to calm me down when he thought I was going into shock, it could have meant nothing other than concern for my health.

Hell's bells, what if he doesn't forgive me?

When he dropped a release form on the table, handing me a pen and instructing me to, "Sign the bottom so we can get you home," I smiled weakly, I was as nervous as cat around a bunch of rocking chairs waiting for him to say something more. I grabbed the pen he'd handed me and noticed my hand was shaking. I took a deep breath to calm my nerves, but it didn't work. As I tried to write, my hand still shook, giving away my state of mind. Before I could finish signing my name, however, his large warm hand closed over mine, and he leaned in placing his other hand on the table boxing me. I felt the heat from his body surrounding me, and his warm breath in my ear as he whispered, "I promise you, whoever this guy is, he won't come anywhere near you, I'll protect you."

God, he was such a great guy, which made me feel even worse about walking away from him last night.

"I'm an idiot," I answered in reply.

"I doubt that, but why don't you tell me why you think you're an idiot."

I turned my head, looked up into those intense honey-colored eyes, and let it all hang out.

"First off, I'm a terrible friend because I put my work before my oath not to do research without the girls. Then I labeled you as arrogant and bossy and maybe even a little bit bullheaded, when, truth be told, all you were trying to do was keep me safe. I'm used to controlling my own life that I put my own needs above those of my friends, and then you, this great guy, who was only trying to protect me, and I walked away from you last night as if your feelings didn't count. Not only am I an idiot, but I'm a slimy slug leaving a trail of goo wherever I go." Dallas chuckled while I drew my next breath, then I let it out in a gust of mortification.

Definitely an idiot.

"I'd say the fact that you realized all that and are willing to admit you're wrong means you're not an idiot."

"Maybe," I responded, then took another deep breath and rushed out, "I'm sorry I walked away from you last night. I'll understand if you're not interested anymore, but I hope more than anything that you'll reconsider."

Dallas stared at me for a moment, not giving anything away with his blank expression.

His reply to my question . . . "Sign the paper and I'll take you home."

Right, I guess I had my answer. He'd protect me if I needed protection, as for the other; I'd screwed that up by being an idiot.

We drove to my house in silence. Dallas seemed to be mulling something over if the way he was biting his lower lip was any indicator. I could see from my peripheral that he looked at me a few times, while I kicked myself for being so stupid. I needed to get my car, but the police had cordoned off the whole block until they could finish investigating, which is why Dallas was taking me home.

When he pulled his car into my driveway, I grabbed the handle and opened the door. When I turned to thank him for the ride, he was peeling his large frame out of the car so I jumped out as well.

"Thank you for the ride, Dallas," I told him as I came around the front of his car. When he stuck out his hand and mumbled, "Keys," I stared at his large hand.

"Nicola, give me your keys. I'm not about to let you walk in there without checking first."

Nodding, I pulled them out, dropped them in his hand, and followed him up my steps and into the house when he opened the door.

"Stay here and don't move," he ordered and this time I listened. It didn't make sense that someone was after the girls or me. But nowadays, who really knew who you pissed off just driving down the street. And after seeing Toni laid out that way, I wasn't about to argue.

It took him more than ten minutes to check my house thoroughly and when he was done, he came back into the foyer and handed me my keys. He looked down at me; his honey-colored eyes with their flecks of green studying me.

"Which bathroom did that asshole touch you in?"

"Um," I responded, confused, and then figured he needed to know for their case against him. I dropped my purse on my oak entry table and said, "This way."

When I reached the bathroom in my master bedroom, I stood to the side and motioned him in. Before entering, he looked around my room and took in my king size, wrought iron bed that was dressed out in a floral print and a lace bed skirt, my soft pink walls with a hint of coral to them, and the frilly coasters that I'd draped over my lap shades. He also took in the antique chest of drawers in a warm honey oak and my overstuffed floral chair with its down pillows that I sunk into while I read. I'm sure if he wasn't already done with me, the site of all that frilly, floral romance that I'd created had him thanking his lucky stars he'd gotten out while he still could.

When he turned back to me, I noticed he'd rolled both lips between his teeth, which told me he was trying to keep from laughing. Whatever, I liked my room and since I lived alone, I didn't have to worry if some macho-man detective liked it or not.

"Show me where you were standing when he came in," he finally asked so I walked into the bathroom and stood at the counter.

Dallas moved in close behind me and stared at my reflection for a moment, holding my eyes. Awareness spiked between us—dark and hungry. Without warning, he buried his face in my neck and his hands came up to my breasts kneading them gently as he ran his tongue up my neck.

162

"Is this what that bastard did to you?" he whispered.

My breath hitched as he pinned me further into the sink, his teeth grazing my shoulder, my neck, his tongue trailing its path, soothing the skin. He pulled his hands from my breasts and I mourned their loss as he pulled one side of my sweatshirt off my shoulder. He began the same sensual trail with his mouth as one hand grabbed my hair yanking my head sideways. The other found its purchase on my breast again, his strong hand stirring my body to life as he continued his attack on my neck.

My legs went weak as his mouth moved from one side of my neck to the other, his hand still kneading and working my nipple, my hair still held tight in his firm grip.

"Did he touch my pussy?" he growled suddenly as his hand left my hair and moved south cupping my core over my clothes. I inhaled sharply, my head slamming into his shoulder, while the heat from his hand and the tantalizing way he worked my nipple had me grinding against his erection.

"Dallas," I moaned as his finger found my clit through the fabric and began to work it with the precision of a man who knew his way around a female body.

"I'm gonna make you forget he ever laid a hand on you," Dallas whispered. "You're mine now. I'm the only one who touches this," he rolled my clit to make his point, "or touches this," he pinched and then rolled my nipple, making me groan, "Or tastes those sweet lips," he finished and turned his head to capture my lips.

My head was spinning by the time his hand moved up and in between my loose sweatpants and panties, his fingers hitting its mark twice before they disappeared further between my folds. Dallas hissed, "Jesus you're drenched," and drove his fingers in and began a torturous tempo. He kept his thumb on my clit while his fingers played my core like a fine instrument, all while I whimpered my approval.

Without warning, he growled low and withdrew his hand. I cried out at the loss before both hands tugged my sweatpants off and pushed my shoulders down so I was leaning over the sink. Then he kneeled, spread my legs, and put his warm mouth right where I need it most.

His tongue went to work and I closed my eyes, relishing the feel of his facial hair against my silken skin. I was so primed from his hand that it didn't take long for his tongue to bring me to completion. I cried out when I climaxed, but I could still hear Dallas grunt his approval as he kept at me until a second wave erupted like lightening in a summer storm.

When my legs sagged with exhaustion, Dallas flicked my clit one more time, causing a tiny tremor of arousal. He nipped the inside of my thigh, my butt, kissed my hip, then rose from the floor and pulled me to him. When I sagged against his front, he picked me up and carried me to my bed, laying me gently on the covers as I caught my breath.

He didn't lay down with me. Instead, he grabbed the blanket off the foot of the bed and draped it over my half-naked body before sitting down on the side. Dallas ran a hand through my hair until I opened my eyes. When I looked at him, I felt a warm flush run up my neck. He must have caught the color rising to my cheeks because he grinned a half-grin as he watched my face turn pink.

"You still think I'm not interested in you?" Dallas asked as he leaned down, cupped my face with both hands, and kissed me twice before pulling my bottom lip between his teeth.

"I'm beginning to see the light."

"Good, 'cause I have to get back to the office. But I didn't want to leave before I had your full attention."

"Oh, you have my attention, detective," I assured him as I wrapped my arms around his neck.

"I want you to stay here today and keep your alarm on. I'll get someone to bring your car to you. I don't know how late I'll be, but once I'm done, I'll come to you."

"Do you really think that someone is after us, or are you just being cautious?"

"Right now I'm not ruling anything out. Promise me you'll stay here with your alarm engaged."

"Ok, I'll stay put today. But I have a book club signing I have to go to tomorrow that I can't cancel."

"We'll work something out for tomorrow. I just need time today to sort through this mess," he explained.

"Ok," I acquiesced since he was being accommodating.

Smiling at how easy he gained my cooperation, no doubt, Dallas kissed me once more before rising from the bed. I sat up and wrapped the blanket around my waist saying, "Hold on I'll walk you out." I ran to the bathroom and grabbed my lacy panties from the floor. Once I'd pulled them on I turned to leave, and I found Dallas leaning against the door, his eyes focused in the vicinity of where my ass had been.

"Jesus, I didn't see what you were wearin'. I'd have taken you hard against the sink if I'd known."

I looked down and saw my black lace boy shorts that sat low on my hips and made my butt look curvier than it was. "These old things," I teased as I sashayed past him looking for my robe. I got about a foot past him when a strong arm grabbed my waist and hauled me back into a large erection.

"You feel this?" he hissed in my ear as he grabbed my hand

and placed it over his steel-like erection "I have to spend the rest of the day with that ass burned in my brain, and the taste of you in my mouth. When I come back tonight, you're gonna help me work it out."

Alrighty then . . .

"Um, you're pretty sure of yourself," I answered, wishing later was now.

"Babe," he replied, "You give me a couple of hours and I'll make that sweet body of yours burn."

"Only a couple of hours?" I scoffed.

"For starters."

"Really?" I asked in awe.

"You better fuckin' believe it."

Twelve

After leaving Nicola, Dallas had one destination in mind and it wasn't his desk. He turned down the hall that led to the office that Agent Parker had sequestered. When he reached his door, he didn't knock; he grabbed the knob and opened the door, walking straight in and around the desk, until he had Parker within his grasp. Not giving a fuck if he got suspended, Dallas reached out, grabbed the agent by his jacket, and yanked him out of his chair.

"Tell me you didn't set her up. Tell me you didn't use her account without her knowledge and bring this fucker to her door?" Dallas thundered.

Parker had been expecting this confrontation ever since he'd heard about Nicola and her friends. Parker wasn't about to provoke Vaughn for the simple reason he knew if he was in the same situation, and had a woman he cared about in danger, he'd react the same way.

"I'll give you two seconds to take your hands off me then I'll explain," Parker threatened.

Dallas didn't need two seconds he needed answers. Shoving Parker back, he moved to his door and slammed it shut, leaning against it. He crossed his arms then took a deep breath to calm his rage, while he waited for Parker to pull off his suit jacket and loosen his tie.

After he'd let Nicola walk away from him the night before, giving her space to sort out her head, he'd gone home. Between wondering what the hell Parker was thinking trying to enlist Nicola for his investigation, and fighting the urge to drive to her house, he hadn't slept. Wide-awake he'd come into work early. From the moment he'd heard the 911 call over his police ban Dallas hadn't been able to take a deep breath. Even now as he stood there waiting, his lungs felt constricted. These murders were connected to Nicola and her friends he had no doubt. What he needed to know is if it was because of her online accounts, and the FBI's interference with them, or something else.

"We received a request from your captain two months back asking for assistance," Parker began. "We studied the file and then handed it over to one of our computer experts. We were able to ascertain that your Shallow Grave Killer found his victims through the online websites Plenty of Fish and Sub Seeking Dom. This guy is good, Vaughn, he covers all his bases. That's why you haven't been able to pin him down. However, your last victim, Stacy White-Cline, she'd changed phone carriers about a week before she disappeared and her old phone was found at her home. When your computer techs uploaded her files, they found a mobile app called Kik that she used to communicate with your killer. The killer's profile was taken down about the time she disappeared, but we were able to trace it back to the original source."

"Then bring the bastard in," Dallas responded immediately.

"We would if it linked back to an individual."

"Who the fuck does it link back to?"

"The Tulsa Police Department," Parker answered, and

watched Vaughn closely for his reaction.

Parker came to Tulsa with an open mind. Knew when he started investigating, he'd have to consider everyone a suspect. However, after talking with Vaughn he'd instinctively known that the man was innocent. He'd lay is reputation on the fact that he was dealing with a clean cop. He'd talked with enough of his fellow detectives to know Vaughn worked outside the law. Parker knew he did what needed to be done to catch killers, short of manufacturing evidence like some overzealous law men had done in the past. With that in mind, and in the light of what had happened this morning with Nicola and her friends, he decided to bring Vaughn into the fold, so to speak.

Parker wasn't there for the Harvest Killer case like he'd told Vaughn. Though he wished he were, that psychopath needed to be exterminated with extreme force as soon as humanly possible. Parker was there to investigate the possibility that one of Vaughn's own was a serial killer.

Parker watched as Vaughn sucked air into his lungs, then let is out slowly. Moving from the door, he covered the distance quickly and got nose-to-nose with him.

"Are you tellin' me I have what amounts to the devil in my house, in my fuckin department?"

"No, what I'm telling you is that whoever is committing the murders routed his activity through the department's computers. I can't tell if it's internal or external yet. And without more evidence, I have to conclude it's internal until I can prove otherwise."

"All right, we'll get back to that in a minute, right now I want your word you didn't hack into her account and attract this fucker."

"I'm not in the habit of bending the law, Vaughn. Until

Nicola agrees to cooperate, I won't touch her accounts."

"Accounts? As in plural?"

"Yeah, she has one on Sub Seeking Dom as well. That's why she we noticed her when we were digging through the websites. Didn't she tell you?"

"No," Dallas bit out, "but she's taking them both down tonight." Dallas studied Parker, gaging the truthfulness of the man. He saw no sign of deceit. "Christ, if you didn't contact this guy through her accounts and she hasn't talked with anyone but you, according to her statement, then I don't know what the fuck I'm dealing with. I don't believe in coincidence, Parker. That fact she and her friends knew both women—"

"Agreed," Parker interrupted. "If it were my case I'd go with that conclusion as well. Let's assume the connection isn't Nicola and her friends for a minute, but the first victim. She was a loan officer, correct?"

"Right," Dallas responded.

"Check and see if she denied a loan to anyone who was irate about being declined, or loaned at too high an interest-rate causing the owner to be foreclosed on. It could be that your yoga instructor saw something she shouldn't on Friday and he came back to keep her quiet."

"The evidence suggests rage was involved, that it was personal. The way he hacked her to pieces doesn't fit with keeping her quiet."

"Was the second kill more aggressive than the first?"

Moving to the corner of the desk, Dallas leaned his hip against it and nodded. "Yeah, it was extreme, off the charts rage."

"He might have let loose with the second because he enjoyed the kill so much he got off on it and couldn't stop."

"Developed a taste for it? Jesus, that's all we need, another psychopath roaming the streets. Can you throw the file at one of your profilers so I can see what I'm dealing with?"

Parker considered the request and figured it would go a long way toward inter-agency relations. Feeling charitable, Parker shrugged and told Vaughn, "Forward the file. I'll put my guy on it and see what he comes up with."

Nodding, Dallas stood from the desk, but he wasn't going to leave until he had more answers.

"You wanna tell me why you pushed my buttons last night?"

Parker smiled. Vaughn was sharp, but he wasn't about to give him the full truth.

"Not particularly."

"You were testing me and I want to know why."

"In due time," was the only answer Parker was going to give. There was one aspect of the investigation Vaughn didn't need to know until the killer was found.

Nodding, Dallas clenched his jaw and then turned to leave.

"She's an intriguing woman."

Dallas paused and looked back at Parker, his hackles rising at the interest in the man's voice.

"You don't find women like that where I'm from," Parker continued

"Nope," Dallas agreed, "you find women like Nicola in your dreams. Lucky for me, I found her first. It'll be unlucky for you, if you so much as look at her again." Dallas held the agent's eyes for a moment, making sure he got his point across, then turned on his heels and left.

Dallas was scowling when he left Parker's office, though he grinned when he heard Parker laugh. He knew the man might be interested in Nicola, but he was also a man who knew better than to step on toes.

When Dallas reached his desk, Reed was waiting for him. He tossed his keys to his partner, and kept right on walking toward the exit. Reed followed without questioning where they were headed.

"You're driving."

"Where are we going?"

"To pick up Nicola's car and return it to her."

"Seems I missed a lot at the crime scene this morning, are you on a first name basis with the woman finally? No more Sandra Dee?" Reed asked as they headed toward the elevator.

"Jesus, you're worse than June when it comes to news," Dallas chuckled.

"Who the hell do you think I'm getting' this information for?"

Dallas pushed the button on the elevator, then turned to Reed and grinned.

"I know that grin," Reed hooted. "Just so I know, am I bringing you back to the station once we get Ms. Romance Writer's car back to her, or are you stayin?"

"I need my bike, so no, I'm not stayin' . . . this trip," Dallas added.

Reed's slow grin told Dallas he got the message. He didn't say more. Right now, he needed to focus and find this killer, so Nicola and her friends could breathe easy.

***

"Where the fuck are you?" Dallas roared over the phone.

"How did you get my number? I don't remember giving it to you," I kind of slurred.

"I got it off the card you left Bill. Now, where the fuck are you?" he repeated.

"Oh . . . we're, um, at Smokey Joe's counting balls. They were having a charity bingo night so we took a cab so we could drink," I giggled since I'd consumed three shots and three drinks in the course of three hours. To say I was relaxed and having fun with Angela and Janeane would be an accurate assessment of our current state of relaxedness.

I'm sure you wondered how I got from point A to point B, but have no fear I'll enlighten you.

All this happened after Dallas dropped off my car like he promised, while Mom and Dad as well as Bo and Finn were at my house freaking out about me finding a body. They'd hung out half the afternoon until Dallas came by with my car. Dad took one look at Dallas and breathed a sigh of relief, and mother's eyes had glazed over at the sight of my dark warlord, no doubt imagining the wedding she'd get to plan if this worked out between us. I'd made the introductions expecting he wouldn't stay long, only to be hauled off to my bedroom for a "private" conversation. He told me, in between a make out session that included plenty of groping, that he'd be at my house no later than ten, and to wait up for him. Well, as you can imagine, when my mother heard he was coming over after work she'd shooed my father and brothers out the door, spouting off that a man doesn't need company after a long day at work. Yeah, I know, but you can't help but love her.

Angela came over early in the evening, since her husband was out of town and we discussed the whole killer-after-us scenario and decided that Toni and Melissa's deaths couldn't possibly tie back to the five of us. I mean, we didn't really know them. In fact, for all we knew they could have known each other. If the killer had gone after one of the five of us, I could see the cause for alarm, but these women weren't our friend's per se, more like acquaintances. We knew them obviously, since Angela worked with Melissa and we all took the same yoga classes with Toni. Not to mention, we all bought our coffee at the same coffee house, but so did thousands of other people. If anything, it linked back to the coffee house or the yoga studio, since Toni worked there and Melissa took classes as well. The way I saw it, Dallas should be protecting Kasey not me.

I know that doesn't answer how that got me from point A to point B. Patience, my little grasshoppers.

Here's the deal. Janeane held a nasty grudge when she was pissed. And by nasty I mean digs her claws into it and won't let go until she is good and ready. Which is what she was doing with the whole, "You broke your oath" fiasco. So when she called while Angela and I were hanging out at my house, throwing back a few shots to calm down, saying, "*I'm at Smoky Joe's come play bingo with me. You gotta meet Mrs. Slocume from my law office, the woman is a hoot and has the most gorgeous pink hair,*" I knew I was in a pickle. You see, I knew I'd promised Dallas I wouldn't leave, so I was torn between trying to mend fences with Janeane and not breaking my promise to Dallas. Then Angela pointed out that I had no problem breaking my word to them, which made me feel about two feet tall. Hearing that, my guilt won out over any caution I may have had about staying home with a killer on the loose. Not to mention, my slightly inebriated writer's brain heard "Slow Cum" instead of Slocume and I knew we had to go so we called a cab and left.

I'd known Dallas a week; these women were my best friends and had been half my life, there really was no other option—hoes before bros. Since Angela needed me and Janeane was willing to speak to me, it was my duty to go per the BFF manual. Pissed off cop or not.

I figured I'd go with Angela, make sure she got home safe, and then head back home in time for Dallas to arrive. Unfortunately, between three shots and three drinks in three hours, not mention Mrs. Slocume, the hip grandmother with shaggy pink hair, who screamed out Orgasm whenever she bingo'd, I lost track of time.

"You wanna explain why you're at Smokey Joe's Tittie Pit when you promised me you wouldn't leave your house?"

"Ok, here's the deal. Janeane was mad at me and I've only known you a week, so when I heard Mrs. Slow Cum was here and that she had pink hair I couldn't say no to her, understand?"

"You're tellin' me that you and your friends are riskin' your lives by being out unescorted while there is a killer on the loose, because of a woman with pink hair?"

"That and men in chaps. We've seen more balls tonight than at a porno convention," I explained, but got nothing back but dead air.

"Dallas?"

"Give me a second . . . I could handle the pink-haired woman named Mrs. Slow Cum, but the image of men walkin' around with their balls hangin' out is gonna take a second."

"Dallas, I'm pretty sure they're gay."

"Nicola, I'm pretty sure I don't give a fuck."

"You know, *you* should learn to relax. Chasing bad guys is gonna make you old before your time."

"If you woulda been where you were supposed to be, I'd be workin' off some of this stress with that gorgeous body of yours."

Well then . . . I couldn't argue with that.

"Um, give me an hour and I'll be home."

"Stay put I'm comin' to you," Dallas ordered before he hung up abruptly.

Angela had been listening to my conversation and was grinning from ear to ear when I laid down my phone. We were waiting for the next round of bingo to start, while Mrs. Slocume or Bette as she called herself, an outrageous older woman from Janeane's law firm, who indeed had pink hair, danced in the aisle.

Bette was not like any other grandmother I'd ever met. She was tall, lithe, dressed classy, and had dyed her short, shaggy, silver hair pink. Dressed in a white-linen pantsuit, silver trench coat, and sliver spiked-heels, she'd had us rolling in the aisles all evening and kept up with us drink for drink. All while slapping gay men's asses when they passed our table.

"Tell me about this new man in your life," Bette asked as she plucked a cherry from its stem.

"He's a detective, and has the dreamiest honey-colored eyes," I informed her.

"Oh, you poor, romantic child, eyes aren't important in the least," Bette chuckled. "He must be well-endowed, dear, that's what is most important. It's *my* considerable experience that unless they're well-endowed to begin with, you're in trouble when they get older."

"Sorry?" I laughed.

"Shrinkage, my dear. If they start out small, they end up the size of a twelve-year-old boy."

"You made that up," Angela laughed.

"Did I?" Bette smiled. "My Frank, God rest his soul, was a virile man, but as he grew older and gained weight there was shrinkage. I believe it has something to do with blood flow. Anyhow, everything stops working properly when they hit fifty then it's a fast ride to celibacy or a bumpy ride until it stops working once and for all. It's God's last laugh over men and their superiority complex. They've controlled women since, well, the beginning of time, but women can have an orgasm until the day they die. You tell me, ladies, would you rather be a man with a limited sex life or a woman who can go to her grave moaning in ecstasy?"

Do you see what I mean?

"Woman," Angela, Janeane, and I agreed laughing.

We'd no sooner stopped laughing when the next round of porn bingo began. We each had cards, but instead of numbers, the cards had phrases.

SEXY BINGO

role play	sex on the first date	69	skinny dip	sex w/ your best friend
sex today before party	sex in a elevator	one night stand	ass licked	sex in restaurant
doggie style	bondage	best sexual escapade	wet spot	3some
use toys	experimented with food	minute man	swallow	watched porn
sex in the park	ate pussy	fell asleep having sex	sex in a car	ever been choked

Each woman had twenty-five penis shaped chips, and each man had twenty-five vag shaped chips. However, most of the men wanted penis shaped and most of the women wanted vag shaped chips. This made sense, of course, since the charity bingo was put on by the LGBT community. Instead of warding off men's advances all night, we'd been warding off women's advances all night. I'd never been propositioned by a woman before, and though it was flattering, it made me giggle.

How porn bingo was played was simple. Each round was over when you had two winners. It didn't matter if the same sex who won, there just had to be two winners. Those two were then called up to the stage and a bad porno was played without the sound. The two winners were required to ad-lib dialogue and the one who had the most applause at the end of the round won a gift certificate to a local restaurant or store.

There were gay men dressed in chaps, bare assed, of course, and they were circulating amongst the crowd bringing drinks to everyone while we played. They had drag queens calling out the phrases as a ball was drawn, and in between rounds, they performed to the delight of the crowd. Oh, and you had to shout out "orgasm" if you had a bingo. Bette had bingo'd twice and won both of her challenges. Angela, Janeane, and I had yet to bingo, and with Dallas on his way, I figured my chances were waning.

On the other hand . . .

"Orgasm," I cried out when I covered "wet spot" on my card. I was the second winner of this round so I crawled off my stool and headed toward the stage.

The first winner was a woman who, from the way she was checking me out, was batting for the other team.

"Aren't you just the cutest thing," Rue Bella announced to the crowd, while she looked me up and down. "Tell me sugar, do you save all that sweetness for the men or the women?"

As if on cue, Dallas walked into the bar, so I grabbed the microphone and shouted, "I save it for dark and dangerous warlords."

Dallas didn't know what I was talking about, since I hadn't shared any of my dreams about him, but the half-grin he gave me told me he caught my meaning. He walked to the bar, raised his hand for a beer, then leaned against the long oak counter and watched.

"Ok, sugar, you've seen how this works all night. Put your game faces on and give the crowd a show they won't forget anytime soon."

At that announcement, the girls and Bette started chanting, "Nicola, Nicola," as a bad porno called Edward Penishands began to play. My opponent got down to business quickly and decided to improvise as the man on the screen. However, I froze when it came to my lines. One reason was because the screen was huge and all that nakedness right in my face made me laugh. The other reason was that Dallas was in the crowd making me nervous.

"Um, you're very big," I laughed because obviously, when the screen is twenty by twenty any penis would be huge.

"I know just how to use it, baby doll," my opponent.

"Um, that's nice?" I replied, completely at a loss for words. Then I peeked at Dallas and saw that what few women here, who weren't gay, were trying to talk to him.

Hmm.

"I bet you do know how to use it, my handsome warlord. I'm sure those big, bulging muscles and strong, firm thighs could sweep me off my feet, my lord," I continued breathlessly staring directly at Dallas. He'd been watching me, ignoring the ladies around him and when I uttered that line, he'd choked on his drink. I smiled at Dallas when he shook his head in warning, then laughed when his narrowed eyes darted around the room as people turned to look at him. I nodded slowly, letting him know he wasn't getting out of this, and watched as his corded neck tipped his head back in acceptance. Then I continued before the other woman had a chance to gain some ground.

"You know, I've waited a long time for a man like you to come along, one who knows exactly how to make a woman burn. I knew the first time I saw you, nay, the moment I looked into those honey-colored eyes, that you were the mightiest warlord of them all."

At this point, Dallas titled his head back down and watched cautiously as I'd exited the stage and made my way toward him. The closer I got, the taller he stood, until he was ramrod straight in front of me.

"Um, can she leave the stage like that?" the other woman asked.

"Honey, I'm thinkin' she can do whatever the fuck she wants," Rue Bella replied.

Ignoring the other contestant, I looked Dallas up and down, then put my hand on his chest, and said, "Of course, my maiden sensibilities tell me to run from you. Aye, I can see that you might be too *big* for me to handle. Yet, I'm sure a mighty warrior as yourself knows how to use a slow, but firm, hand when the maiden is so pure."

I finished my dialogue and rubbed my hand over his chest and down his stomach, but was halted by his hand before I could go further south. I looked up into those honey-colored eyes, when he stopped me and my breath hitched when I saw them staring back at me— intense and hungry. A tad uneasy that I'd made such a spectacle, I started to turn back toward the stage since I was finished. However, Dallas had other ideas when I tried to leave. He grabbed my waist and halted me, then swung me back, dipped me low across his arm claiming my mouth. The whole bar erupted into applause as Dallas pillaged and plundered my mouth, and I held on for the ride of my life. When he was done, he pulled back, kept his eyes pinned on mine, and then softly whispered, "What did we win for that performance?"

"I had my heart set on dinner for two at Mahogany Steak House."

Smiling at that, he then whispered, "Babe?"

"Yeah?"

"Maiden sensibilities?"

"I'm fairly pure," I scoffed.

"I got a memory from this afternoon that says otherwise."

"Don't be crass."

"Don't be cute."

"Whatever, I was winging it."

"I'll let you in on a secret," Dallas mumbled, "it worked. I intend to take a slow, but firm, hand with you as soon as I get you home. Though, probably firmer rather than softer for the shit you just pulled."

Hell's bells, he wouldn't, would he?

I narrowed my eyes and studied Dallas closely, then decided by the gleam in his eyes and the twitch of his lips that he absolutely would.

Thirteen

You know how in romance novels, or even movies, the woman goes to the bathroom to "freshen up" before sex. Giving her a moment to compose herself, maybe even have a pep talk about stomach in, boobs out, don't moan too loudly or too softly—don't use your teeth on the wrong body parts. No? Well, that was *my* previous experience with men. Dallas, however, was a beast of a different color, a horse of a different breed. Any thoughts I had about being shy, insecure, or hesitant about jumping in the sack too quickly, melted into oblivion when I opened the door to my house and got about two steps in before Dallas was on me. There was no warm up, no, "Do you want something to drink," or "Maybe we should sit and talk?" One minute I was in the foyer, and the next I was being backed down the hall with an occasional pit stop against the wall. Pictures fell, the cats scattered, and I had no time to worry about what underwear I was wearing, or if the push-up bra I had on shows me in the best light. Why? Because it was mouth-on-mouth, hands tugging hair, strip your clothes off on the way, thank God I'm on the pill so I can jump his bones, goodness. And for your information, he wore black boxer briefs. Yep, all that man in tight boxer briefs.

***

Moonlight filtered in through the blinds, casting a soft glow throughout the room. The light danced off his face casting him in shadows, making his dark features almost look sinister. I hadn't been wrong when I thought he looked like a warlord ready to plunder. He was doing just that. He'd tasted every inch of my body, brought me almost to the brink of shattering, and then rolled me over and told me, "I wanna be in you the next time you come."

Now, I was on top (my favorite position), riding him hard while he slammed up to meet me with each downward stroke. My head was back and I was moaning as his large, larger-than-I'd-ever-had, cock, filled me, stretching me to my limits. Dallas grunted, "Give me your mouth, baby," as one of his large hands grabbed my neck. Following instructions I leaned down, gave him my lips, sliding my tongue into his mouth, and kissed him like he asked. When I was out of breath, I pulled back and caught Dallas watching me. I thought right then, the way the moon highlighted his body, the way his bottom lip was fuller than the top, and the way his eyes seemed to reach into my very soul, that he was the most beautiful man I'd ever seen.

Normally, I was shy during sex, but the way he held my eyes, his strong hands drifted whisper-soft across my skin, as if he was memorizing my every curve, emboldened me. His intense stare and the way it burned into me made me feel sexy, beautiful even. I hadn't even climaxed yet and the way he played my body, touched and caressed me, made him the best lover I'd ever had, bar none.

I was reaching for it, trying to find that bliss that burned white-hot, but Dallas wanted control again. He pulled me off suddenly, moved me to my knees, moved in behind me, and slammed back inside.

"Hands on the headboard," Dallas ordered. I reached out and grabbed hold as his hand slid down and around, finding the spot that took me to heaven.

I learned quickly the man was efficient, and that he wasted no time when he wanted something. Luckily, for me, what he wanted was me in his bed and my cries of passion ringing in his ears.

'Dallas," I whimpered as the warm burn I'd been looking for started to build.

"Find it, baby," Dallas growled, so I slammed back into him repeatedly while he rolled my clit with one hand and the other worked my nipple, pinching and pulling until a moan broke free deep in my throat.

Dallas grabbed my hips as I rode out my orgasm, pounding deep, bringing what had started to die out back to life. I'd never had multiple orgasms during sex, only ever with a mouth or my favorite toy. However, Dallas seemed to know how to work a female body, to make it sing, to make it fly.

The second climax hit me harder than the first and it wasn't so much a moan as a shriek that spilled from my lips. Yet, even over my own noise, I still heard, and felt deep inside, the rumble of his own groan as he surged in, held, and then spilled inside of me.

It was beautiful, better than I could have imagined in my writer's brain. On paper, sex was like choreography of sorts. Choosing which way they flip or what position they should use. However, this wasn't a book; this was messy, sweaty, excruciatingly beautiful, and bone-tiring sex.

Sated, we tumbled to our sides. Dallas reached down, pulled the blanket from the foot of the bed, and covered us both as we tried to catch our breath. I rolled until my head was resting on his chest; my legs tangled with his, and listened to the thundering sound of his heartbeat.

"You ok?" Dallas asked as he ran his hand up and down my spine.

Nuzzling my head into his chest, I kissed him and answered with, "Mmm."

Dallas chuckled at my inability to speak and the low tones vibrated in my ear as my lids grew heavy from exhaustion. I could have drifted off to sleep within a minute and I was thinking about doing just that, but he squeezed me once and I lifted my head to find him looking down at me. He leaned down, took my mouth, and gave me the sweetest kiss I'd ever had. Then he stunned me.

"Get under the covers, baby. I have to hit the road."

You have to what?

I wanted to blurt out, "I'm sorry I must have misunderstood," but I didn't want to be *that* woman, the kind that questioned everything, the kind that acted like a leech—clingy. He had his own place, a job, and he might have a cat or dog that needed feeding. Hell, there were any number of reasons why he had to leave, yet, I, figured it was me, of course.

Oh, don't groan at me for thinking that. I'm a novice at this stuff. I write these guys, I don't actually know what goes on in their heads.

He squeezed me again to get me to move. I untangled from him to let him up. He tucked me in (which was nice even though I needed a shower now), before he pulled on his jeans and tagged his shirt and boots off the floor. He pulled out his phone and checked his messages before leaning down to run a hand gently down my cheek. I held my breath thinking this is where he'll say, "You're the best I've ever had."

185

I was sadly disappointed though, when his intense eyes slightly softened before he asked, "What's your alarm code?"

What's my alarm code?

Why is it never like it is in books, where the hero spews forth words of love or flowery poetry that made the heroine weak in the knees? He should have said something romantic like, "Waited my whole life for someone like you," not "What's your alarm code."

"Um, five four five two," I answered feeling morose.

"I'll let myself out and set the alarm. You've got my number now so I want you to check in with me tomorrow after your book signing and let me know where you are okay."

"Okay," I whispered back, wondering why I had to call him. Aren't the heroes in a story supposed to pursue the heroine? Yeesh, one lunch and a romp in the hay and already he wants *me* pursuing him.

"Hate to leave, babe, but duty calls," he mumbled, then brushed his lips across mine twice, then whispered "Later," and he was gone.

Duty calls?

I should call *him*?

Snape jumped up on the bed while I was thinking "wham bam thank you ma'am" had been the order of this evening and asked him, "Did you hear his phone ring or vibrate, Snape?"

"Meow."

"Yeah, I didn't either . . ."

***

"What's so important that you needed my help?" Dallas asked Reed as he approached the tarp covered body.

Reed looked up at his partner then looked at his watch. He'd called him over an hour and a half ago to tell him they'd caught a case. He'd never known the man to take this long to arrive on a crime scene.

"You get lost?" Reed asked.

"I was taking Nicola and her friend home from a bar when you called."

"Were you now?"

"Yeah," Dallas answered cautiously, "I was searchin' her friend's house when you called, makin' sure she was secure then I had to take Nicola home."

"That still doesn't account for an hour of it," Reed grinned.

"Are we here to work or here to gossip?" Dallas asked with a sigh. He didn't need reminders of what he'd been doing. Never in his career had he postponed leaving on a call if Bill needed him. But after what Nicola had said at the bar, the minute she had opened her door and the scent of vanilla had wafted up from her hair, he'd lost control of his brain functions. His neurons hadn't started firing again until his head hit her pillow and she'd curled her body around him like a kitten. Even then, he hadn't wanted to crawl out of that bed, he wanted to lay there with her until he'd recovered, then roll her to her back, and begin a slow seduction all over again. He could still hear her mewling cries rambling around in his head and all he wanted to do was turn around, head back to her house, and crawl into that king sized bed until she was breathless and screaming his name.

"I'm thinkin' work, but your face is tellin' me, you're someplace else," Reed grinned.

"Victim?" Dallas snapped, not about to admit to being so weak for a woman's touch that he couldn't focus.

"You're not gonna like this one," Reed stated, instinctively knowing when to stop pushing. "You know Jerome Warner, the kid Nicola took out?"

"Are you tellin' me he's out on bail already and is now lyin' dead in the street," Dallas asked surprised.

"Nope, I'm tellin' you that the only witness to his crime is lyin' in the street, due to a drive-by shooting."

Dallas moved quickly to the sheet-covered body and pulled it back. Staring wide-eyed back at him was the seventy-six-year old man who'd bravely testified that he'd seen Warner pull a gun during a drive-by shooting that ended the life of a five-year-old girl.

"Goddammit," Dallas seethed. "First a kid and now an old man, who fought in a war, so this bastard could live free, just to get killed."

"Warner is still in jail, so he couldn't have killed the man."

"Right," Dallas replied in disbelief. "You know as well as I do the punk is responsible for this man's death, whether he pulled the trigger or not."

"Oh, I know that, partner, but without this man to testify, your kid walks free. And with him behind bars, he's got the perfect alibi. The kid may be an idiot, but he's not dumb."

Gently covering old man Jeffery's face, Dallas stood and looked around at the crowd that had gathered. He saw indifference on all the faces to the fact that this old man had died doing what was right. He also saw fear that if they testified to what they'd seen, they too would be lying in the street covered with a coroner's sheet.

"Tell me something, Reed," Dallas demanded. "How many of those gawkers do you think know who did this and won't lift a finger to see justice served?"

Reed scanned the crowd and saw the same thing Dallas had seen, fear, and indifference. "I'd say most of them know and none of them will."

"Yet, we'll spend most of the night and part of tomorrow interviewing everyone."

"It's the way it works," Reed agreed.

Dallas looked at Reed and thought about what he'd left behind to stand over the body of a man who'd risked his life twice to do what was right and for the first time since becoming a cop, he wished he hadn't.

"I'll start on the left and meet you in the middle," Dallas mumbled before heading toward the gathering crowd.

***

One of my favorite places in the world to be in is a small and intimate bookstore. Actually, any bookstore sends my heart racing, but there's something about a smaller bookstore that makes the experience special. With the larger warehouse stores and their designer coffee taking over, the smaller stores that have been home to generations of booksellers are hard to come by. In Tulsa, the smaller stores have all but disappeared. Thankfully, one bookseller has remained in business by selling some new, but mostly used, books.

Gardner's Used Books has a vast space filled with classic tales, fiction and non-fiction, children's books, and even a music section where you could dig for hours hunting vintage vinyl treasures. A huge, green, Incredible Hulk greets you when you walk through the door, and aisles and aisles of books. But it's the aroma of coffee mixed with the smell of ink and paper that makes me dizzy with glee.

Gardner's supports local writers and because of that, they offer our current titles on a special shelf to ensure customers know they are supporting our work. In addition to supporting local talent by promoting their books, they decided to host a book club for the first time this month, allowing authors to read from their books and answer questions from readers.

My mother liked to accompany me when I had book signings. With her children raised and my father at work most days, she had the time to tag along. Be it at home or out of town, she's been my travel companion, and biggest fan, since my first book was published.

Today was no different.

At fifty-six, Maggie Royse retained her girlish figure and good looks that had caught my father's eye all those years ago. She still wore her blonde hair longer than most her age and hadn't fallen into the trap many women of a certain age do, by letting herself go. Her style was casual, hip, but not so hip she looked like she was trying too hard. As the wife of a doctor, she knew that she needed to keep her look fresh in a world where women couldn't care less if a man was married. Not that I thought for a minute my father would cheat (yes, I'm Daddy's little girl), but mother was realistic and thought if she wanted to keep her man focused on her, she needed to take care of her appearance, and of him. Daddy adored my mother and from the looks he gave her and the hand that always seemed to make it to her ass if she was close, I'd say she gave him good reason.

Anyhow, mother was with me and as always a big help restocking books if the need arose or taking payments while I chatted with my readers and took pictures. She was talking with the owner of Gardner's and I was seated at a long table with four other authors from the surrounding area.

Earlier, during a question and answer session, I couldn't take my eyes of a woman that I could swear I met before. She'd asked whether or not Broderick and Rebecca, the couple in my upcoming novel "Highlander's Pride," would unseat Douglas and Heather from "Highlander's Bride" as the most passionate couple I'd ever written. Now she was handing me a book and I had the oddest feeling she was dissecting my every answer, maybe even looking for flaws. She was attractive, somewhere in her late forties, I'd guess, with dark-brown hair, a curvy figure, and green eyes that seemed to miss nothing as she took in the room.

"You can make that out to June," she smiled as she scanned my face, hair, and body.

"It's nice to meet you, June. Thanks so much for reading my books," I replied as I signed her copy making sure my curly Q's were attractive as I wrote her a note of thanks.

"You seem to know a lot about relationships. I suppose you've been married for a while?"

"No, I've never been married," I smiled back. "But my parents have a great relationship. I learned from them how to pick your battles, the give and take in a marriage, and how to trust someone with your heart."

"I'm shocked you aren't married as cute as you are. Surely you must have men begging you for dates," she inquired.

An image of Dallas popped into my head followed by sweaty limbs tangled with mine, hot breath on my neck as he pushed me up against a wall, and the memory of how he made my body burn. Feeling a blush creeping up my neck, I mumbled, "Um, no, no one begging me for dates."

"Are you interested in marriage?" she asked, almost as if I was under interrogation.

"Um, to the right person," I responded as I dotted my I's and crossed my T's before closing the cover and handing it back to her.

"But you haven't met him yet?" she continued like a dog

with a bone.

I started to answer her with "maybe," but the lady behind her moved to her side and handed me her book. "It was nice meeting you, June, thank you for coming,"

"One last question before I go," she blurted out.

"Ok."

"Do you have a problem with guns?"

"What?" I squeaked, looking around the room, wondering if there were any brawny sized men close at hand.

"You know handguns, shotguns."

"Um, is there a reason you're asking me this?"

"Definitely . . ."

"And that would be?"

"Well, *if* you and Dallas work out and get married, eventually you'll have guns in the house. You need to be prepared. If he's anything like my Bill then there will be lots of guns. I've learned to live with them and our girls know not to touch them. I've even learned to shoot too, so when you're ready, we could go to the range together, maybe blow some pop bottles up."

"You're Detective Reed's wife aren't you?" I knew I'd recognized her from somewhere. She's the same woman from the picture on his desk.

"Oh, sweet joy!" my mother gasped. "What's this about her getting married?"

Hell's bells.

"I am, I married the man over twenty years ago, and I wouldn't change a thing. If you tell him that though, I'll deny it."

"It's wonderful you've been married this long, but what's this about Nicola getting married?" my mother continued, her breaths coming quicker at the thought of marrying me off.

192

"Mom," I tried to jump in when June turned to look at her.

"Hi, I'm June, and you must be Nicola's mother," June replied, sticking out her hand to my mother.

"Nice to meet you, June, but *what's* this about her getting married?" my mother shrieked as she grabbed June's hand and started pumping it excitedly as her eyes glistened with uncontrolled euphoria.

"I'm not getting married," I interrupted, knowing this would end badly if I didn't get my mother under control.

"Not yet, but we'll work on it," came June's answer and she and my mother moved to the side and began scheming.

I had at least twenty women waiting in line, which meant I couldn't jump up and curtail whatever was happening between my mother and Bill's wife. As if she'd forgotten why she was here, my mother, disappeared with June into the café attached to Gardner's, while I struggled with signing books and taking payments at the same time. By the time the line had shrunk in size, I had a bad feeling that bridesmaids dresses and location for the wedding had been discussed.

After I'd handled the crowd, packed up my books, and loaded them into my car, I went in search of the two women. I found them in a booth drinking coffee, chatting away as if they were best friends. Flopping down in the seat next to my mother, I turned and scowled at her.

"Thanks for the help," I said when she turned to me, but she didn't look the least bit chagrined about leaving me shorthanded.

"You'll thank me later, sweetheart," mother laughed, unfazed by my mood.

"June," I said, ignoring my mother, "Dallas and I have only just started dating. It's a little early to be planning our wedding."

"Don't crush my hopes, Nicola," mother bit out on a sigh.

June had been watching my mother and me as we interacted with a knowing smile.

"Nicola," June jumped in, "Dallas has been single for two years and in all that time he's been on four dates of which all ended with him not calling for a second. The way he rushed out of my house when you called the other day told me you were different."

"See, you're different, sweetheart," my mother spouted, vibrating at the thought of marrying me off. "Wait, why did he rush out of the house?"

Oh, boy.

My brothers and I had agreed not to say anything to my parents because they'd worry for no reason. Now the cat was out of the bag. Looking at my mother, but coming up empty, June saved the day with a knowing look and replied, "She was having a cookout, and her grill wouldn't light."

"Oh, a cookout, that's a wonderful idea. I'll talk to your father and see if we can't organize one this weekend. We can have you and Dallas, the twins, the girls and you're welcome to come as well, June."

"Mother, I don't think—"

"It's all settled, Nicola. The sooner Dallas gets to know everyone the sooner he'll feel like part of the family."

"But—"

"Humor your old mother," she snapped, "I could be dead before any of my children get married at the rate you three are going. The least you can do is give me this."

"She's good," June replied, laughing at my mother's obvious manipulation.

That she was.

"Fine, but I can't guarantee Dallas will come. I think he's on

194

call this week."

"Nope, it's Bill's week to take after hours calls."

"Dallas isn't on call?" I asked, thinking about how he had to race off last night.

"Nope, they take turns if anything comes in after hours. It's Bill's turn this week."

"Oh."

Duty Calls? How could I have been so stupid? I laid there like some lovesick fool waiting for pretty words from a man who was just trying to leave quickly.

"Nicola, are you ok?" my mother asked.

"Hm? Oh, yeah, just worried about Kasey is all," I lied. "I need to hit the road mother; I have a ton of stuff to do."

"I'll walk you to your car," she answered as I scooted out of the booth.

"June, I look forward to visiting with you at the barbecue, if you can make it."

June smiled, and then stood to walk out with us. "I wouldn't miss it," she replied with a wink.

I didn't need to be walked to my car; I needed a swift kick in the ass for jumping into bed so quickly with a man I barely knew. Warlord my ass, he was a wolf in sheep's clothing and he couldn't wait to get away from me.

That's what you get for living in your head, Nic. You see the world through rose-colored glasses, turning every man you meet into a potential knight in shining armor. Mom was right!

"Hell's bells."

"Did you say something, sweetheart?"

"Um, yeah. I said, um, Taco Bell for dinner."

Yeesh, don't look at me like that; it was the best I could come up with on short notice. The last thing I needed in that moment was my mother's "I told you so."

Fourteen

In case you're wondering, romance writers aren't immune to affairs of the heart. We may write dashing heroes who are tested by feisty heroines, but that doesn't mean we all live in castles while living happily ever after. Our ability to dream up imperfect heroes, who are perfect for the right female, made us creative not experts. We don't always use the best judgment when it came to our day-to-day lives, just like the rest of you. What made complete sense in a book might not make complete sense when you're the one living it. Take for example the fact that I was now under the impression that Dallas had lied about why he left and that I was indeed just a one-night stand. If one of my heroines had jumped to that conclusion, I would have clucked my tongue at her and thought, "Silly woman, talk to him first before writing him off." However, that was Grace Martin the writer, not Nicola Royse the woman.

My insecurities about not having a voluptuous body like my friends, or not having enough sexual experience for a man like Dallas, had led me down the path of "I suck in bed" and "he got a good look at my body and thought, yikes." Of course, that train of thought had me ignoring my phone when Dallas called. I figured I could be just as nonchalant as the next twenty-first century female. Women were no longer held to a double standard about sexual partners (lies), so more and more of us were sleeping with whomever. I could be just like the next woman. I didn't have to pounce on the phone when the guy called for another booty call. I could see it for what it was—a night of passion the likes I'd never known, nor would see again in my lifetime.

You see, I'd ignored all that he'd said to me on Monday about him being lucky and chalked it up to flowery words that he'd used to get me in the sack. Why else would someone like Dallas be attracted to someone like me?

Yeah, yeah, I learned later that evening I was stupid, you don't have to roll your eyes at me. Honestly, you'd think as many times as I'd written this type of misunderstanding that I would have seen it for what it was. Petty insecurities that I shouldn't have, but all of us do, no matter how gorgeous we are. It didn't matter if you were a one or a ten on the beauty scale; women always find something wrong with themselves, while men just see us for who we are. Too bad we couldn't all see ourselves as easily as men did.

So, here's how it all went down.

Picture it . . .

Since the fair-haired maiden was licking her wounds in light of her discovery that the dark hero was nothing more than a cad, a rake, and a scoundrel, she decided to prepare her favorite comfort food upon the hearth. Double dark chocolate fudge brownies so rich they'd cure any heartache. While she whipped up the batch of double dark, delicious delights, she ignored her phone when it rang. That might have worked to keep the warlord at bay, but she'd been so busy wallowing in her self-pity when she arrived home, that when she came through the side door to her kitchen, she'd forgotten to lock it and set the alarm. Normally, that wouldn't have been an issue because A) she lived alone and B) it didn't stop the twins. However, as she was reminded later, there was a killer on the loose so C) it was just plain stupid.

Thus, there she was in her kitchen, heavy hearted and mixing a double batch (heartache required double) of brownies, when a very male, very pissed off voice seethed in her ear, "You don't answer your fuckin' phone, you don't lock your fuckin' door, and you didn't call me like I told you to do."

As you can imagine, that scared the living daylights out of her, so when she turned and screaming, the mixing spoon in her hand came with her, splattering the front of his shirt with precious double-dark chocolate fudge brownie delight.

He looked down at his shirt and scowled while she felt her temper rise because A) she was a one-night stand and B) he can't order her around!

In a moment of sheer lunacy, she decided he needed more fudge on his clothes for being a cad, a rake, a scoundrel, so without a second thought she grabbed a handful of mix and splatted it upon his chest. The dark hero was so caught off guard by her childish maneuver that he in turn wiped the mix from his shirt and smeared it on her exposed chest. That, of course, sent her into a conniption because honestly, how dare he?

More mix was smeared as tempers flared and before she could say, "Mayhap you should leave," the dark hero grabbed her by the waist and buried his face in her chest. That, of course, got a rise out of her. So much so, it sent her tumbling to the floor in hopes the rise could be extinguished. Shirts were ripped off and mouths were clashing when the kitchen door banged open and the idiot knights came bounding in.

"What the fuck?" said Frack, while Frick started laughing,

but the dark hero didn't think it was funny. He covered her chest before he stood, then shoved them out the door with the angry warning, "If my bike is in the drive, you fuckin' knock first," before he slammed the door in their smiling faces.

When he turned around and caught the fair-haired maiden standing there laughing, he stalked across the kitchen, grabbed her by the waist, ran his tongue up her chest, and then put a shoulder to her stomach and pitched her up and over his as he headed for the shower.

Get the picture?

***

"Babe," Dallas grunted.

"Mmm."

"That's the fifth shirt you've ruined. If this works out between us, I've got a bad feeling I'll need a new wardrobe."

Glancing down at his face, I gazed in wonder at his dark beauty as he looked up at me. We were lying on my bed, tangled together after having just tumbled out of the shower. A shower that left me very satisfied and very clean in all the right places, thanks to Dallas.

"If you'd quit sneaking up on me, I wouldn't ruin your shirts."

"If you'd called me like I told you to do, I wouldn't have rushed over here when you didn't answer your phone."

"You rushed over here?"

Dallas' brows pulled together and his eyes flashed like fire right before he rolled me to my back, pinning me to the bed.

"There may or may not be a killer out there after you and your friends. Until I have this bastard behind bars, I want you checkin' in with me so I know where you are. If you don't check in with me, I'm gonna hunt you down until I find you.

Are we clear?"

"You were worried?" I asked for clarification.

"I hadn't heard from you all day, you didn't call me when you were done, and you didn't answer when I called, so, yeah, I was worried."

Thinking that was the nicest thing a man had ever said to me, I curled my arms around his neck and leaned up pressing my lips to his.

"Sorry," I whispered against his lips, and then watched in fascination as the honey color deepened to a dark amber.

"Jesus, you're sweet," he murmured against my mouth right before he touched his tongue to my lips causing me to open for him. Rolling to his back, his lips molded tight over mine as he plundered my mouth until I shivered. If I'd been standing that would have been a kiss that weakened my knees, just as he said he could.

Pulling back from his mouth, I lay astride his body; legs tangle together, the veil of my hair falling around our heads as I noticed a small scar to the right of his left eye.

"How did you get this scar?" I asked, running a finger across the pebbled skin.

Dallas seemed more interested in the swell of my breasts, which were pressed against his chest, than my question. Leaning forward, he ran his tongue between the valley of my breasts before husking out, "Murder suspect cheap shot me with an elbow."

It's funny that what he did for a living had never sunk in until that moment. I'd knocked a guy out with a door, but until I saw that crescent shaped scar, the danger of his job hadn't penetrated my brain.

"Your job is very dangerous," I whispered, looking at the scar. It wasn't a question really, more of a statement of fact to myself.

"Driving a car can be dangerous," he mumbled against my neck.

"This is true," I gasped as he nipped my ear, "especially if my mother is driving."

Dallas smiled against my neck, while his hands burned a trail down my side, over my ass, and, hello . . .

"Always wet for me," Dallas growled as he parted my folds and slipped a finger inside.

Breath escaped my lungs as he rolled me to my back and attached his mouth to my nipple. His tongue teased as I arched up against him, burying my fingers in his hair. I felt his cock lengthen against my leg while he applied pressure to my clit, finding a rhythm that had me mewling like a kitten. Dallas covered my mouth and absorbed my cries while I shuddered around his fingers and liquid fire turned my body to mush.

Floating in a cloud of orgasmic contentment, I slowly tuned into the fact that Dallas was chuckling against my throat.

"What's so funny?" I panted.

"You light up like a Christmas tree when I touch you."

"Don't be arrogant," I warned.

"Babe, it's kinda hard not to be arrogant when you're wet the minute I touch you," he explained.

"You're being crass again."

"I told you if you didn't stop bein' cute, I wouldn't stop bein' crass, since you bring out the "rake" in me."

"Rake?" I laughed in astonishment that he knew that word at all. Rolling to his back, Dallas tucked me into his chest and began playing with my hair.

"Yeah, a man with loose moral values, who's devilishly handsome, and preys upon innocent maidens," he informed me unnecessarily.

I looked up, caught the glint in his eyes as he looked down on me, and knew he was teasing me about the books I write.

"Are you making fun of my profession?"

"Nope."

"Have you ever read a romance novel?"

"Nope."

Narrowing my eyes, an unfathomable thought occurred to me and I blurted out, "Please tell me that you read for God's sake."

"Do police reports and arrest records count?"

This was not good.

"One, two, three, four, five—"

"Why are you countin'?"

"I always count when I meet people who say they don't read."

"Why?" he asked, but I didn't miss the way his lips twitched in amusement.

"To keep from bashing them over the head and yelling, "What are you, stupid or something? Books kick-ass!"

Dallas threw his head back laughing, rolling to his back, and taking me with him even though I didn't think it was the least bit funny.

"It's not funny," I groused

Ignoring my anger, Dallas pulled me further into his body and buried his head into my neck while he continued to roar with laughter.

"Dallas this is serious," I complained.

Still laughing.

"I'm not sure this will work."

His whole body shook with it.

"Stop laughing," I shouted with indignation.

"Can't," he choked out on a gasp of air.

"Why not?" I snapped.

"Cause you're still bein' cute."

***

With everything that had happened that week, the girls and I had agreed to postpone working on the book for a few days. We decided to get together on Thursday, but with Dallas in my life, I'd almost forgotten that I was supposed to meet the girls after work until Angela had sent me a text. Dallas had stayed the night, leaving early to head home and change clothes before work. I'd gotten up with him, said goodbye, and was now on the back deck drinking coffee as I watched Snape and Simi twitch their tails as they stalked a bird across the yard. There was a cool breeze as the sun slid higher in the sky and the sound of birds serenading boisterously.

Sipping coffee while a tranquil smile pulled lazily across my mouth, memories of the night of passion I'd shared with Dallas flitted across my mind. I'd started the night thinking he had used me for sex and then lied about why he was leaving. But after he'd come over, mad that I hadn't kept in touch with him, worried that something had happened to me, I knew then I'd made a mistake. He was a cop and they worked long hours, just because he didn't go to the crime scene didn't mean he didn't have work to do, so I let it go. Thinking about his strong arms holding me close as we laid in bed talking about anything and everything, I smiled again. He was easy to talk to for such an overbearing and arrogant man, one who was fast becoming entrenched in my heart.

Opening my computer as I watched Snape stalk his prey, I logged onto both my POF and SSD accounts to delete them.

Per Dallas' orders. Out of curiosity, I decided to scan through my messages on both accounts. I found nothing of interest on POF and deleted the account, then scanned through the messages on SSD. I was about to search for the delete account function, when a message from a man who called himself MasterX caught my eye. The subject line was the same as a message I'd ignored on POF so out of curiosity, I clicked on the message titled "Gotcha." The message mysteriously read, "Now you see me, now you don't," but nothing else. Confused by the message, I chalked it up to spam, and was starting to close it when my screen started jumping and numbers and words ran across the screen at hyper-speed. Panicked because my whole life was on that computer, I watched painfully as the screen flashed bright white and then went black as if my computer turned off.

"No, no, no," I shouted as I punched the power button and watched it turn on.

It took more than twenty heart-pounding minutes before the home screen pulled up because the computer installed updates for some reason. And when it did, I could tell from my missing icons that my computer was different. Searching for my book files, it only took me a few short heart-breaking moments to see that they were gone. It was as if my computer had been factory reset.

It wasn't so much that my books were missing since I stored them on external hard drives. Not to mention my editor received a copy every time I finished a day of editing. It was that all my notes for "Property Of" were gone, along with my schedule. I searched my history and it was wiped clean as well, not a single app or software I'd installed still remained. I didn't have a clue how this happened either, it's not as if I'd downloaded a virus attached to some illegal software or pirated book. I only used my computer for correspondence, writing, and Facebook.

Frustrated and beyond angry, I turned off my computer while speculating how this could have happened. I wasn't computer savvy in the least and decided my best course of action would be to take it to the Geek Squad and have them run a full diagnostic check-up.

***

Everyone met at Gypsy's after work except for Kasey for obvious reasons. Dallas had informed her that as of right now the only link they had to Toni and Melissa's murders was Om-Oklahoma. Until she could decide whether or not to move the business she was staying closed, handing over her books, and wait for the court order for her to hand over her client list.

Considering everything that had taken place in the last week, none of us were really in the mood to discuss the book. Instead, we caught Kristina up on porno bingo and they all wanted to know how things were progressing with Dallas. I'd regaled his sexual prowess while admitting I'd overreacted to his leaving so quickly. They'd nodded in agreement, swooned when it was appropriate, and sighed when I started receiving text messages asking where I was. When I told him I was at Gypsy's his response had been quick.

"I'll be there in 10."

Ha, a man of few words.

He made it in five.

With my back to the door, I was listening to Angela talk about Melissa's funeral, when I felt a hand hit my neck. I looked up and melted a little as I saw two honey-colored eyes coming closer. Both his hands captured my face as his thumbs made a gentle sweep of my cheeks before he touched his lips gently to mine.

"Hey," he whispered against my lips.

"Hey yourself," I whispered back.

Three sets of lungs sighed for added effect as butterflies danced in my stomach.

"Be right back," he breathed in my ear before trailing his fingers across my neck. I turned and watched him as he made his way to order coffee and appreciated the back view as much as the front.

"That man could singe your panties off with just one look," Kristina stated.

"That is true," I chuckled, "they haven't stayed on long all three times we've been alone."

"Hussy," Angela gasped.

"Whore," Janeane agreed.

Peeling my eyes from Dallas' backside, I looked at my three friends and responded, "It's about damn time don't you think?"

"Way past," they replied in unison.

We were giggling about Janeane's plans to play hooky from work the next day for a much-needed day of relaxation, when Dallas walked up. Smiling at our coffee clutch, he pulled up a chair and sat down, draping his arm across the back of my chair. He said, "Ladies," as they smiled back, then pulled me into his side as he sipped his coffee.

"You're very direct and to the point, even in your text messages . . . A man a few words," I teased.

Dallas grinned as he raised his coffee to his mouth, but paused before taking a sip, saying, "Nic baby. . . I don't wanna blow up your phone with texts, I just wanna blow your mind," and then winked before taking a sip.

"Um, consider it blown," I mumbled to myself as I watched his lips form around the side of the lid and remembered what that mouth had done to me the night before. My eyes must have unfocused during my daydream because Dallas leaned in and asked, "Jesus, what are you thinkin' about now?" Blinking to focus my eyes, I blushed instantly then watched a knowing grin tug across his mouth.

"Nothing," I stuttered.

"Liar," he mouthed.

I needed to get my head out of the gutter before I made a fool of myself, I blurted out, "Since you're here now, I can tell you all at the same time. Mother called me today and she's throwing an impromptu barbecue on Saturday at noon. She wants all of you to come."

"Speaking of your mother," Dallas broke in with a grin, "Bill told me you met June yesterday."

"I did. Is she always so forward?"

"Always," he smiled brightly before moving his hand to my neck and lightly caressing the nape. I shivered as whisper-soft touches caused me to lean further into his side and shiver. The gentle rumble of his chuckle told me he felt the shiver and knew the effect he had on me.

So much for playing it cool when I'm around him. *Pfft, if I played it any cooler he'd know I was a besotted mess.* It hadn't taken him a week to get under my skin, and at the rate he was burrowing under, I'd be hopelessly in love with him by the end of two.

"I'll be done with work in a couple of hours. If you can hold off eatin' until then, I'll take you to dinner," Dallas asked.

"Ok, I'd love that," I answered as he ran fingers through my hair, leaning closer by the second. Oblivious to my friends watching, or even caring, Dallas seemed fixated on my mouth. He was leaning in for a kiss that I didn't mind giving in public when his phone rang stopping his descent. Sighing, he pulled out his phone from his back pocket and scowled at the number.

"Give me a second," he stated briskly as he stood from his chair and walked away. His brows furrowed and his eyes glittered dangerously as he spoke on the phone. I watched with interest when he rolled his eyes to the ceiling, then his free hand wrapped around his neck, annoyance written all over him as he bent his head and looked at his boots. He gritted out, "I'm done and you know it, so don't call again," to whomever was on the other end. Anger flared across his face and his jaw ticked in agitation as the caller responded, so Dallas hung up without another word. As he made his way back to our table, his phone chimed with a text. He looked down, read the message, then bit out, "Jesus," right before he shoved it into his back pocket.

"Problems?" I asked when he stopped by my chair.

Dallas looked down, but not at me, and I could see he was lost in thought. He seemed to stare right through me for a moment, then his eyes cleared and he focused on my face right before he shook his head no, muttering; "Duty calls. Walk me to my bike?"

"Sure," I answered, wondering what had him preoccupied, but I knew better than to pry. It had to be work related, so I knew he wouldn't answer.

Reaching down, he took my hand and pulled me from the chair. Hooking his arm around my shoulders, he walked us outside. At his bike, he shoved his coffee into one of two drink holders that hung from his handlebars and I giggled at the sight. It hadn't occurred to me until just then how he got his coffee back to the station when he needed two hands to drive. Dallas leaned against his Harley, pulling me in between his legs. I wrapped my arms around his neck and smiled as he scanned my face, his own serious as he searched for something. Finally, his face gentled for a moment as he took me in.

"It's been a long time since I had somethin' sweet in my life," Dallas replied pulling me closer to his body.

"I'd like to think I'm more like chocolate covered peanuts." Smiling, Dallas cocked a brow for an explanation.

"I'm salty and sweet."

A slow grin pulled across those sexy lips, before he leaned in, nipped my lip, chuckling, "Considering the positions I've had you in I'd say you're more like chocolate covered pretzels."

Before I could admonish him, yet again, for being crass, he boxed in my face with his hands and kissed me until my legs were like noodles. Ripping his mouth away, I staggered back while he climbed on his bike. When he started the engine, he winked at me with a devilish grin, and told me, "Later, babe," before he gunned the engine and drove away.

As I rounded the building, a spark from a lighter caught my attention. I glanced briefly in the direction of the man who was lighting a smoke. His head was covered with a baseball cap and his eyes covered with sunglasses. He was tall, well-built, and looked up at me when I passed, so grinned a slight hello, then forgot all about him as I walked back into Gypsy's.

It would be much later when I realized I should have taken a closer look at that man, read the warning signs for what they were. He hadn't smiled when I grinned at him, but had a setline across his mouth. It wasn't indifference, I'd read in his face, but barely held back hostility I would realize later. That's the funny thing about hindsight, when you looked back on events—it's never around when you need it.

Fifteen

The moment he stepped into the bedroom while she took off her clothes, she'd stiffened—she knew he was there. His heart didn't pound as he stared back at her. The thought of the kill didn't excite his blood as it did in the beginning. It calmed him with the certain knowledge that the drug he craved would soon be at his disposal. She shook her head and backed up as she took in his mask-covered face and the knife he held. She tried to dart to the left to escape him, but his knife slashed across her back halting her escape. There was no escape from Dark Prince when he hunted you, only pain, only death.

She screamed, "Why?" when he lifted his knife again. Dark Prince cocked his head, his lips pulling in a sarcastic grin, before he uttered, "Because I'm your master. Because you disobeyed me."

Muted prisms of color danced across the wall as he sheathed his knife. The effects from a crystal star and the warm glow of a streetlight held his eye. Glancing down at her face, which was contorted in terror, he let the power he held over life and death roll over him. This one had been easier to kill than the others had; she'd been too terrified to fight. It was unfortunate that his adversary would soon know to be on alert. However, the thought of the fear he'd inflict, to know they'd live in constant terror waiting for his arrival, heightened his exhilaration for the game. His game, the one they brought to him by offering him the woman of his dreams, only to snatch her away. He was their master, and by right, only he could end their association as he saw fit. He chose death.

✱✱✱

I decided to hang at Gypsy's with the girls until Dallas got off work. Janeane had scurried off not long after he left going on about a hot date with a movie and a bowl of popcorn. Kristina had left next to run home and change before meeting her husband for dinner and finally Angela had to run to pick up food at the store for dinner. Alone and wondering if I should just head home and wait there for Dallas, I was stopped from leaving when Bo called.

"Hello?"

"I hear we're having a family barbecue to welcome Dallas to the family," Bo laughed.

"I suppose you and Finn are coming so you can challenge him to a duel."

"I wouldn't be doing my job as your big brother if I didn't try and send him running for the hills," Bo explained.

"He's a cop, Bo; I think he can handle anything you and Finn dish out."

"He's held up so far, I'll give him that much; we'll just have to push him to the limit on Saturday."

God save me from overprotective brothers.

"Bo, I really like this guy, can you—" my phone beeped breaking into my train of thought so I put Bo on hold and clicked over.

"Hello?"

"Are you at home?" Dallas inquired.

"No, I'm still at Gypsy's waiting for you."

"Do you like beer?"

"Yes."

"Do you like burgers?"

"Yes."

"Then meet me at McNellie's in twenty minutes and we'll eat and play a game of pool."

I smiled because I loved McNellie's Public House. They had the best sweet potato fries and largest selection of beer I'd ever seen.

I answered, "Ok, see you in twenty minutes," then clicked back over to Bo.

"Bo, I have to go, I'm meeting Dallas at McNellie's."

"McNellie's? If you bring me back some sweet potato fries, I'll consider going easy on the man."

"No way, you're on your own if you want food. I'll talk to you on Saturday at Mom and Dad's.

"Right," Bo answered, "gotta run."

McNellie's Public House is an Irish bar in downtown Tulsa with a limited, but excellent, pub menu and a beer selection with over three hundred and fifty choices and counting. If you like Lager, Ales, or even harder to find Lambic beer, then McNellie's was the place to go. Built in 2004 by a fresh-out-of-college entrepreneur, McNellie's was styled after Irish pubs the owner had frequented while on an extended trip to Ireland. Their menu was limited, but what they had got an A plus rating from me. However, the best part of the pub was the game room upstairs with its pool tables, dartboards, shuffleboard, and video games. You could eat, then go upstairs with a pint of Irish ale with your friends and ease the night away playing darts. This is what Dallas and I were doing when I heard a booming voice shout, "Yo, Nic, small world."

The drink I'd been taking lodged in my throat when I turned around to find not only Bo standing there, but also Finn and my parents. I narrowed my eyes at the bastard, and then smiled warmly at my parents while I calculated how long we'd have to stay before I could sneak out the door with Dallas.

My father came forward first, putting out his hand to Dallas and shaking it while Dallas greeted him with, "Sir, nice to see you again." Then he turned his bright blue eyes on me and I walked into his arms.

At fifty-eight, my father was still a handsome man. Originally from Oslo, Norway, he'd come to the states to study at John Hopkins in Baltimore, Maryland. Once he'd completed his residency and was about to return home, he decided to take one last cross-country trip with friends. Fascinated with American culture, Dad wanted to travel the Old Route 66 highway toward California. Fortunately, for mom, Old Route 66 cuts right through Tulsa and they'd stopped to rest for a day. Obviously, since Dad was still here, you can guess the rest.

He made the acquaintance of a local beauty and fell deeply in lust with her. While he continued his trip to California, he couldn't stop thinking about the blonde-haired beauty. She'd given him her number before he left, so each night he would call when they checked into a motel. When it was time to return to Baltimore, then back home to Norway, all thoughts of leaving had vanished. Instead of getting back in the car and traveling back across the US, he jumped on a plane and headed for Tulsa. That was thirty-four years ago and they were still blissfully happy.

"Hey, Daddy," I whispered as he engulfed me in a bear hug.

"Hello, my little one, how are you feeling today? Well, I hope."

"Fit as a fiddle," I replied on a squeeze.

"Good, good, my little pixie," he replied with a smile wrapping me into a side hug. I had the distinct feeling he was claiming me in a way in front of Dallas, letting him know no matter what happened in the future between us, I was *his* little girl first, last, and always.

"I see you play darts, Mr. Vaughn. How about we throw some and you can catch me up on this mess my little girl stumbled into on Tuesday."

Yep, definitely putting Dallas on the spot.

Dallas grinned and threw his arm out to let dad know he should lead the way. Seeing that, Dad let me go and moved toward the dartboard while I mouthed "sorry" to Dallas. He didn't seem bothered by the request however, he just winked at me before he turned and followed my father.

"How are things going with Dallas?" mother whispered in my ear.

"We aren't getting married, mother," I replied with a sigh as I turned toward her and my brothers.

"Got any brownies left?" Finn snorted when my eyes landed on him.

"No!" I bit out then motioned toward my mother with sharp, angry eyes.

"Don't worry about me sweetheart, your father and I acted out the movie 9½ Weeks when you and your brothers were staying with Momma and Daddy one weekend. A little food play is very healthy for a relationship."

Finns grin vanished quickly upon Mother's admission to sex in our kitchen. Personally, I wanted to throw my hands over my ears and singsong "I'm not listening," but all I could think about was the fact Finn and Bo had told her.

"You told her?" I seethed at my brothers.

"I need a drink and some bleach," Bo muttered as he walked off, heading for the bar.

"It's not a big deal, sweetheart," Mother laughed.

"Right, knowing that you and the boys talk about my sex life isn't a big deal at all," threw out.

"Don't be such a prude, Nicola Grace. It's a perfectly natural part of a relationship. Your father and I enjoy a healthy...."

"Jesus, mom," Finn groaned as he walked away following Bo's lead.

"That should teach them not to embarrass you any time soon," Mom laughed as she watched Finn go downstairs.

"I need a drink, no, I need a bottle. Please tell me Daddy doesn't know about the brownies?" I begged as I turned back to Dallas and my father. Dallas had a serious look on his face as my father spoke and I wondered what my father was saying.

"Why do you think your father wanted to play a game of darts?" she grinned.

Hell's bells.

That did it; I could sabotage my own relationship without the help of my family. Whirling on my heels, I stomped over to where Dallas and Daddy were playing darts and grabbed Dallas' hand, saying, "Night, Daddy, we're leaving."

Dallas didn't stop me when I started tugging him toward the stairs, but I could hear him chuckling as he followed. When we got outside, he walked me to my car, telling me to follow him to his house. Ten minutes later, we pulled up in front of a small, brick Gingerbread Bungalow with an arched porch and big windows. There was minimal landscaping which didn't surprise me since Dallas was single and worked most of the time. His interior was minimalist as well. Way minimalistic. From what I could see, the ex-wife got all the good stuff in the divorce and left him with the hand-me-downs. A flat screen TV and one old brown leather couch and matching recliner were all the living room held, apart from the pictures on the mantle. The living room sported a highly ornate fireplace that was indicative of the houses built in the 1920's. In fact, his home was full of architectural details that, if he had the time and money to spend, could boost his home's value and make it feel more like a home than just a place he crashed.

Dallas walked through his sparsely furnished dining room that held only a small table with a single chair, into to his galley kitchen. I followed and leaned against the opening to the kitchen. He opened his fridge and pulled out two beers popping the tops off both before turning and handing me one. As I sipped my beer, I looked around his kitchen, took in the gold appliances with matching gold counter tops, and smiled. My brothers would love to get their hands on this place.

"You live very sparingly," I commented.

"Yep, I don't spend a lot of time here other than to sleep, so there's no need to have a bunch of crap."

"Do you work all the time because there is nothing waiting for you at home?" I inquired with interest.

Dallas took a pull from his bottle, his eyes watching me closely as he swallowed. Something about his mood seemed different since we'd left McNellie's and it put me on guard.

"I know now where you get your old-fashioned sensibilities from," Dallas told me after he finished his sip.

"Sensibilities?" I laughed.

"Isn't that what you call them in your books?"

"Yeah, but my books take place hundreds of years ago, some even a thousand."

"It occurred to me after talking with your father that your love for all things, I'll call it provincial, seem to come from him," he answered drawing closer.

"Oh, God, what did he say?"

Dallas looked around his house as if he was taking an inventory, when he was done, his eyes came back to mine and he paused before answering.

"He asked what my intentions were toward his daughter. Asked if I was serious where you were concerned, could I provide for you and any future children? Made it clear that as your father, he couldn't give permission to a man, any man, that is, to marry his daughter if he didn't think she came first in that man's eyes."

Instead of being embarrassed by my father's old-fashioned attitude, not to mention, it was way too soon for that type of talk, I was nervous. I had a feeling after that statement Dallas had brought me to his home to show me just what I'd be getting myself into being married to a cop.

"Is that why you brought me here tonight, to show me a house that isn't a home because you work too much, that if we *were* to get married someday, this would be my life?"

"You know I've been married before. She left because I worked too damn much and didn't make enough money to provide her with a huge home."

"Please don't insult me, Dallas, I'm not your ex-wife," I replied sharply because it hurt that he'd lump me in with someone who would cheat.

Dallas scanned me from head to toe, but his eyes weren't giving anything away. For some reason it felt like he was slipping through my fingers while I stood there, and I didn't get what had happened in a few short hours.

"You came from money, I can never give that to you," he stated blank faced. "You're accustomed to the finer things in life."

"You think money matters to me?" I bit out, insulted that he thought I could be that shallow. Money never bought anyone happiness. Those who've had it know that, and I'd trade a simple home full of love over a mansion any day.

"Money always matters in the end when there isn't enough. You grew up wanting for nothing; I grew up with parents who lived paycheck to paycheck. I'd never have gone to college if it weren't for my football scholarship."

"You know, that's called reverse snobbery, Dallas. You're, you're . . . well, I'm not sure what you're doing, but for some reason you're holding my parents wealth against me."

"I'm not holding it against you I'm trying to make it clear before this goes any further between us that I am who I am— I work too much and I'll never be rich."

I didn't know whether to scream or cry. It felt like he was saying goodbye. Clearly, whatever my father had said had Dallas stepping back.

"Dallas," I ask breathlessly, afraid of what his answer might be, "what do you want? Forget that my parents provided a comfortable life for me when I was a kid. Tell me what it is that you want."

Drawing a sharp breath through his nose Dallas looked down and stared at his boots while he worked his jaw. I took a step back and leaned against his dining room table for support, afraid of what I might hear. After a few moments of deliberation, he raised intense eyes to me, but still didn't speak.

"Dallas?" I whispered my heart rapidly firing because I couldn't read his face. He rolled his lips between his teeth as he stared at me, deciding what it was he truly wanted. Taking another sip of his beer, he nodded as if he'd made up his mind then laid down his beer, moved in front of me, putting both of his hands on my face, as he looked deep into my eyes.

"What I want," he told me firmly as he swept his thumbs across my cheeks, "is to own that part of you that you've never given away, the part that can only be mine. I want to put my hands on you and feel the way you shiver from just my touch, to slide inside of you and hear you moan. I want to make love to you every day until the world slips away, until it's just you and me. I want to wrap you in my arms and protect you because you brought somethin' sweet back into my life when all I've tasted is sour for far too long. That's what I fuckin' want. That said," he went on moving his hand to my shoulders, kneading the muscles gently, "I don't want you to wake up one day and feel like you've settled. I need you to be certain before we go any further 'cause the way I feel right now tells me if we continue, I won't let you go."

Blood was roaring in my ears, as I stood there shocked by his admission. Who knew a man like Dallas had it in him to spout tender words of love. I opened my mouth to tell him I'd waited thirty-two years to give that part of me away to someone who was loyal, protective, and possessive of his woman. A man like him who could make me feel cherished and wanted. So much so, that I knew if we were together fifty years from now, I'd still feel cherished and wanted.

Maybe he was right; maybe I do have old-fashioned ideas. I'd probably be frowned upon by feminist's if they knew that the thought of having a strong man to take care of me filled me with hope for the future, instead incensing me that he thought I couldn't take care of myself. As for his ridiculous idea that because I came from money I'd lose interest or fall out of love, well, that was just insulting. I *definitely* didn't know whether to scream or cry. However, something told me, with a man like Dallas, I needed to get used to these conflicting emotions.

Bearing that in mind, I was ready to let him know that he could set his concerns aside. If we stayed together, he wasn't the only one who would bring money to the relationship. I wasn't rich by any standard, but I made a comfortable living off my books. Although right now, I just needed him to accept that I was not like his ex-wife, because something told me that deep down this was where his hesitation came from.

"Dallas," I got out before his phone rang interrupting my thoughts. He automatically reached for the phone to check to see who was calling. I figured it was engrained in him to answer his phone after so many years in law enforcement. Death didn't wait for conversations to be finished, and considering with death came devastated families, I didn't hesitate to let him answer when he looked up at me. "Go ahead and answer this can wait until you're finished."

Giving him privacy, I walked around his living room while he took the call. On his fireplace mantle were three pictures in decorative frames that only his sister could have purchased. All of them were of his niece and nephew at different ages. Picking one up and inspecting the smiling faces of two curious children, I heard Dallas rattle off questions to the caller as he came back into the room. When he said, "Be there in twenty," I knew he had to leave. He swiped off his phone and placed it on his dining room table before he came over to me.

"Let me guess, duty calls?" I smiled.

"Duty calls, no rest for the weary, or cops," he smiled back. "Think about what I said and call me tomorrow when you have an answer."

"I don't need to—" he interrupted my reply with a kiss that was quick and hard just like the first. A claiming kiss, one that told me what he hoped would be my answer.

"I gotta go," he mumbled against my lips, keeping me from saying anything else.

"Ok," I answered back, letting the topic go for now since he seemed determined for me to think about what he'd said.

Dallas grabbed my hand, locked up his house, and walked me to my car. He kissed me gently one last time before he got on his bike and drove away.

When I arrived home, I fed my cats, crawled into bed, and realized when I reached across the open space that I already missed having Dallas in my bed. I missed being able to curl around his body sated after passionate sex. I missed having his strong arms wrapped around me while he played with my hair. I missed the rumble of his laughter as I laid my head on his chest while we talked. In fact, I slept so restlessly without him that by sunrise I was wide-awake thinking didn't need to wait to call him because I'd already made my decision.

That said, I jumped in the shower, fed my cats, and picked up coffee and muffins at the Starbucks drive-thru on my way to his house. I figured telling the man I was slowly falling for that I wasn't going anywhere should be done in person. I also thought if I got there early enough, I might get to show him just how much I cared before he went to work. This was all running through my head when I knocked on his door while staring at a black SUV in his driveway. I was sure Dallas had told me his other vehicle was a truck.

When the door opened suddenly, I turned with a smile and

coffees in my hands. However, when I saw who opened the door, I wasn't thinking anything at all, except why had a tall, curvy blonde with sex hair, sleepy eyes, wearing only a man's T-shirt answered his door.

"Can I help you?" she yawned.

I stepped back and looked at the house number thinking I'd come to the wrong house. That is until I looked past her and saw Dallas' old furniture.

"Um, who are you and where is Dallas?" I bit out.

"I'm his wife if you must know and he just left for the office. Who, may I ask, are you?"

"You're not his wife," I answered, looking over her shoulder for Dallas while dread slowly sank in.

"Well, technically, ex-wife, not that it really stopped us from hooking up," she replied with a smile.

"You're lying," I whispered, because I couldn't find my voice past the knot forming in my throat. I didn't know what was going on here, but I'd written this scene before and after my last mistake with Dallas I wasn't going to jump to conclusions.

"Why would I lie about being his ex-wife?" she yawned again. "Wait, are you seeing Dallas, too?"

That did it; I pushed past her looking for Dallas or a clue to why she was there. There was no way the man who said those things to me last night had come home and been with this woman.

"Is there something I can help you with?" she chuckled as I stormed down the hall and looked in his bedroom, finding only an unmade bed.

Turning around I marched back into the living room and asked, "Why are you here?"

I watched as a slow grin pulled across her mouth, her eyes twinkling in hilarity as she answered, "It's true Dallas and I are divorced, but we are still addicted to each other. We scratch the itch that others can't reach if you must know. We even have a code for it. I used to joke with him it was his duty to screw me until I couldn't walk, so whenever one of us is in the mood, we call or send a text and say, "duty calls."

My eyes closed slowly as I thought about how many times in the past week he'd left me saying, "duty calls." My stomach wanted to get rid of the muffin and coffee I'd snacked on during the drive over when I thought about how I'd trusted him. When my eyes opened, she smiled sweetly, ran her hand down my arm as if she felt sorry for me, and told me, "I can see by your reaction he's used that excuse before. I'm sorry, Hun, but if you don't believe me, he forgot his phone when he left and I can show you the sexy pictures I text to him all the time."

Cool as can be, she walked over to his dining room table and picked up Dallas' phone. With mirth in her eyes, she sauntered back like the model she was, all arms, legs, and swinging hips, before scanning through his messages. She enlarged the screen once she'd found what she was looking for and with a cat-like smile, she showed me lingerie clad pictures of herself. One after another after another. My lips started trembling so I turned my eyes away, unable to look. I'd woken this morning with excitement about my future with Dallas and now I was plummeting to the depths of despair. I was at the finish line of the relationship before it had even started and I wanted a redo to last week making sure I never ran into the man.

How can someone become that important so quickly that all you wanted to do was find a hole and crawl into it?

Looking around his home as if I was lost, his ex, with her perfect model body, who I figured would be hard to forget, stated, with contained glee, "Sorry to break it to you this way but I thought you should know before you got your hopes up. We'll never stop sleeping together, married or not. I'm duty, and I'll always call."

Sixteen

Up all night and running on nothing but coffee and fumes, Dallas walked into his house to shower and grab a bite to eat. For once in his career, he wasn't upset by what he found when he taken a call about another drive-by shooting. No witnesses, of course, but he was inclined to hang a medal on the chest of whoever had taken Jerome Warner out. The world would not mourn that loss, and was safer for having him gone.

He spotted his phone that he'd forgotten the night before and checked to see if he'd missed a text or call. Walking into his bedroom while he scanned his phone, he stopped short when he saw his bed wasn't made. Making his bed daily was a habit, something that was drilled into him by his mother, therefore his hackles rose when he saw crumpled sheets. He'd stayed the night at Nicola's the day before, so he knew he hadn't been in his bed for two days. Looking around the room, he caught sight of one of his T-shirts thrown on the end of the bed, one he hadn't worn this week, and he picked it up. The smell of perfume drifted up as he sniffed the shirt. He knew that fragrance, knew it intimately because it used to make him hard when he'd smell the subtle perfume. Smelling it now, he was pissed.

She'd still had a key.

Scanning through his text messages, he saw he had at least five new ones from Brynne since he'd left. All pictures in different degrees of undress. She had contacted him for the first time in two years the night before; professing her undying love to Dallas saying she wanted him back. It had taken all his self-control to keep from laughing when he'd heard her crocodile tears. Then the text messages had started. He'd ignored them all, which is probably why she'd been persistent with the pictures hoping the memories of her body would sway his mind.

Two years ago, unhappy with how much Dallas worked and made as a cop, she'd found a replacement for him. One who made twice as much as Dallas did.

He and Brynne had married young and bought the house Dallas currently lived in with dreams of flipping it so they could buy a bigger house once kids came along. Renovations on a cop's salary were slow but steady. However, not steady enough for Brynne. She'd complained constantly that she wanted a bigger house. Coupled with his promotion to detective and his constant calls in the middle of the night; the tension in their household rose to a fevered pitch. So much so, that Dallas stayed later and later at the office and Brynne went searching for another man.

He'd met her new husband one time, on the day he showed in court to finalize their divorce. He knew when he met the man she had him on a short leash and would be bored quickly. However, he never dreamed when she decided to trade up again, she'd come sniffing around Dallas. He neither wanted the attention nor gave a fuck that she was calling. He'd been done long before the divorce was final and intended to keep it that way.

Scrolling through his recent call list to find her number, Dallas hit dial and waited for her to answer.

"It's about time you returned my call. You know, ignoring all those pictures I sent could give a girl a complex," Brynne breathed sensually into the phone.

"You still have a key?" Dallas gritted out, wanting to end the call quickly.

"No, but I remember where you hide the spare." Dallas could hear a smile in her voice as she tried to taunt him with her sexuality. She had that in spades with her long legs and flaxen hair, but Dallas found out recently that a tiny woman with jade-green eyes and a cupid-bow mouth appealed more to his baser desires.

"I'm only gonna say this one time so you'd better listen carefully, Brynne. No more calls, no more texts. I don't want you comin' to my house and I don't want you crawlin' into my bed. You lost that privilege when you fucked another man."

"Dallas, baby, I miss you. I know you still have feelings for me or you wouldn't be this mad."

"What feelings I had for you died when you wrapped your mouth around another man's cock," Dallas growled.

There was silence on the other end of the phone. He could hear Brynne breathing hard, formulating a comeback for her actions that wouldn't mean shit to Dallas.

"You worked all the time and I had needs, Dallas. You weren't here to take care of them. What was I supposed to do?"

"Jesus, this excuse again?"

"It's not an excuse, it's a fact. It's your fault we broke up," she whined.

"I'm not havin' the same argument with you again. Go back to your husband if he'll still have you, I'm done, been done for two years."

"But he's not you," she whispered into the phone.

"And you're not Nicola. I've found a woman who's so goddamned sweet that after you I feel like I've won the lottery. If you think I'd give that up for you, you'd be wrong."

"You bastard," she shrieked. Not one to reign in her temper before speaking her mind, fortunately for Dallas, Brynne let loose before she could check herself, giving him a heads up to what she had done. "You know Dallas you really shouldn't leave your phone lying around," Brynne hissed, "you don't know who might look at it. Maybe even "sweet" blondes with big green eyes." Dallas caught her meaning as soon as the words left her mouth, and knew immediately that she'd met Nicola here at his house. *Jesus, she'd been in my bed, in my fuckin' shirt.*

"What the fuck did you do?" Dallas seethed.

His answering reply was dead air.

***

Devastated after finding out about Dallas and his ex, I ran home and packed a bag so I could check into a hotel and lick my wounds for a day or two. I didn't want to talk to anyone; I just wanted to hole up where no one could find me and order room service. I couldn't bring Simi and Snape to the hotel, which meant I had to drop them off with Mom and Dad, while I ate my weight in ice cream.

My parents lived on a quiet street in Maple Ridge, an older neighborhood in midtown Tulsa full of historically maintained homes. In the early days, Tulsa was the center of the universe for oil and gas production and was aptly named, "The Oil Capital of the World." This distinction quickly brought oil tycoons, such as Waite Phillips, J. Paul Getty, and William G. Skelly, to Tulsa. The insurgence of these tycoons and others into the small city of Tulsa required stately houses to be built with modern conveniences. Due to Maple Ridge's close vicinity to the Arkansas River and downtown Tulsa, those stately homes were built on the winding streets trimmed with cherry blossom trees. Most of those mansions were built in the popular Art Deco style of the time, giving Tulsa a treasure trove of architectural gems. Mom and Dad lived in one of those gems and it was my mother's full time job, in her opinion, to maintain the historical home for the generations to come. Their three-story Art Deco home, with its red-tiled roof, soft yellow exterior, and large black shutters framing the windows, stood at a corner of Madison Avenue. This house was my touchstone, the place where I grew from a child to an adult. Nothing signified family, security, or love more than that three-story home on that quiet street, but somehow, as I sat in my car with tears streaming down my face, I didn't think it could help me this time.

I had my lie all figured out as to why I was leaving the cats on such short notice. I'd tell them my editor called and I had to fly to Chicago to work out some bugs with Highlander's Pride. This would kill two birds with one stone. A) I could cancel the barbecue without having to explain and B) no one would worry or come looking for me, this way I could be alone. I could hole up until this emptiness in my chest healed over and then come home as if nothing had happened. I knew eventually someone would ask about Dallas, hopefully by then I'd be able to explain without bursting into tears that we didn't mesh. Don't ask me why I was hiding Dallas' deception other than I knew I wouldn't be able to handle the pity in their eyes if they knew.

My experience with men should have taught me better than to think someone like me would be woman enough for someone like him. No, that's not exactly true, based on what his ex-wife had said *no* woman was enough for Dallas, no one but her.

"Oh, God, after he fucked me senseless he couldn't wait ten minutes before he threw on his jeans to go to her. Was I really that bad in bed?"

A fresh wave of tears streamed from my eyes and I buried my head in my hands.

"Meow," Simi called out from her kennel, letting me know that she felt my pain.

"I'll be fine guys, just give me a minute," I sniffed.

Reaching into my purse, I grabbed a tissue and blotted my eyes. Pulling down the visor to inspect the damage, I groaned when two red eyes stared back at me. Taking a deep breath to steady my frazzled nerves, I jumped when my phone started ringing. I pulled it out and saw that Dallas was calling and immediately turned off my phone. He'd probably talked with his ex by now and knew the jig was up. I didn't want to hear about how he had a weakness for her. I didn't want to think about all the lies he'd told. I wanted to crawl into a bed and pull the covers over my head until it sunk in that there were no real men anymore.

A loud rap on my window made me jump. My mother was standing at my door, peering down at me with concern in her eyes. I should have known she'd see me out the window and come out to check on me. Pasting on a bright smile, I opened my door and got out.

"What's wrong?" my mother asked.

"Nothing. Why would you ask?" I lied.

"You're sitting in your car and your eyes are red. Oh, God,

did you have a fight with Dallas?" she blurted out, her eyes wide with worry that I let another man get away.

My fake smile faltered just a little when it hit me that my mother expected me to do something that would send Dallas running for the hills. She was wrong, of course, he sent *me* running for the hills instead, but it added an additional crack to my already broken heart. Was there something about me that screamed, "She can't keep a man?"

"I haven't seen Dallas since last night, mother, he was called away on a case. I'm here because my editor called and I have to fly to Chicago unexpectedly. I need you to watch the cats," I explained. "Sorry about the barbecue, can we reschedule for another time?"

"Why are your eyes red?" she inquired ignoring my explanation as if she knew I was lying.

"Allergies. I woke up this morning with my eyes swollen shut," I lied rather convincingly, considering I was making it up as I went.

"Oh, well, hand me one of the carriers and I'll help you in with it. Do you need me to drive you to the airport?"

"No. I don't know how long I'll be gone. It'll be easier to have my car waiting for me, rather than bother you when I return." I had to admit, I was making this stuff up while we spoke. She seemed to believe me so I wondered why I got into so much trouble in my youth. It must be all those years writing. Maybe my ability to piece together stories quickly meant I programmed my brain to come up with a plausible answer on the fly.

I said goodbye to my two feline children, stopped at the liquor store and bought a bottle, then headed downtown to the Mayo Hotel and booked myself a room. I spent the day watching movies, ordering room service, and taking shots to ease my pain. By eight o'clock I was foxed (that's drunk in regency speak), lying on my bed flipping channels looking for something to watch that wasn't about cops or love. The former reminded me of Dallas and the latter reminded me that I sucked at finding a man to love. Settling on a rerun of Jerry Springer, I waited anxiously to find out if Daisy's baby was indeed fathered by Duke.

"Daisy and Duke," I snorted. "Daisy Duke. I wonder if they have an old Charger. What did the Duke Brothers call that car?" I wondered out loud. Grabbing my purse, I fished out my phone and turned it on. While looking for the google app so I could research the name of the Dukes of Hazard's car, I glanced at my text message icon and noted I had fifteen new texts. Under the influence is my only excuse for opening my messages to see who was looking for me. Though reading them easily was questionable. Blinking several times to see who had texted, I saw Angela, my mother, Dallas, and Bo. Grabbing my half-empty bottle of Jose Cuervo Gold, I took a swig for courage before swiping to see Dallas' text.

"We need to talk, call me."

"Um, no, we don't," I slurred at the phone.

"Babe, call me."

"In your dreams pal and don't call me babe," I shouted at the phone.

"Where the fuck are you?"

"Having an illicit affair with a bottle," I giggled.

I went back to the home screen, swiped Angela's text, and tried to focus on her words.

"Dallas called me looking for you. WTF is going on? Call me ASAP."

"I'm having an illicit affair with a bottle," I repeated to my phone, "It's very rude of people to bother me."

I went to tell her just that, but my hands didn't cooperate and I dropped my phone. Reaching down to pick it up I hit the back function by accident and had to go back to my messages. I swiped Angela's message again, or so I thought, and used the voice function to type for me since I couldn't read the keys, *"I'm having an illicit affair. I won't be home for several days 'cause I'm getting foxed with a handsome golden Latino named Jose. Yours respectively, Nicola Grace Royse."*

It took all of thirty seconds for my phone to start ringing so I answered it without looking to see who was calling since I knew it would be Angela.

"It's very rude of you to call me while I'm entertaining a gentleman," I slurred.

Dead silence, yet heavy breathing, could be heard down the line.

"Angela?"

"You wanna repeat that?" Dallas growled in my ear.

I didn't repeat what I said I didn't want to talk to him at all. I swiped end call immediately when the knot in my chest started aching again. All those hours of drinking to help ease the pain were shot the minute I heard his voice. The tears started streaming, followed by big gulping sobs. Jesus, I hadn't snot sobbed like this in years. Probably since I was a little girl. Leave it to Dallas to reduce me to a big puddle of mucus in one short week.

When my phone started ringing again, I turned it off and burrowed under the covers. Exhausted from crying and coupled with the alcohol clouding my head, my lids became heavy as I watched the fading light of the burnished sun slowly setting through my window.

That's the last thing I remembered, until I heard pounding

on the door. Covering my head with a pillow, I tried to ignore the pounding in my head as well as the pounding on the door. The sound of my door opening scared the bejeezus out of me, so I sat up and tried to get out of the bed as a deep rumbling voice bellowed, "Where the fuck is Jose?"

Turning around at the sound of Dallas' voice I watched in shock as he opened the door to the bathroom and searched it for the imaginary Jose. When he stormed back in, I almost laughed when he bent at the waist and looked under the bed. Furthermore, I did crack a grin when he opened a closet that no man I knew could fit in. When he turned around and glared at me as if *I* had done something wrong, it sunk in that he was pissed and he absolutely had no right to be.

"What are you doing here?" I snapped.

"Where the fuck is Jose?" he roared.

He didn't deserve an explanation, but I gave him one anyway. I picked up the half-full bottle of Jose Cuervo and handed it to him. When he read the label, recognition of what I'd meant in the text dawned on him, and his tight mouth and angry eyes softened. Not that I cared, he was still a cad, a scoundrel and a rake of the highest order.

"We need to talk about Brynne," he started cautiously as he placed the bottle on the nightstand.

"I think everything that needs to be said she explained quite elegantly, if not visually, to me yesterday morning."

"She lied," was his pitiful excuse.

"Oh, well, that makes this awkward. You see I came by yesterday morning to tell you that you were right, that I did need a man who could buy me my heart's desire. When she told me that you two were still sleeping together, I was quite relieved," I lied. If he was going to string me along, I could too. The only problem was, the more I spoke the more he smiled.

"Do you always hide in a hotel and refuse to return phone calls when you break it off with someone?" he questioned with a grin.

"Um."

He had me there dammit.

"Babe, she lied. She's got a wild hair up her ass that she wants me back, so when you showed up yesterday morning, she got rid of the competition."

"Why was she in your house?"

"She used the spare key. I suspect she thought if she climbed in bed with me, I'd overlook the fact that she cheated."

"But you have nearly nude pictures of her on your phone," I reminded him.

"Yeah, pictures she sent me all on the same day, which I didn't get because I left my phone at home."

"But she told me you have a code for when you're supposed to hook up. She said you refer to it as "duty calls."

"Jesus, that bitch. Nic baby, I've said "duty calls" since I was a kid and she's heard me use it a million times. I watched some cop show when I was a kid and one of the detectives said it. Since all I ever wanted to be was a cop, it stuck, and I've used it ever since."

"Are you telling me she lied about all of it?" I asked incredulously.

"Babe, honestly, do I seem like the type of man that would share a woman?"

I studied him for a moment and thought about how he'd been with me the last week, how easily he was jealous of other men and it hit me like a bolt of lightning; he wasn't the type of man who shared. In fact, if I'd thought about that trait yesterday morning instead of automatically believing what

236

she'd said, I would have known she was lying.

"No, you aren't," I finally answered as the hole in my chest started to close. "She lied and I'm an idiot for believing her."

"Then get over here," he growled.

I'd stood while we were talking and the bed separated us. When he issued the order for me to come to him, I put a foot to the bed and launched myself at him. He caught me as I wrapped my legs around his waist and buried my head in his neck. Overcome with relief, tears flowed once again, but for the right reasons this time. He'd cared enough to hunt me down and win me back. God, I'm an idiot. I should have answered the phone when he called and listened to what he had to say. With deep regret at how I handled this situation, I whispered, "I'm sorry." What else could I say? I'd put us both through the wringer because of my foolish pride.

"Don't," he murmured in my ear. "She's a good liar and I have no doubt she was convincing."

"I should have talked to you," I cried.

"Yeah, you should have, but considering I thought you were with another man from a fuckin' text, I can understand why you'd believe her considering the pictures."

"And the fact she was in your shirt."

"That too," he agreed with a sigh.

"With sex hair and sleepy eyes," I continued as I pulled back and locked eyes with him.

"Jesus, she's a piece of work," he bit out before wiping a tear from my cheek.

"She said you were addicted to each other and that she was "duty" and she would always call."

"That should have clued you into the fact she was lying," he replied with a smile. "The only thing I'm addicted to is your lips and heart-shaped ass."

"You're addicted to me?" I asked breathlessly.

Without warning, Dallas dropped to the bed, still holding me close. When he let go, he yanked the shirt from my body before he leaned down and placed a kiss where my heart lay.

"I'm addicted to your heart," he answered against my chest, his tongue darting out to taste the skin. "To your ass," he ran his hand down my side, watching it go until he reached my knee and pulled it up so he could cup the cheek of my butt. "To your big eyes," he explained, leaning down to kiss my lids, "and this sassy mouth," he finished, biting my bottom lip.

I guess you could say that in that moment I knew without a doubt that I'd spend the rest of my life with this man. That I fell in love with him on the spot for giving me tender words that I knew he meant, but didn't give often. He was a man's man for God's sake; they don't easily spill forth words of love or hearts and flowers. So I tucked them away in my heart and the hole sealed over for good.

"Dallas?" I whispered against his lips.

"Yeah?" he whispered back before he kissed his way across my jaw and up my neck.

"I think I'm falling in . . . like with you."

Dallas stiffened for a moment only to relax further into my body. He pulled back and looked at me, his eyes like molten gold as he scanned my face, looking for the truth of my statement. Our eyes locked and held for a moment, an electric tension seemed to bounce between us and we both held our breath waiting for what I wasn't sure. When I was about to laugh and say I was joking, since his silence was more than I could bear, he leaned down suddenly, ran his nose up my neck, and exhaled on a shudder before whispering, "Good, I like you a fuck of a lot too."

Seventeen

"You need to call your mother and let her know you're all right," Dallas mumbled as he ran whisper-soft touches down my back.

"She thinks I'm in Chicago," I explained running my own fingers through the hair on his chest.

"Babe, she didn't buy that excuse for a minute. When I called looking for you, she laid into me."

"What?"

I sat up and looked down at Dallas, momentarily caught off guard by this announcement. "What did you tell her?" I fairly shouted. Rolling from the bed, I grabbed my phone and turned it on.

Dallas had found me at seven a.m. with the help of Agent Parker, who'd illegally searched and found that I'd checked into the Mayo Hotel. Dallas had then flashed his badge to the manager, who'd reluctantly admitted him into my room, under threat of jail time if he didn't, with a passkey. It was now ten a.m. and the thought that my mother and father had been worried about me for almost twenty-four hours made me ill.

Dammit, I should have kept my phone on and answered my messages and none of this would have happened.

I'm sure the twins were in an uproar by now as well. I loved my family, but they all perceived me as being unable to take care of myself, which meant they overreacted about every little upset in my life.

"I told her the truth as I knew it."

"I bet that went over well," I grumbled as I checked my messages.

"Actually, she offered to beat the shit out of Brynne for me, since a man can't lay a hand on a woman," he chuckled.

I paused and looked back at him, my eyes wide at the thought of my tiny mother raising a fist toward anyone.

"You're joking."

"God's truth," he smiled.

Shaking my head, I typed out a message stating all was well and that she should stand down the Royse men. I figured other texts were in order so I responded to Bo and Finn's messages. They'd been blunt, as always, they wanted to know if they needed to teach Dallas a lesson, which made me laugh. It's truly scary they hadn't realized yet that Dallas would always be the one doing the ass kicking and not them.

Just as I was about to toss the phone on the bed, it rang. Expecting it to be my mother, I was surprised when instead it was Janeane's mother, Mrs. Dee. Puzzled that she was calling since I hadn't talked to her since she'd moved to Arizona, I swiped answer and put the phone to my ear.

"Hello?"

"Nicola? It's Mrs. Dee, dear. Have you heard from Janeane? I've been trying to reach her since Thursday night, but she isn't returning my calls. I thought maybe she'd gone out of town with you, or one of the girls, and was hoping she was with you."

Don't ask me how I knew, but I did, the instant that she said Thursday night, it all clicked into place with the force of a speeding train. Melissa was killed after meeting us at Gypsy's, Toni was killed after meeting us at Gypsy's, and now Janeane hadn't been heard from since we'd seen her at Gypsy's and when I checked my messages everyone had texted me about my location but Janeane.

"I need to call you back, Mrs. Dee," I mumbled before I ended the call, her soft voice asking, "Please have her call me," as I blindly swiped the phone off.

"Babe?" Dallas asked, concern etched in his voice as I began to shake.

"Janeane hasn't . . . Oh, God, Dallas," I wailed as I turned my eyes to him for help.

"Nicola, talk to me," Dallas insisted as he threw on his jeans and made his way over to me. He crouched down in front of me, took my lowered face in his hands, and prompted me to look at him. "Talk to me," he ordered again.

Like a child who thought if she covered her eyes then no one else could see her, I didn't want to say the words out loud because I knew if I did, they would become true.

"Nicola," Dallas barked out while giving me a tiny shake.

I looked up and grabbed his arms, willing myself to speak. "Janeane hasn't . . . Janeane hasn't been heard from since Thursday night," I cried out finally.

Dallas hissed, "Fuck," standing immediately, pulling his phone from his pocket. "I need her address, babe."

"Dallas, they all died after meeting us at the coffee shop, didn't they?" I asked, looking up at him.

"Don't go there, she could be out of town," he replied as he dialed 911.

"She wasn't going out of town she told us she was watching movies and paying bills this weekend."

Dallas didn't answer me because he was barking orders

into the phone. I repeated Janeane's address twice as he asked for officer assistance. After that, he called Bill instructing him to wait until he got to the station. I rushed around and put on my clothes while Dallas finished his call and put on the rest of his clothes. When my bags were packed, he took my hand, led me to the elevator and down to my car.

"I want you to go straight to your parents' house and don't leave until I get there to take you home."

"Dallas what if—"He kissed me hard, interrupting my thoughts, and said, "Promise me, you'll go straight to your parents."

I nodded I would, but my eyes filled with tears because the grim look on his face told me he was expecting the worst. Seeing my tears, he grabbed my neck, pulling me to him swift and hard, pressing a kiss to my forehead for a long moment.

Then, without another word, he turned and headed for his bike but waited for me to get inside my car and leave before he drove away.

He didn't say he would find her, he didn't say I'll call you when I know she's ok, he wanted me tucked away safe from harm because he knew what he would find. It was then I let all the fear I had for my friend out and began to cry uncontrollably as images of Janeane whirled in my head like a movie. Janeane in high school, college, our road trip to Stillwater, porno bingo just this past week, all mixed with the images I still had of Toni's ravaged body. When Janeane's beautiful face blended with Toni, my stomach recoiled. Pulling over, I threw open the car door and emptied my stomach onto the street.

***

"Fuck me," Bill bit out, as he and Dallas stood frozen in place, staring at the mutilated body of Janeane Dee. Dallas didn't hear his partner. Blood was pounding in his head, drowning out all the noise while his heart pushed it to his brain in panic. He'd spoken to this woman not two days ago and had laughed with her the night he'd picked Nicola up at the bar. She was kind, she was funny, she was gorgeous, and she was now very dead. Normally, he approached a murder scene with the practiced indifference required to work in homicide. But those skills left him the moment he found one of Nicola's closest friends gutted on her bed.

"You're gonna have to recuse yourself from the case," Bill muttered. "The connection is no longer the yoga studio, but Nicola or one of her friends, and that puts you smack dab in the middle."

Dallas closed his eyes and tried to block out a vision of Nicola laying on her bed, her tiny body opened from sternum to pelvis, her insides spilling out onto that floral quilt she used to cover her bed.

"You think I'm gonna trust anyone else to work this case when it involves the woman I . . ." Dallas stopped himself before he said the words that had been rambling around in his head since he'd made love to her this morning.

Jesus, when did that happen?

He thought about her green eyes, her cupid smile, and the way she laughed when she was lying in his arms. The way she bit her lip when she was nervous, the way she whimpered his name when he had his hands on her, and he knew without out a doubt it had happened the moment she'd spilled coffee on him and smiled.

"You can't be objective when it involves someone you care about and you know it. Do you think if some fucker was after my June I wouldn't be stark raving mad?" Bill asked.

As if he had a sixth sense, FBI Special Agent in charge Dane Parker walked into the bedroom. He took in the scene with the calm detachedness of a Fed and turned to Dallas.

"That's three in a week. This makes it my jurisdiction, Vaughn."

"You aren't takin' this case from me," Dallas growled. "No way am I takin' a chance on an agency that is overworked and prioritizes their cases based on the number of kills. Not when it involves women being slaughtered and especially when it involves Nicola."

Parker knew Vaughn was hanging on by a thread because he'd seen it before. So, he waded in cautiously.

"You know that I'm better equipped to find this guy. You also know that you can't be objective and remain on the case."

"What do you expect me to do, just stand back and wait for you to prioritize this guy over The Harvest Killer and The Shallow Grave Killer? No fuckin' way," Dallas seethed.

"I expect you to use your head and protect Nicola, while I find this sonofabitch."

Vaughn took a step toward Parker but Bill stopped him with his arm across Dallas' chest.

"Easy, now, partner. We can play nice with the Feds if it catches this fucker." Dallas shot his eyes to Bill and leveled the man with a stare that would have intimidated most men. "You know we're right," Bill went on unfazed.

Dallas' natural instinct was to tell them both to go fuck themselves, but he knew if he pushed, he'd be sent home and locked out of the investigation completely. He couldn't lose what little control he had over the situation.

"I'll only step back if you stay on the case," he growled at his partner. Bill looked to Parker and the agent nodded once before exiting the room. "You find this bastard or I will," Dallas bit out as Lieutenant Cross entered the room.

"You keep your nose out of this. Do you hear me Vaughn?" Cross fumed, levelling his finger at Dallas. There weren't many men brave enough to put a finger in Dallas' face. Lieutenant Cross was one of them. "You work the Warner case, while the Feds handle The Shallow Grave Killer and whoever the fuck this motherfucker is, are we clear?"

Beating back the need to rail at someone, Dallas reined in his temper long enough to grit out, "Clear," before he pushed past his lieutenant, leaving Janeane in Reed's care.

Having stopped at the station in order to ride with Bill to the scene, Dallas searched for a patrolman who could give him a lift to Nicola's parents' home. Catching sight of an officer directing traffic, he was about to head toward him when a hand landed hard on his shoulder.

"You need a ride?" Parker asked as Dallas turned around. He didn't hesitate, "Yeah. Are you offering?"

"I'm offering. I wanted to pick your brain one last time before you're officially off the case."

"Then lead the way," Dallas answered, following Parker to his SUV.

✱✱✱

One of the great things about a close family is that they rally around you without hesitation. A family can be those who share your blood or friends you've made along the way. There is no prerequisite for being in a family, only that you love them unconditionally. Such was the case with my parents, my brothers, and my friends. The girls had been in our lives for fifteen years, and as often does, they became daughters to my parents. So when I came rushing into my parents' house, my mother immediately took charge and called the twins, my father, Angela, Kasey, and Kristina. It took less than an hour for my parents' home to be filled with my family. We paced, we texted Janeane, praying she would call one of us, but mostly we held on to each.

My father stood guard at the front door as if he could keep the world at bay by sheer force of his will. The twins were huddled together talking, their attention straying from time to time to look at me. I could see in their eyes that they were angry, maybe even terrified that with Janeane's disappearance, and Toni and Melissa's murders, I could be next.

We were as close as siblings could be. When you added in the fact that we were triplets, I knew if the positions were reversed and one of them was in danger, I'd be terrified too. We were an extension of each other, not whole without the other, and if this madman had his way, he'd rip their world apart. Knowing that, and knowing how they must be feeling, I moved to Bo and Finn and wrapped my arms around them both.

"Nothing's gonna happen to you," Bo vowed against my head.

"Janeane is probably out with some guy and refusing to answer her phone," Finn added.

I nodded against Bo's chest, but whispered, "I love you both. Please don't ever forget that."

"Shut it," Finn growled. "You're a pain in our asses and you will be until we're old and gray."

"Whoever this sonofabitch is he won't get near you, do you hear me? We'll drag you off where he can't find you. Maybe

246

go to Oslo and visit Gran while Dallas finds this guy, then we can come home," Bo insisted.

"Ok," I answered not sure of anything other than trying to breathe. I looked around the room and watched Angela with her husband Kevin. The worry on both their faces also mirrored those of Kristina and her husband Jake. Turning my eyes to Kasey, who sat alone, staring out the window, lost in some memory, no doubt, that involved Janeane, I mumbled, "Who will look out for Kasey?"

Finn stiffened when I said that and hissed, "Fuck," as if it had just occurred to him that it wasn't just me who was in danger, but all the girls as well. "We'll take her with us," he answered without hesitation.

"To Oslo?"

"Why not, she's closed down until this mess is sorted out."

"Finn, she has the boys. She can't just pick up and leave. Besides, it would take weeks to get passports for all three of them."

"Then you go with Mom, Dad, and Bo to Oslo and I'll take Kasey and the boys to the mountains. We can lay low in Durango if need be," Finn stated with a shrug.

"You'd do that for me?"

"No, but I'd do it for her," he grinned before he winked.

"Thank you," I exclaimed with a hug.

"I'd do anything for you, brat, and you know it. But this is all speculation and I'm certain that Dallas is gonna walk through that door, followed by Janeane, and we'll all want to kill her for putting us through this."

"God, I hope you're right," I replied, feeling a smidge better that he sounded so sure.

Mom came bustling in right then carrying a tray of mugs filled with coffee and cookies. Not one to sit still, she'd always handled times of stress by cleaning or cooking. She was handing coffee to Angela's husband when a black SUV pulled up in front of the house. Everyone froze as the doors opened and Dallas climbed out, followed by agent Parker. My heart started pounding as they walked up the path, my eyes focused on Dallas' face. I couldn't read his expression, but the scowl on Parker's face caused my eyes to fill with tears.

Dad opened the door before Dallas could knock and stopped him in the foyer. The three men spoke in whispered tones, but when my father closed his eyes slowly, I knew that Janeane was gone.

"NO!" Kristina shouted her face ashen when Dallas walked into the room.

"Tell us," Angela cried out as she stood from the couch only to sit back down as if her legs couldn't hold her.

Dallas didn't say anything as he stared back at me, the muscles in his jaw working overtime as he tried to control his anger. Then all hell broke loose when my mother dropped the mug she'd been holding and whirled around looking for me. She started crying, Kasey started wailing, and I just stood there feeling numb.

Bo barked out "Pack your bags. We're leaving tonight," as Finn headed for Kasey.

I just stood there staring at Dallas and tried to make him say, "She was out of town."

He didn't cooperate.

Dad drew mom into a hug, Kevin tried to calm Angela down, and Jake was rocking Kristina while she sobbed, and I just stood there thinking that this was the worst joke Janeane had ever pulled. How dare she put us through this for a laugh?

My laughter mixed with tears silenced the room. Everyone

turned and looked at me as I gasped for air, leaning over to catch my breath at the hilarity of this cruel joke. Dallas moved toward me, but I put up my hand to stop him. He, of course, didn't listen because he had to play his part, you see. Even her mother had been in on it. I couldn't believe she'd do something so cruel.

When he was in arms reach, he yanked me forward until I fell into his chest. "I've got you," he whispered in my ear as he tightened his hold.

"This is a cruel joke," I cried out, trying to break away from him, my hands pushing at his chest then lashing out at his face.

"It's not a joke," he whispered in my ear as he pinned me to his chest. "I've got you and I won't let go."

"It's a joke," I shrieked.

"It's not a joke," he lied again holding me tighter, holding me up lest I crumble to the floor.

Shaking as if I'd been set outside in snowstorm without a coat, I stiffened and cried out, "NO!" when three sets of hands pulled me reluctantly away from Dallas. Looking up, I found Angela, Kasey, and Kristina with matching expressions of devastation. I shook my head no, but they ignored my denial. They pulled me toward them until we'd wrapped our arms around each other and our heads were pressed together. With deep shudders and broken cries of anguish, the four of us held on to what was left of our sisterhood of friends.

***

Life is short, people say. Live each day likes it's your last. Those who are young don't understand the meaning of those words because their whole life is in front of them, their dreams yet to be realized. Those who are old or aging quickly understand it well, for in a blink of an eye their best years are behind them. Those who are dying from some disease that ravages their bodies, shortening what should have been long and fruitful lives, understand those words with every breath they struggle to take. And some, unfortunately, understand it all too well when a heinous monster takes what doesn't belong to him, ending the life of someone close to them who never hurt a single soul in her entire life.

These were the thoughts running through my head while I sat in an interrogation room with Angela, Kasey, and Kristina. If I had a pen and paper in hand, I'd be furiously writing down my thoughts, my feelings, and the anger that boiled inside of me. Once the shock had worn off, the anger came, and all we could think about was how to find this bastard— this devil who'd stripped us bare and ended the life of someone we loved.

Bo had tried to whisk me off to Oslo, but there was no way in hell I was leaving. I owed it to Janeane to help hunt down this monster, *we* owed it to Toni and Melissa as well because clearly their lives ended because of something one of the five of us knew or did. Therefore, after the tears had stopped for a moment we turned to Dallas and said, "How can we help."

"Start at the beginning," agent Parker asked as he opened a file and pulled out a pen. "You were at Gypsy's having coffee when Miss Webster came in."

"Right, I worked with Melissa," Angela replied.

"So she came over to say hello, correct?"

"Right," we all agreed.

"Was there anyone who seemed like they were watching you, watching her?"

I thought hard before answering, but couldn't recall a

single person so I shook my head along with the girls.

"Did she sit down with you or was it a brief encounter?"

"She sat down," Kristina jumped in.

"How long before you left?'

"Maybe twenty minutes, we were all on our lunch hour," Angela explained.

Tapping his pen against his paper, Parker took in the four of us and sighed. He leaned back into his chair; one arm slung over the back, casual, relaxed, just a friend having a conversation. But his green eyes were working overtime, taking in our posture, our expressions. He was reading our body language while he looked for telltale signs that we were lying or holding something back that could be important. I knew this because I was a people watcher as well. I studied those around me because I tried to write human nature as authentically as I could.

"What did you discuss?" he threw out before leaning forward and writing something in the file.

I looked at Angela, trying to remember, then over at Kasey as she also tried to recall.

"We were discussing your book," Kristina finally jumped in.

"That's right. You'd just come up with the title and we were telling her about the plot," Angela mumbled.

"And that Dark Prince guy, remember? Wasn't that the day we all rushed over because he'd sent a new message and we didn't know how to respond?"

"Right, Janeane called me and I was with Kasey griping about . . ."

"Griping about?" Parker asked quickly, fully alerted to my pause.

Jesus, me and my big mouth.

Looking at the girls, I sighed. In the grand scheme of things, it didn't matter anymore. This information wouldn't help catch the killer, but I doubted he would move on until I told him. Therefore, I leaned in, hoping I could keep this between him and me. "I was griping about Dallas because I thought he was married and he'd flirted with me," I whispered.

"So you were griping and then what happened?" Parker asked with a grin pulling at his lips. When he looked over my shoulder at the two-way mirror, I knew Dallas was behind the glass listening.

"We went to Gypsy's to wait for the girls to arrive, then Janeane read the message he'd sent."

"And this, what did you call him? Prince?"

"Dark Prince," Angela explained. "Nicola is writing a book and we were online looking for catfish to interact with."

"So this Dark Prince was a catfish?"

"No," I shook my head, "he's a dominant we interacted with on Sub Seeking Dom. We'd messaged with him the night before, but he was too demanding for our research, so we cut him loose."

"Demanding how?"

I looked at my friends with wide eyes, then took a deep breath and explained how we'd made up a fake woman to attract men of a certain type and how we'd pretended to be a submissive looking for a Dom. We told Parker about the request he'd made and that Janeane had stripped down to her bra so we could send him a picture.

"So you severed ties with him because he demanded more than you were willing to give?"

"That's right. He wanted Taryn, that's the name we'd given the fake woman, to, um, masturbate for him, and take a picture."

Parker stopped writing when I replied, and sat back in his

chair. He was fascinating to watch when the wheels started turning. You could see him assimilating the information we'd just given him in the blank stare he directed over our shoulders.

"Give me your screen name and password for the account," Parker asked suddenly his face no longer blank, the wheels spinning rapidly behind his eyes.

I looked at the girls expecting one of them to answer, but we all looked back at each other.

"Janeane set up the account she never gave us the passwords," Kasey explained.

"Did Janeane communicate with this man again?" he asked swiftly.

"Not that I know of, but we only plotted the book at Gypsy's. She wouldn't have had any reason to talk to him again. In fact, we haven't talked about the book since last week Friday."

Parker's eyes shot to the two-way mirror for an instant before he leaned in and with a deadly calm, asked, "Let me get this straight, Janeane signed up for the account, communicated with this man and on the day you broke ties with him, Melissa was killed and now Janeane is dead. Tell me ladies," Parker asked sharply holding each of our eyes before continuing, "on the night that Toni Roseneau was killed, did you happen to meet at Gypsy's?"

Eighteen

"Did you find Janeane's computer?" Dallas asked Reed as they exited the surveillance room once Parker finished his interrogation.

"Tech guys have it now," Reed answered.

Parker exited the interrogation room with eyes on Dallas as he headed for his office. Both Reed and Dallas followed, none of the three men speaking until Parker's door was closed. Rounding the desk, Parker pulled off his jacket, and sank into the chair while moving the mouse to bring his computer to life.

"Tell me, Vaughn," Parker asked without out taking his eyes off his computer screen, "did any of the Shallow Grave victims have accounts on Sub Seeking Dom?"

Dallas looked at Reed then back at Parker, immediately following his train of thought.

"If this sonofabitch is the Shallow Grave Killer then he's changed his MO."

"If he's Shallow Grave he's had access to all five women's addresses since last Tuesday when they gave their statements, assuming he knew they gave them. However, it doesn't seem likely since I've had my tech guys monitoring the server for remote access into the system. My guess is, whoever this killer is, and I'm leaning toward Shallow Grave, he's been stalking them from the coffee shop."

"Remote access?" Reed asked in confusion. "Are you saying that Shallow Grave has been accessing our system?"

Still typing, Parker didn't look up from his screen and succinctly laid out the FBI's discoveries associated with the Shallow Grave Killer. By the time he was done sharing what they knew about the killer, Reed was red-faced with rage.

"You're tellin' me this fucker has been piggybacking off our system to avoid detection?"

"Not piggybacking, remote accessing, in case he was detected, it would lead back to the department. Think of it as a 'fuck you' to the police. A catch me if you can message."

"Jesus, Mary, and Joseph," Reed growled.

Parker ignored Reed's outburst as he picked up his phone and dialed Humphreys over in tech to relay to him they needed the Dark Prince's SSD account hacked.

Dallas was searching his memory for what he knew about the Shallow Grave Killer, looking for anything that would shed light onto this new information. When Parker slammed his phone down Dallas looked at the agent and waited.

"It seems Ms. Dee's computer has been wiped clean," Parker stated calmly. "My guy says factory reset was initiated at nine seventeen p.m. on Thursday."

"Tell me you can recover the files?" Reed bit out.

"Already recovered them, but it seems the Taryn Rivers POF and SSD accounts were cancelled and her history wiped clean before the reset."

"If the time of death is before the reset, when we find this fucker and link him back to the Dark Prince account will that hold up in court?" Dallas asked.

"One way to find out," Parker replied as he picked up his

phone and called the DA's office. As the phone rang on the other end, Parker covered the mouthpiece looking directly at Vaughn and told him, "You're off this case. I've already given you more information than I should," as he indicated with his head that Dallas should leave.

Reed slapped Dallas on the shoulder, a move to let him know he'd keep a close eye on the investigation. Dallas scowled at Parker, the frustration clear on his face, before turning and exiting the room.

There are five stages of grief. First comes denial: it's a way to protect yourself from overwhelming emotions, to safeguard yourself so you don't shutdown from the shock of loss. Then comes anger: it's a way of redirecting your grief, also a safeguard for our fragile psyche to cope until we've come to better terms with the loss. Next comes bargaining: this is the "If only" stage, or bargaining stage if one is dealing with terminal illness. You bargain with God that you'll do this or that if he will only spare your loved ones or yourself. Most of these stages are on repeat and you flux in and out of them for weeks and months. I moved to the "If only" stage once Parker left the room when it became obvious that he thought that all of this started with us communicating with Dark Prince. Though, I wasn't alone in this, the girls also felt responsible since they'd insisted that they be involved with the book. For every "It's all my fault," I threw out they in turn threw back, "We forced you. If it's anyone's fault, it's ours." I kept thinking back to our first meeting, and of how if I'd only kept my mouth shut Janeane would be alive. How if I hadn't taken that stupid oath, the one that said if I broke my promise it would bring about the destruction of our sisterhood, Janeane would be here and the rest of my friends wouldn't be in mortal danger. Deep-down I knew there was only one person to blame, the monster who'd taken all three women's lives, but the fact remained—my book had brought about this mess and I needed to fix it.

Starting now.

Once Parker had left the room, I convinced the girls we should all leave town until Dark Prince was caught. I called Finn and he confirmed he would take Kasey and the boys to our family cabin in Durango. Angela and Kristina spoke with their husbands and both were set to leave town after Janeane's funeral.

That just left me.

I wasn't going anywhere.

I started this nightmare and I would be the one to draw the bastard out. With that in mind, I hugged the girl's goodbye at the elevator as they left, and headed for my car that was in the parking garage. Dallas had driven my beetle to the station since his bike was here, so I had transportation to leave. I had one destination in mind, the only link we had to the killer—Gypsy's.

***

"Answer your fucking phone."

That was the third text I'd received from Dallas since my phone started ringing off the hook. I guess you could say I'd added a new stage in the grieving process; this one was labeled "*revenge.*"

With a new laptop in hand and a 9mm Smith & Wesson in my purse, I was at Gypsy's creating a new account on Sub

Seeking Dom. My intent was to draw Dark Prince out and stop this maniac, who had stolen one of my best friends, my sister of the heart, before he could take any more away from me.

I was calmer than I'd ever felt in my life. I was focused; I had one purpose only, seek and destroy this bastard. Unfortunately, what I also was was stupid. I'd parked my car right in front of Gypsy's, not thinking about hiding the damn thing. And a powder-blue VW beetle is easy to spot if you're a cop, on a bike, searching for your missing girlfriend. I'd no sooner typed in my new screen name than the lid of my laptop was slammed shut. I looked up, saw angry, but compassionate eyes directed at me, but I ignored them and raised the screen again.

Without a word, Dallas leaned over, unplugged my laptop, pulled it from my hands, and began wrapping the cord around it. When he was done, he took hold of my hand, pulled me from my seat, and started heading for the door.

"You can't stop me," I told his back as he led the way.

"I can stop you," was his arrogant reply.

"I have to stop him."

"We'll get him."

"He can't hurt them."

"I won't let him."

I tugged back, the calm I'd held onto was leaking out, only to be replaced by panic as we walked down the sidewalk.

"I have to do this," I shouted, trying to wrench my hand from his.

Dallas whipped around and tugged my arm until I fell into his chest. "You're gonna get in your car and then I'm gonna follow you home. We've got detectives on the way with a court order to review the security tapes and to interview the owner. There is no way in hell he's gonna show up tonight and there is no way in hell I would ever allow you to be a sitting duck," Dallas seethed.

His tone of voice managed to reach through my panic until I could think clearly, then I felt myself slipping right back to stage one of grief.

"This isn't real, there isn't a monster out there trying to kill my friends," I argued.

Dallas wrapped his arm around my shoulders and put his lips to my forehead. I grabbed two handfuls of his shirt and held on while he held me on the sidewalk next to my car. After I gained control, I pushed back and he let me go. Stepping off the curb, he opened my driver's door, threw my laptop on the passenger seat, and helped me into my car.

"Are you okay to drive?" he asked before closing my door.

Nodding, I barely looked at him as he closed the door. I started my car, pulled out, and headed for home with Dallas close on my bumper. When we got to my house, he took my key, opened the door, and drew his weapon from his holster. The fact that I was in a situation that required a gun to be drawn in order to enter my own home should have made me laugh. Instinctively, I knew it would one day, but right now; the crushing despair I felt all but swallowed me whole.

***

Dallas made a sweep of the house checking doors, windows, closets, and under beds. He saw no sign of forced entry, so he headed for the foyer where he'd left Nicola. When he rounded the corner, his jaw tensed when he took in the sight of her. Her shoulders were shaking as she clutched her purse and laptop; her eyes were closed as silent tears fell down her face. Dallas was accustomed to seeing those broken and grieving after a loved one was taken too soon, but he wasn't there to view the aftermath. The time shortly after he had broken the news, to watch helplessly as the families coped with the tragedy. The utter helplessness that came from losing someone they loved in such a barbaric way. Yet, he knew instinctively that if he let her withdraw, to slip into depression for the unfounded guilt she felt, that she'd be hard to reach. And he wasn't about to let that happen. She was his to protect and that included protecting her from her own guilt.

Since he'd seen Janeane lying on her bed, he'd been in a cold sweat of fear that this bastard wouldn't be stopped before Nicola was dead. For a man who spent his days in pursuit of justice, a man who wouldn't hesitate to put his life on the line for the average citizen, he knew he wouldn't hesitate to kill for the woman falling apart in front of him. Right now, he needed to reassure himself that she was safe needed to give her something to feel beside gut wrenching pain, needed to touch her and feel the warmth of her skin because her heart was still beating. That she wasn't cold and rigid because some monster had taken her from him.

When Dallas reached Nicola, he pulled her purse and laptop from her hands and dropped it on the entry table before bending at the waist and lifting her into his arms. She buried her head in his neck, her arms curling around it as he walked down the hall to her bedroom.

Without a word, Dallas placed her on the bed, reached behind him, and pulled his shirt from his body followed by his jeans and boots. Once he was naked, he reached out and grabbed Nicola at the nape of her neck, drawing her up until their mouths met. She opened for him without hesitation, attacking his mouth as if she hadn't just had him that morning. With their hearts beating rapidly, Dallas ripped off her clothes and revisited the curves and planes of her body, memorizing the smell of her skin, the pulse points which told him she was alive, breathing—his.

When his mouth found her silken folds, her scent further ignited his blood, which called to him to claim her—to make her body burn with life, to remind him she was still living, still breathing. Her hands buried in his hair, anchoring him to her hot center as he teased her sensitive clit, causing it to swell until she was gasping for release. He took her close to release, then eased off until she was mad with passion, chanting, "Please, please, please" while she lifted her hips closer to his mouth. He wanted her incoherent when she finally burst free, wanted her thinking only of the pleasure he was giving her, wanted her sole focus on him and what he was doing to her body.

Dallas rolled, taking Nicola with him. With his hands on her ass, he raised her up until she was hovering just above his mouth. His tongue snaked out and flicked against the bundle of nerves, smiling when she jerked with a moan. He inserted two fingers inside her silken depths and curled his fingers until he found the spot that turned pleasure from an almost living breathing thing to an otherworldly experience. His cock hardened painfully as he watched her hands slide up her body until she reached her breasts and began tweaking her rose-colored nipples. Then she moved a hand back and he growled deep in his throat when the delicate hand reached back and wrapped around his throbbing shaft. When she bucked on his face and released another deep moan, he lifted her from his mouth until she was positioned over his cock and surged up as she slammed down. She climaxed immediately, tightening around his throbbing cock like a velvet clamp, but she held back, pain cloaking her desire, choking her, numbing her body to the healing a release could give her.

Rolling them both again, Dallas pumped into her core, his mouth on hers, his tongue matching the rhythm of his thrusts while her moans turned from staid to erotic as she fought to feel something other than hollow. Raising her leg so he could sink further into her, Dallas grunted low each time he felt the head of his cock touch her womb. With one hand on the bed, he pulled back, moved his other hand to hers, and placed it where they were joined.

"Focus on this," Dallas grit out, determined to hold off until he'd punched through her pain and she felt something other than loss.

Nicola whispered, "Yes," as the mounting despair she felt mixed with her need to be claimed by Dallas, to drown in the possession of her body so she couldn't think.

"*This*" Dallas hissed as she wrapped her hand tighter around his cock, "is all that matters in this moment," Dallas ground out.

"Yes," she whispered, then begged, "Please, I want to feel something other than pain."

"Then let it go and give it to me."

"I'm scared," she cried out.

"Don't be," he fired back.

"You'll leave me too, and then I'll be empty."

Dallas paused for a moment, holding her eyes with his. He saw her fear, her pain, and the anger that was choking the life out of her.

"Give it to me and I promise I'll guard it with my fuckin' soul. I swear, I'll fight the demons back and keep you safe."

Nicola whimpered, her breath catching as she stared back

at him, hope settling across her face instead of anguish.

Dallas saw the moment when she let go, trusting him to carry the load, trusting him with her heart, trusting him to keep her safe. The tears flowed faster than before, but the line that had been drawn sharply across her forehead since that morning melted away. She let go, giving it all to him. It was the single most beautiful thing he'd seen in his thirty-four years—complete surrender of her mind, body, and soul.

With a growl of possessive triumph, Dallas pulled her up, claimed her mouth, and then rammed back into her until they were both burning. Then, with a shattering intensity, he took them both over the precipice.

***

Yellow crocuses pushed through the winding gardens in my backyard. Their golden color bringing life to the brown beds as the days grew warmer; evidence that spring was upon us, followed by the sweltering heat of an Oklahoma summer. Jason Aldean was right when he said the skies here were beautiful, watercolors that took your breath away.

Staring at the burnt orange of the rising sun, mixed with robin's egg blue of the sky, helped settle my nerves, and grounded me in a way nothing else could. This was God's country, from the rolling plains of the panhandle to the highest peak of the Ouachita Mountains in eastern Oklahoma. God came first here, followed by family and country. We weren't a bustling state, but laid back with a smile for our neighbors and a helping hand if one needed it. It's one of the reasons my father chose to stay here, and one of the reasons I chose not to move when my writing career took off. That being said, right now, sitting on my back patio watching the rising sun on those water-colored skies, I wished like hell I'd left. If I had, none of this would have happened, yet, at the same time, I knew that God didn't make mistakes— he was in control. For whatever reason, God guided me to stay, laying the groundwork for the events that happened this past week, and I knew that in the end He would show me why my friend had to die. That ultimately gave me the comfort I needed to shift the blame from myself to the person who was responsible—Dark Prince.

Now we just had to find him and make him pay.

With my eyes on the horizon, I opened my computer and clicked on my OneDrive account through Microsoft. When my computer crashed a few days before I was in such a panic over losing my files that I'd forgotten I had uploaded them all to my online office account through Microsoft. I'd taken thorough notes on the man in the beginning because I thought I would base my killer on him. Knowing now that he probably was, sent a chill through my veins. Shivering as I opened my "Property Of" file, I began reading my notes.

I heard the door to my patio open, but didn't turn to watch Dallas walk outside. I was concentrating on my notes when a hand brushed the hair from my shoulders. Warm lips touched my neck and an even warmer hand cupped my breast, swiping a thumb across my hard nipple, I closed my eyes and let his strength flow through me, warming my cold body.

"I don't like waking up to an empty bed," Dallas whispered in my ear before his hand left my breast to tilt my chin up so he could kiss my lips.

"I couldn't sleep," I whispered back against his lips before opening my mouth for him and taking my fill. When he was through kissing me good morning, instead of taking a seat in the chair beside me, he plucked me up then sat down forcing me on his lap. I leaned my head against his shoulder while he ran his hand through my hair in a lazy absent-minded way. Kissing my forehead, he reached out for his coffee that he'd placed on the table next to his phone, while I settled deeper against his body and held on.

"What are you working on?" he mumbled in my ear.

"I took notes on Dark Prince and I was hoping there was something in them that might help find him, but there wasn't. Just impressions, things I remembered him writing."

"We can give them to Parker, he might see something you don't," Dallas replied, still running his fingers through my hair.

"I thought I'd lost my notes when my computer crashed the other day. But I forgot I had my files set to upload automatically to my online account."

"Your computer crashed?"

"Yeah, it was the strangest thing. I was shutting down my POF and SSD accounts, and all of a sudden, my computer went crazy and shut down. When I turned it back on, everything was gone as if it had been factory reset."

Dallas tensed when I said that so I pulled my head from his shoulder and looked up.

"Did you download anything right before this happened?"

"No, I had just opened a message on SSD and then seconds later it crashed."

"Fuck," Dallas bit out as he leaned forward and grabbed his phone from the table. "Do you remember who the message was from or what it said?"

"Um, Master something and the subject line was . . . Oh, my God. Dallas, the message was titled, "Gotcha" and it said, "Now you see me, now you don't.""

Nineteen

Dallas stood quietly listening as Parker updated Reed on the investigation. The amount of information the FBI had gathered in twenty-four hours was staggering and made his blood boil. After Nicola had explained about her computer the day before, he'd called Parker who had sent one of his agents to retrieve it from Mega Watts, a local computer repair company. He'd then turned it over to his tech support who recovered the computer files, logged into her SSD account, and determined that the man behind MasterX, in layman terms, had embedded a code into the message he'd sent Nicola and when she clicked on it, it triggered a Trojan horse, and a factory reset. The why of it, Parker figured once they'd traced MasterX back to the TPD server, was to get rid of any information she may have had on Dark Prince. Tracing MasterX back to the TPD servers proved that the man stalking Nicola and her friends was also The Shallow Grave Killer and for once in his career, he wished like hell that they'd been wrong. They knew who the killer was, but they weren't any closer to his identity than they had been in close to two years.

"How the fuck is this guy getting around our firewall?" Bill ground out, red-faced with anger that the sick sonofabitch was using the TPD as a shield against them.

266

"It's not uncommon; just about every government agency has been hacked. Trust me, if we could find some of these guys we'd give them jobs with the FBI or CIA, that's how good they are, most without high school diplomas. It doesn't take an MIT graduate to get around a system; it just takes time and knowledge."

"How does this help the investigation?" Dallas jumped in. "If you're saying that most of these guys aren't found since their fuckin' brilliant, how the hell do we find this bastard if the FBI can't find him?" Dallas fumed.

"He'll eventually make a mistake and then we'll have him," Parker placated, which pissed Dallas off.

"Nicola doesn't have time for him to make a mistake," Dallas seethed trying to reign in his temper, "neither do Angela, Kasey, or Kristina."

"Vaughn," Reed interrupted in a warning tone to get him to back off. Parker had allowed him to sit in on their meetings, but Reed knew if he pushed, the agent wouldn't hesitate to leave him out.

Frustrated and out of time, Dallas moved to the door and pulled it open sharply, exiting the room before he lost control. He needed to find this guy. It took a criminal to know a criminal so he figured it took a computer hacker to know another one. Grabbing his weapon and shoving it into his holster Dallas headed for his bike. The only man he knew that might be able to help him was his go-to guy when he needed information under the table Greg Powers with Aztec Custom Computers.

Twenty minutes later, he'd pulled up in front of the stone building that housed Aztec Custom Computer Company. Dallas had been referred to Powers by a detective in narcotics a few years back. Dallas helped Powers brother-in-law out of an ugly divorce by keeping tabs on the wife. In exchange for his help, Powers provided Dallas with information only a skilled hacker could obtain. Normally Dallas called Powers when he needed information, but today he wanted an up close and personal conversation with the man.

Dallas entered the front of the business and saw Powers sitting at a desk covered in computer components. In his early fifties with a lean build and sharp eyes, Powers looked up when he heard the door open but did a double take when he saw Dallas. There were two other employees working up front, so Powers stood and motioned Dallas into the back with his head, neither one of them saying a word. Dallas followed, closing the door behind him after he entered the back room and then locked it for privacy. The only other way in to the room was from an outside door, which meant their privacy was assured, so Dallas got down to business.

"I need to find someone who has the ability to hack into the TPD servers."

Powers grinned at that and replied, "I can hack into their servers."

"All right, where were you last Thursday night around nine p.m.?"

"Out to dinner with my wife after parent teacher conferences, why?"

"Then I need to find someone other than you who can hack the TPD server."

"Are you looking for a specific person? 'Cause there's probably thousands in the Tulsa area with the expertise to hack their system."

"Jesus," Dallas mumbled when Powers imparted that bombshell on him. "I can't go into details, you know that. But

I need to find a man, who is between 25 and 45 with enough expertise to get around the online firewalls that protect TPD's servers."

As he was talking, Dallas heard the side door to the warehouse open and turned quickly out of instinct to see a man carrying a large box, his face hidden from view. Dallas turned back to Powers, to protect his identity, when Powers hollered out, "Just leave it by the door for now, Micah. Detective Vaughn here needs our help."

Powers face suddenly pulled into a scowl and he called out, "Where are you going?" just as the name Micah registered to Dallas. He turned back around just as the door slammed shut and the lock was thrown into place. He turned on Powers when a jolt of awareness sent his heart pounding and bit out, "What was that man's full name?"

"Micah Shockley, why?'

"Sonofabitch," Dallas roared as he pulled his gun from his holster running for the door. The side door to the warehouse was a double key entry lock, which halted Dallas' pursuit. Before he could raise his gun to shoot out the lock, he heard the squealing of tires in the back alley. Turning back quickly, Dallas pulled out his cell and dialed Reed as he ran back toward Powers.

"Does Shockley have the experience to hack the TDP server?" Dallas shouted as he waited for Reed to answer.

"Micah? Yeah, he's my top guy," Powers explained, confused at what was happening.

"Has he done work related for me?"

"Do I *look* stupid? Jesus, Vaughn, what the hell is going on?"

Before Dallas could respond to his question, Reed answered his phone and immediately started in on Dallas for walking out of the meeting. Dallas unlocked the door to the outer office and rushed through heading for his bike. When he got outside, he cut Reed off.

"The Shallow Graver Killer is Micah Shockley. Pull his arrest record from last week, find out what the fuck he drives, and get it out over the wires. Then send a unit to his house until Parker can get his team there," Dallas growled.

"Jesus, are we talking about that ass-wipe you arrested last week?"

"Yeah, the same ass-wipe who put his hands on my woman, the same ass-wipe who works for a computer company and is "brilliant" enough to hack into the TPD computers. I don't know what the hell he was doin' in Nicola's brother's employ last week, but I'll track one of them down and haul them in for questioning. Shockley showed up at Aztec and did a runner as soon as he saw me. Powers confirmed he's one of his top guys."

"Jesus, Joseph, and Mary! Are you tellin' me that sonofabitch is the Shallow Grave Killer and he works for your hacker?"

"Yeah, that's what I'm saying. We had him Reed and we fuckin' turned him loose because he had no priors."

"Jesus, Joseph, and Mary," Reed repeated.

"Find Parker and tell him I gift-wrapped him the killer. You also tell him if he doesn't find him first, I'll send Shockley to him in a body bag."

"Who's the contact as Aztec?" Reed asked, he was all business now.

"Powers, Greg Powers. I can't investigate this, Reed. You need to get your ass over here right now."

"I'll be there in thirty, tell Powers to lock up until I get there."

"I'm gonna head to Nicola's. One of her brothers is there

keeping an eye on her while I'm at work. I'll bring him and Nicola in as soon as you're done with Powers."

"Roger that. I'm heading to find Parker now. Keep your line open 'cause I'm sure he's gonna want to talk to you."

"Don't forget to notify Cross," Dallas reminded him and then hung up and headed back inside Aztec to inform Powers he'd possibly been employing a serial killer.

***

I sat in shock after Dallas told us he was positive that the man who killed Janeane was the same man who'd molested me. He kept talking, but I barely heard him when he asked Bo how Micah Shockley had come to be his employee. I was too busy trying to pull up his face. So much had happened since that day and his face was a blurry intoxicated memory. I remembered he was tall, broad, good-looking, and he had a goatee that framed his white teeth. He had black hair, and black eyes that had focused too long on Janeane's breasts. Then I remembered how he came up behind me in the bathroom, pinning me to the counter, his hands trapping my breasts, clamping down hard until it hurt as he hissed in my ear.

Closing my eyes to block out the memory, I opened them when I heard Bo shout in his phone at Finn.

"Where the fuck did you meet Shockley?" I could hear Finn answering, but I had feeling I already knew. "Finn said he approached him at Gypsy's because he overheard him say he owned a construction company. It was right after you and the girls left. Says it was the same day Melissa died. Finn told him to come by the office and fill out an application. On Sunday, Shockley walked into our office as we were loading tools. We figured the best way to see if he was qualified to work for us was hands-on training, so we brought him along."

"Tell Finn to bring Kasey here and we'll head downtown together so you can give your statements to Parker," Dallas ordered.

"He's known all this time where I lived and he hasn't come after me, why?" I asked Dallas as Bo finished his call with Finn. Dallas clenched his jaw clearly pissed at the thought that Shockley could have been watching me and pulled me into his arms, resting the side of his head on top of mine. "How did he get out of jail so quickly?"

Dallas raised his head as I pulled mine back and looked up.

"He had no priors so his bail was set low and he was bonded out by noon the next day," he explained.

"If he wanted to kill me, why would he risk going to jail just to assault me?"

"He's a psychopath, Nicola, they act impulsively. He saw an opportunity to harass you and he took it."

"Ok, then how does he keep his job if he's watching out for us at Gypsy's?"

"His boss said he's contract labor and works from his home."

"Answer me this then, how did he find us in the first place? How did he know we hung out at Gypsy's?"

"I'm not a tech guy, baby, but I'd say if the only place you messaged to him was at Gypsy's then he traced you back there somehow."

Thinking about books I'd read and movies I'd watched where the government or hackers hunt you down via a computer, it hit me then what he'd done.

"He tracked us through the IP address," I blurted out. "We

only communicated with him when we were at Gypsy's so the internet provider would have linked back to the coffee shop."

Moving out of Dallas' arms, I started pacing searching my memory to see if I remembered him there.

"If he was watching us from inside, I would have seen him," I stated.

"Nic baby, he knew what you looked like. He could have sat in his car and waited until one of you came out."

The image of a man in a baseball hat hiding behind sunglasses lighting a cigarette popped into my head and I froze. "You're right, he was watching from outside," I mumbled, "I remember seeing him now. He was outside watching us say goodbye at your bike the night Janeane died."

"I'll inform Parker and see if there is any tape outside Gyspy's," Dallas replied, his voice strained with anger, no doubt pissed that he'd been that close.

I wanted to cry that I'd looked right at him without really seeing him. If I had, maybe I would have recognized him and Janeane would still be alive. But I didn't, she was gone, and all I felt was rage.

Dallas' eyes followed me around the room as I paced, they had a sharpness to them, the way his brow was furrowed as if he was contemplating something. Perhaps he was watching me closely because he expected me to fall apart at any moment. However, I was tired of feeling scared, so I fed off the anger instead and head for the door.

"Are you ready to go?" I called over my shoulder, "We need to get downtown so I can get back on time. The girls and I are getting together tonight to put together a photo album for the funeral."

Bo and Dallas looked at each; brows raised high in surprise then back at me and smiled. They followed me out the door as I made my way to Bo's truck each placing a kiss to my head as they passed me.

Typical men, they thought women were fragile. We may falter sometimes in the mist of extreme circumstances, but we always bounce back tougher than we were before. Having a face and a name to put to the killer made him less frightening, less . . . ominous. He was just a man for God's sake. He could be stopped by bullets, brought down easily by someone like Dallas or Bo. As long as I kept them close and the girls were protected, we had nothing to fear.

***

The haunting melody of "Fields of Gold" sung by Eva Cassidy, a talented singer who lost her life to cancer before her career took off, stayed with me after the funeral. The girls and I had put together a slide show of Janeane for her parents to be played at her funeral. "Fields of Gold" was the final song. Janeane had discovered the singer years before and loved her eclectic mix of music. It seemed appropriate to include one of her songs since like Eva, Janeane was taken too soon.

The day was gray like all of our moods, rain threatened, which seemed appropriate. The low rumble of thunder broke the silence as we stood and watched as they lowered Janeane to the ground. Clasping our hands, Kristina, Angela, Kasey, and I stood at the head of her grave and quietly sang "Old Irish Blessing." The five of us had met in high school, specifically during concert choir our sophomore year. Our choir director always had us end our final recital of the season by singing the poignant song. It spoke of God's blessing until you meet again in life, but today it spoke of farewell to our friend until we meet her again. It seemed fitting that we send a second-generation Irish-American off with the blessing, and in my heart, I knew she was harmonizing with us.

It had been two days since we found out that Micah Shockley was The Shallow Grave Killer and he was still on the run. Described as a loner who had moved to Tulsa from Minnesota, the FBI was now looking at cold cases there to see when his reign of terror began.

The girls and I were never alone—escorted to work by their husbands, Kristina and Angela refused to leave town and cower. Kasey decided she wouldn't let the bastard kill her dreams either, so she hired another yoga instructor and opened Om-Klahoma again. Loyalty brought back her regular customers and macabre fascination brought in new ones. Within two days of opening her doors again, she had close to fifty new customers.

They say tragedy brings people closer together. This nightmare was no different. Dallas and I were inseparable when he wasn't at work, with Bo acting as bodyguard during the day so he wouldn't have to worry. Our nights were spent wrapped around each other, the need to be close, to know the other was still living and breathing paramount to anything else.

Janeane's death also opened the eyes of Finn. Feelings that I think were dormant for Kasey surged to the surface and his devil-may-care attitude turned possessive. He wouldn't let Kasey out of his sight. Where she went, he went. Her ex-husband had been deployed, so she couldn't send the boys to him while we waited out the conclusion of this gothic tragedy. Therefore, he moved into her home, drove the boys to school, and drove Kasey to and from work while he managed his construction company by phone with Bo. I was the only one who didn't need to leave the house to make my living, so during the day while Dallas was at work Bo worked from my home while I sat at my computer and wrote what was in my heart. "Property Of" was no longer a fictional book, but a non-fiction true-life crime novel; one I had no desire to write. All things considered, I was in no hurry to write again period.

A hush fell over the crowd as we sang the last note of Old Irish Blessing. Releasing our hands, we turned into a group hug and held on as the sky began to weep along with us. Moments later, I felt warm hands turn me until I was wrapped in a cocoon of strength. I grabbed hold of Dallas' suit jacket and held on as I buried my face in his chest, absorbing his heat, the calming effect he always had on me when I was in his arms.

It seemed like a lifetime ago since I'd run into Dallas, spilling his coffee. Yet, in actuality, it had only been a little over two weeks since that faithful day. Nevertheless, the extreme circumstances we'd been thrown into fast-tracked my feelings for Dallas. I was no longer "in like" with him, I was in love. I didn't have a clue how he felt. We'd been so busy looking for Shockley and planning Janeane's funeral that by the end of the day the only energy we had was focused on our physical needs. However, one thing this Shakespearean tragedy has taught me is to tell those you love how you feel. I just wished I knew if Dallas was feeling the same way.

Dallas turned me around once I'd gained control, so we could make our way back to his truck and head to the Irish wake that Janeane's family had organized. The Irish celebrate life rather than mourn the passing of someone in an all day party filled with singing, dancing, and booze. Considering how much Janeane loved the nightlife, sending her off with a party was the only way to go.

Normally a wake would be held at a local pub, but with the number of people attending her funeral her family chose to hold it at a friend-of-the-family's ranch just outside of the city. The girls and I had spent the night before hanging lanterns that would be lit once the sun had set, while others cooked and hauled in cattle troughs to fill with beer.

Flying G ranch was located north of Tulsa. Just shy of a thousand acers, the flat plains where the cattle grazed slowly rolled into hills and cliffs that butted up to Skiatook Lake. The log-style home sat at the top of the cliff looking out onto the lake below with a huge covered deck. We didn't have to worry about the weather thanks to the covered deck and the relaxing atmosphere helped put us in the mood to celebrate life instead of wallow in grief.

By the time the sun had gone down, most of the guests had headed home, except immediate family and close friends. The grills had been extinguished, but Irish music was playing as Janeane's extended family who'd flown in from Ireland danced an Irish jig. The girls and I were seated at a table laughing as Janeane's Uncle Ethan from Dublin belted out Danny Boy for the tenth time that night.

"Janeane would have loved this," Kasey laughed as Uncle Ethan held a note until he couldn't breathe.

"She would have, and it makes me realize we should make time for things like this more often. I say we set aside the first Saturday of every month for backyard barbecues," I told the girls. Three smiling faces told me they agreed, so I made a mental note to tell my parents.

Finn walked up carrying Kasey's sons, both asleep with

their heads tucked into Finn's neck.

"We need to get these guys home, babe," Finn told Kasey. I smiled as I watched her face melt a little at the sight of her sons in Finn's arms. Kasey stood, taking her youngest boy, Luca, from Finn while he kept hold of Jackson. We hugged her goodbye then she and Finn walked over and said their goodbyes to Janeane's parents together. When they were done, Finn took her hand and led her through the house to the front door.

"At least something good came of her death," Angela said as we watched them walk away.

"Yeah," Kristina and I agreed.

Dallas was standing at the railing, looking out at the lake, so I got up and joined him. The moon was casting its reflection on the water and you could see boats anchored out on the lake, rocking back and forth with the waves. When I wrapped my arms around his waist, my head turned in order to rest it on his back; Dallas reached up and ran his hand along my arm. After a moment of just being, he finally turned so he could wrap me up. I turned my head to rest it on his chest, his own resting on the top of mine and we stared out at the water. The sound of the water lapping on the shore lulled me into a sense of peacefulness I hadn't had since we found out Janeane had died. I was so relaxed, in fact, that I didn't check myself, and on a sigh of contentment, I whispered without thinking, "I love you, Dallas."

As soon as the words left my mouth, I closed my eyes, hoping he hadn't heard me. Dallas' breathe caught for a moment, which meant I had my answer. I guess I whispered louder than I thought. When he tried to pull me back, no doubt to ask if he'd heard me correctly, I tightened my hold on his waist. When I wouldn't look at him, he brought both hands up and tilted my head back until he could see my face. I kept my eyes lowered afraid of what I'd see until I heard him whisper, "Look at me."

I raised my eyes to his and my own breath hitched when I saw those honey-colored eyes gleaming possessively at me right before he slammed his mouth down to mine. He drew me harder into his body as he tilted his head, further devouring my mouth. I clung to his shoulders while he kissed my legs weak just liked he told me could two weeks before. Just as suddenly as he'd kissed me, he ripped his mouth from mine, bent his head until it was laying on my forehead. With a heaving chest, he growled, "You pick a fine time to tell me."

"It just slipped out," I explained, trying to catch my own breath.

"We're thirty minutes from home, surrounded by family, and you tell me that shit when I can't throw you on a bed and give back to you what you just gave me?"

"I take it back then," I smiled.

"You aren't takin' it back, but we sure as hell are leavin' or I'll drag you up those stairs and find a vacant room."

I rolled my lips between my teeth to keep from laughing while his jaw ticked in frustration at being miles from home.

"I'll get my purse," I finally told him and tried to turn out of his arms. Dallas tightened his grip around my waist, then, with a slow grin, leaned down, and touched his mouth to mine before letting me go.

It took five minutes to say our goodbyes before Dallas threw me into his truck and started heading down the dirt road that lead to the ranch. I wished he had one of those older trucks with the bench seats so I could sit next to him while he drove, but I had to settle on holding his hand on my thigh as he drove through the dark back roads heading for the interstate. I was smiling to myself over his reaction that I loved him right before Dallas barked out "sonofabitch." I looked up at the surprise in his voice, just in time to see headlights as another truck t-boned us. The impact sent my head into the windshield right before our truck flipped, tumbling repeatedly before coming to rest in a ravine.

Twenty

Gray smoke billowed in the moonlight as Parker slowly exhaled. Nicotine helped him focus while he tried to reach inside the mind of a killer.

"You dream about them don't you, you sick sonofabitch. You lay awake at night with your hand wrapped around your cock, getting off on the memory of your kills."

Flipping through the pictures of Janeane Dee, he noted again that her hands and feet were bound to the head and footboards of her bed, and Parker felt his blood pressure start to rise. In all the years he'd work for the FBI, he'd never known any of the victims he investigated. Of course, they weren't faceless to him, but he'd remained detached so he could do his job. This one he knew, albeit briefly, but it changed the rules for him. He'd met Janeane at the police station and had seen her with her friends on the street, when he'd met Nicola for dinner. Therefore, the need to find this killer was stronger than he'd felt in years.

"You like power, the control you have over them, you want them submissive," he whispered as he closed his eyes. "Master," he hissed as he thought back to Melissa Webster's murder and the word written on the mirror.

Parker flipped back to the files of his first victims and noted again that all had been bound by their feet and hands. There was tearing within their anal and vaginal walls, indicating they'd had rough sex within hours of dying.

"Master," he repeated, "You find your victims online and dominate them before killing them. You see yourself as their master, so are they your slaves? Is that what they are, Shockley? You live in an apartment with thin walls and no room to play so where did you take them, you sick fuck?"

Parker laid the autopsy pictures of all six victims at the end of the bed and stood back, staring. The first three had the same ligature marks. Wide bands, probably leather cuffs, had been used to secure them. He scanned the reports again for any evidence found on the bodies. White-Cline had a single hair that was being rushed through DNA, but there were no fibers that would give them a clue where to look. Only traces of crude oil, they determined had transferred from the dirt where they were buried, had been on the bodies.

"Oil refineries leach oil into the ground," Parker mumbled as he scanned the report, "three of them within a mile of the dump sites. Christ, only in Texas or Oklahoma would that evidence mean shit."

Scanning the reports again, he noted that all of the victims' friends and family members had said they were messaging men on dating sites, but at the time they disappeared, they didn't know if they had met anyone. It was the only connection the women had in common, that, and they were all blonde and well-endowed by God.

Parker's cell began to ring as he studied the files so he pulled it out and answered.

"Parker," he said, distracted.

"He's got her," Vaughn roared down the line.

Parker hesitated for a moment, his eyes narrowing as the

words sunk in. There was only one "her" that would have Vaughn panic.

Nicola's green eyes and angelic face rushed into his mind, and he tightened his grip on the phone.

"Where? When?" Parker barked back.

"Twenty minutes ago. The sonofabitch was waiting for us when we left the wake. We were on a back road. He came out of nowhere with his lights off and rammed my truck, flipping us into a ravine," Vaughn bellowed, panic obvious in his voice. "I was pinned. I couldn't reach my fuckin' gun, and he pulled her from the wreck and drove off. I need you to tell me right fuckin' now where he would take her. You have a team of experts who need to pull their heads out of their asses and give me a location," Vaughn thundered.

"Vaughn—"

"Swear to God, if you and your team . . . I can't lose her—" Vaughn gritted through his teeth, hanging onto his emotions by a thread.

Parker stopped listening; he had the ability to tune people out in stressful situations so he could concentrate when time was critical. He filtered through what he knew about Shockley.

He bound them, but didn't gag them—he liked to hear their screams, which means he would need someplace isolated. He wouldn't want to haul the bodies far from the kill site, but they had been found in fields off the west bank of the Arkansas River. Nothing had been found on the bodies but crude oil, which was prevalent in that area because of. . .

"The crude oil," Parker bit out.

"What about it?"

"It was on all three of the first victims, on their backs but not their fronts. Crude oil is raw oil; it's useless until it's processed.

How the hell did we miss that? Vaughn, they were exposed to crude oil before they died. The oil in the ground around the bodies should have been processed, not raw. He had them someplace that's abandoned and deals with crude oil."

"Refineries," Parker and Vaughn shouted in unison.

"He's taking them to the abandoned POCO refinery," Vaughn whispered. "Jesus, he's barely driving a mile from the kill site before dumping them."

"Are you in transit now?" Parker asked as he picked up the pictures he'd laid on the bed and shoved them back into his file.

"I took her brother's truck when they arrived at the scene. I'm about ten minutes out from that location. If you get there before me, you go in silent. I don't want squads coming in blazing. He'll kill her if he knows he's trapped."

"Roger that. I'll call it in and meet you there, I'm at least ten minutes out myself," Parker acknowledged as he headed for the front door. Parker paused when he reached his front door and against his better judgment told Dallas, "He takes his time with these women, Vaughn, he won't rush to kill her unless he's provoked."

There was silence on the other end as Vaughn processed that information and Parker heard him take a deep breath before answering.

"If he's touched her at all, Parker, I'll kill him. So you better beat me there," Vaughn warned him in a voice so low and deadly that Parker knew he wasn't throwing out false bravado.

"If he's touched her at all I'll kill him for you," Parker vowed and he meant it. Knowing the victims made it personal now. Shockley could only play this, one of two ways. Either he gave up without a fight or he left there in a body bag. Either way worked for Parker, but he'd get more satisfaction if it were in a bag.

***

A distant light crept in as the sound of water dripping broke through the fog clouding my mind. My eyes wouldn't focus and my head felt like it had been split in two. Full consciousness seemed to elude me, no matter how hard I tried. My pounding head was pushing me back into a black vortex, spinning me further into its murky depths, submerging me into a place where I only felt peace. Yet, a small voice inside my head kept crying out and urging me to awareness. "Wake up, fight," my subconscious screamed, so I forced my eyes open, blinking several times until a light came into focus.

Turning my head slowly, I made out the shapes of large pipes running overhead and I stared at them. They were cast in an unnatural shadow from the small light glowing from across the room. The stagnant smell of oil assaulted my senses, powerful and overwhelming. I tried to raise my hands to shield my eyes from the light, but they wouldn't move. With heavy lids, I turned my head from one hand to the other and saw large black cuffs imprisoning my wrists. My heart rate picked up, galloping in my chest at the sight of the restraints, and then I felt the bindings on my bare legs.

I was spread eagle on some sort of table that allowed my arms and legs to be bound. The black dress that I'd worn to Janeane's funeral was parted open like a coat. Cut down its length, the gaping center leaving me exposed. Jerking with fear, I started struggling to pull my hands free while the evening came rushing back to me like a tidal wave.

Dallas taking me home in his truck because I'd told him I

loved him. The sound of metal on metal when his truck flipped, landing upside down. Angry hands on me as I was jerked from the truck. Dallas' enraged voice shouting he would kill Shockley while he struggled to break free of his jammed seat belt. And finally, Shockley's raised fist before he punched me in the temple, sending me spiraling into the terrifying darkness as he drove away.

Oh, God, I'm going to die.

"You know it was your hair that caught my attention most," Shockley's emotionless voice called out from somewhere in the dark. "All of Taryn intrigued me, but it was the exquisite color of your hair that sold me."

"You're mad," I shrieked, my scream bouncing off the cavernous room, echoing like a ghost in a forgotten graveyard.

I knew with clarity that it was only a matter of minutes before I also became a ghost.

"And you're a liar," Shockley hissed, his voice closer than before. "You tempted your master with a fake woman."

When he finally stepped into the light, all but his eyes were visible. They were shadowed by the surrounding darkness, but I swear I could see them glowing unnaturally like some sort of demon spawn.

"When your master gives you instructions, he expects them to be followed without question, you fuckin' cunt. When they aren't, your master has the right to dole out punishment as he sees fit. You brought this on yourself," he raged, "and since you can't be trusted to follow my instructions, the punishment is death," he explained without remorse as he stepped fully into the light holding a knife. I struggled to pull my feet out of the bindings as he stalked toward me. He was almost graceful, like a jungle predator taking his time before he pounced on his prey. When he reached the table, he leaned down and tilted it until I was upright staring him in the eyes.

"You, Ms. Royse, have disobeyed me for the last time," he roared in my face, spittle dripping from his mouth. With a quick jab to my side, I felt the knife pierce my flesh like a hot poker. My reaction was instantaneous; I cried out in shock at the searing pain and then I spit in his face.

Nonplussed by my defiance, he reached up, grabbed my hair, and yanked back hard. I glared instead of crying out. I had no doubt he wanted to see my fear as he took my life, but I wasn't about to give him the satisfaction. I started to laugh at him, to taunt him so he would kill me quickly rather than draw out the torture, but he silenced my cackles by slamming his mouth over mine.

Survival is instinctive; your body will protect you from your own foolish behavior because it wants to live. My brain took over in the last fleeting moments of my life and, in a last ditched effort to free myself, my brain instructed me to point my feet and yank hard. My right foot gave way slightly, so I yanked again and it freed from the restraint. Raising my knee up, I wedged it in between our bodies, and kicked him back. When he pulled away to grab my leg, I kicked him with all my might in the groin and then screamed for all I was worth, while I felt the loss of blood slowly weakening my body.

Shockley went down on one knee, breathing deep as I tried to free my other foot. I kept kicking out with my free leg, trying to knock him out, but he was out of my reach. He rose slowly after he'd recovered from my kick, pulling a clear plastic bag from his back pocket. Cold fear coursed through my veins when I realized what he intended. Moving quickly, his eyes blank as a snarl ripped from his mouth, he threw the bag over my head, twisting it tight around my neck cutting off my oxygen. I fought with my free leg to no avail and felt my lungs burn and my eyes bulge as my brain and lungs cried out for oxygen. Stars danced before my eyes as Shockley grabbed my breast squeezing hard as he rubbed his hardened shaft on my leg.

Shockley released his hold for a moment, long enough for my oxygen starved brain to gasp for air before he tightened it again. I was too weak at this point to move, to fight against him and the darkness crept back in. He released his hold on the bag again, and blood rushed back to my brain. It was almost euphoric the way the blood rushed through my arteries, releasing a sense of calm. He pulled his knife from the back of his waistband again, turning the blade toward me. Before I could kick out, he shoved the blade deep into my stomach in a swift strike. Unbearable pain that would have doubled me over if I could have moved caught what was left of my breath as Shockley leered in satisfaction. *This is it; this is the moment when he raises his knife and buries it deep in my heart.*

As if he could read my mind, he smiled sadistically, pulled the bag from my head, and raised the knife high. I closed my eyes and waited for the strike that would end my life, saying a silent good-bye to Dallas and my family. I was almost calm, peaceful in the knowledge that the red-hot pain in my stomach would soon end. Taking a deep breath and letting it out slowly, preparing for the blow that would end my life, I gasped and my eyes flew open when I heard a door slam open and Dallas thunder in rage, "Nicola!" before the rapid fire of a gun caused Shockley's head to explode in front of me.

Through tears and pain the likes I'd never felt, I watched

Shockley fall into a heap to the floor, blood pouring from what was left of his head. I heard Dallas' pounding footsteps as my eyesight blurred and a cold numbness set in.

"Hold on, baby," Dallas shouted as he pulled out a phone, called 911, and began barking orders. I closed my eyes to block out the pain as my head slumped forward. Dallas grabbed my face and ordered, "Don't you close your fuckin' eyes! Do you hear me? You stay with me Nicola, help is almost here."

I could feel the darkness seeping in, pulling me under, and I knew I needed to say good-bye just in case. As Dallas loosened the restraints on my arms and leg, I laid my head on his shoulder and whispered, "Tell my family that I love them."

"You can tell them yourself after we get you to the hospital," Dallas replied, his voice shaky as he spoke.

I tried to nod, but my body wouldn't cooperate. When he lowered me to the ground I cried out, my back arching in pain as he pulled the shirt from his body and applied pressure to my wound.

Parker arrived just as I screamed out, bursting through the door with his gun drawn.

"Look at me, baby, keep your eyes on me," Dallas ordered so I focused on his honey-colored eyes with their flecks of green. They were the most beautiful eyes I'd ever seen, but they were wild looking now, betraying his somewhat controlled movements. He was terrified. My dark and dangerous warlord was shaken to his core.

"Heard your call over the radio, the ambulance is less than five minutes out," Parker stated as Dallas stroked my face. "I see you handled Shockley."

"Yeah, and if you want my badge for the kill, you can have

it," Dallas bit out, "I don't give a fuck."

I tried to keep my eyes open like Dallas ordered, but I was tired, and so very cold. Reaching out I placed my hand on Dallas' face. I felt his warm mouth on the palm of my hand as he kissed it, and I wanted to burrow into his body so I could feel warm again. I was going into shock and I knew it. So, with my last conscious thought, I curled my fingers around his hand and whispered, "Love me, Dallas."

***

"Love me, Dallas."

Jerking awake with a start, Dallas turned to look at the tiny woman lying in the hospital bed. The dark circles under her eyes and the constant beeping of the monitors reminded him that Nicola was alive, but not yet awake. She'd lost too much blood from the knife wounds and slipped into a coma. After coding twice during surgery, the doctors had given Nicola a 50/50 chance of making it through the night. That was two days ago and he'd refused to leave her side for a minute. Her family and friends were in the waiting room, coming in every two hours as allowed, but Dallas had flashed his badge and glared, daring the doctors to throw him out.

They quickly saw the wisdom in letting him stay.

Tangling his fingers with hers, he raised her hand to his lips and kissed the only spot on her hand that didn't have an IV in the way.

"You need to wake up, Nicola," Dallas ordered for the hundredth time and he watched her face for a sign she'd heard him, any movement at all.

Nothing.

Releasing her hand, he rubbed his own across his face,

then stood up, and stretched his back. Dallas was still dressed in the suit pants and white dress shirt he'd worn to the funeral—he had refused to go home to change.

A knock on the door had Dallas turning to find a hospital technician dressed in blue scrubs holding a chart.

"I'm here to take Ms. Royse for neuroimaging."

Dallas narrowed his eyes at the man.

"Why?"

"To check for brain function."

"Her brain is fine, she just needs time to recover," Dallas growled.

"I'm just here to take her for the test, sir, I'm not a doctor."

Dallas saw Dr. Royse in the hallway talking with Nicola's doctor, so he exited her room and joined both men.

"She's not brain dead," Dallas argued.

"We aren't saying she is, but she hit her head in the accident, so we want to take a look and see if there's anything going on that could be prolonging her coma," Dr. Royse explained.

"She just needs rest," Dallas argued again as fear crept in again.

"She should have woken up by now," her father explained, Dallas' own fear mirrored in his eyes.

"She. Just. Needs. Rest." Dallas bit out each word, then turned his back on the men, and walked back into her room.

The technician had started disconnecting the machines, pausing alarms as they rang out so the nurses wouldn't come running. Frustrated with Nicola for being so stubborn, Dallas leaned down and kissed her forehead before moving to her ear so she could hear him.

"Nic baby, I need you to wake up," he whispered. Grabbing her hand, he squeezed hard hoping for some type of sign that she heard him.

Nothing.

"Goddammit, Nicola, open your fuckin' eyes," Dallas ordered, "you're missing out on a love story for the ages while you lay there sleeping."

Still nothing.

Taking a deep breath, Dallas lowered his head to hers and tried to reach her through her greatest love—her books. "Ok, Nicola, have it your way . . . Once upon a time there was a lonely warlord who spent his life fighting one injustice or another. Even though he was disillusioned with life he kept searching for something that made all the shit he waded through daily worthwhile. Then one day, this sexy maiden bumped into him in a coffee shop and smiled at him," Dallas chuckled. "With that one smile, that one single sexy grin, all the filth in my life faded away. Nic baby, if that isn't a fairy tale that deserves a happy ending I don't know what is," he whispered. "You asked me to love you, Nicola, but the problem is I can't tell you that I already do unless you open your eyes and look at me. Do you hear me, gorgeous? I love you, but you have to open your eyes so we can have our happy ending."

Nothing, not even a twitch.

"I need to take her downstairs now, sir," the technician broke in. Dallas reluctantly stepped back and followed him out of the room. Once they were in the hallway, the tech stupidly advised that he wait in her room, so Dallas pinned the man with a look that would have made most men run.

"Or you can come with us," the tech spit out quickly.

"I'm not leaving her side until she wakes up," Dallas stated as he grabbed Nicola's hand and held on. He saw Bo and Finn standing in the hallway, concern etched on their faces mixed with a shit-eating grin that said they'd seen the whole encounter.

Dallas ignored them both and started talking to Nicola as if she were awake. He told her they were headed downstairs for an MRI and that it was a, "Fuckin' waste of money," since she was only asleep. When they stopped at the elevator, he started to tell her about her cats and how they were tearing up her mother's house. When a slight movement had Dallas jerking his head down suddenly, looking at where her hand lay in his. His heart beat swiftly as he watched her pinky twitch, then seconds later her hand moved and she curled her fingers around his own.

"Dallas," he heard Nicola mumble weakly. He turned his head quickly at his name to find two jade-green eyes looking up at him.

"Thank, Christ," he breathed out, leaning down toward her face as relief rushed down his spine and settled in his legs. He whispered, "Welcome back, baby," against her lips, then pulled back to look at her. She had a funny look on her face when her mouth formed the words, "Where's your Kilt, you always wear a kilt."

"My what?" Dallas asked confused.

"Kilt," she replied groggily.

"Are you saying you want me to wear a kilt?"

Nicola nodded slightly as her eyes closed, a dreamy expression overtaking her face.

"Christ . . . will you remember if I say okay?"

"No," she mumbled weakly, sleep almost upon her.

Smiling at her expression, he leaned down and whispered, "All right, babe, I'll wear a kilt for you." When she smiled brightly without opening her eyes, he waited a moment longer for her to fall asleep again and then added without guilt, "When hell freezes over."

Epilogue

Everyone thought romance novelists had exciting sex lives—if they only knew . . . If they only knew, they'd hate me.

Four months later

A soft breeze caressed my body, sending tiny shivers down my spine. I was naked, covered with a fine sheen of sweat as my body heated thanks to Dallas. He slid in and out of me slowly as our tongues danced, tangling in erotic play. Still afraid to lay fully on my stomach for fear he'd hurt me somehow, Dallas held back. Ripping his mouth from mine, he leaned down and ran his tongue across my pebbled scars, the only physical reminder I had of the nightmare so many of us endured. Running my hands through his hair as he kissed his way up my chest, Dallas stopped at my heavy breasts to lavish my nipples with attention.

"I love the taste of you," Dallas moaned as he ran his tongue up the valley between my breasts only to take my mouth again, while his rhythmic thrusts built a fire inside me. His hips pounding at a furious pace, he grabbed my shoulders and pulled me up until I was straddling his thighs. Mouth-to-mouth, chest-to-chest, our arms wrapped around each other's shoulders and we pushed and pulled to a frantic rhythm. Two hearts beat in unison, climbing to that place that threw you off violently, only to burst free in exquisite bliss. I threw my head back as my release shot fast and beautiful through my soul, unleashing the calm and peacefulness I always felt in his arms.

"Marry me," Dallas whispered in my ear seconds after we both cried out, the smell of sex and sweat curling around us like a cocoon.

"What?" I asked breathlessly as my eyes shot to his.

With Dallas still buried deep inside of me, he held onto my waist as he flipped to his back, taking me with him until I was lying on his chest. I lifted up, bracing my arms on his chest as my hair fell around his in a veil. His honey-colored eyes blazed with emotion as he cupped my face with both hands before taking my mouth again in a life-altering kiss.

"I told you once that I wanted to own that part of you that you've never given away, a part that can only be mine," Dallas whispered against my lips when he finished kissing me. "What I didn't tell you was that I wanted you to own that part of me I'd never given away. A part that can only belong to you. You own it now and I don't want it back."

A knot formed in my throat as he spoke, choking the sob that wanted to breach my lips.

"You never gave that piece to Brynne?"

"Never. I was too young to know she wasn't the one I should have waited for. When you ran into me at the coffee house, my soul stood up and took notice. I'd been waiting for you to come along; I just didn't know it until you smiled at me."

"I've been waiting for you, too," I cried, unable to stop the flood that poured down my face.

"Marry me, Nicola, and I'll spend the rest of my life loving and protecting you," Dallas asked again.

Choked by feelings I'd never felt in my life, I couldn't answer, so I nodded emphatically and slammed my mouth over his until he took over, rolling me to my back. His cock hardened while still inside me, so I wrapped my legs around his waist and he began sealing our engagement with slow, tender thrusts.

Nine months later, the first Saturday in April

Beer in hand, Dallas flipped hamburgers as the girls and I sat around my patio table catching up. Kasey's boys were chasing Snape and Simi while Bo and Finn talked with my parents. Bill and his wife June rounded out my monthly barbecue; the last one I'd host as a single woman.

Dallas had pushed for a short engagement, but my mother's wide eyes and fake tears over her only daughter not having a huge fairytale wedding, complete with white doves and a horse drawn carriage, shut him up. I, for one, didn't care if we went to the justice of the peace or Vegas for a quickie ceremony, since I finally had my own real-life storybook hero. However, I will admit, walking down the aisle in a beautiful white gown while Dallas waited for me to take our vows did hold some appeal.

It had been just over a year since Micah Shockley came into our lives and a day doesn't go by that we don't think about Janeane and all that she'd missed. My upcoming wedding should have been a joyous occasion, but a part of me couldn't help thinking about the fact that I should have had four bridesmaids instead of three.

The girls and I still meet once a week at Gypsy's, even though it's a reminder of how we lost our dear friend. But it's also a way to keep her memory alive, since on those days I brainstorm with the girls about my current WIP. I went back to writing historical romance; my taste for writing a contemporary novel died when Janeane did. My current book, due to release in three months, is about a young English maiden named Janeane who meets a golden-eyed Highlander named Duglas, pronounced Doolas. They fall deeply in love and, of course, live happily ever after. I may have given up my contemporary novel, but I hadn't given up using Dallas as one of my heroes. In addition, if I do say so myself, it's my best work to date for obvious reasons. The hero, you see, saves the maiden from certain death.

The past year had been an exercise in adjusting. Such as adjusting to life with a bossy male, who wants to know your every move because he still has nightmares about the night you were stabbed. Or adjusting to your best friend dating your brother (yes, I get phone calls at midnight, hearing what an ass he is) leaving his twin to fend for himself, which meant he spent all his time at my house. But those adjustments came with deep, abiding passion and love that never ceased to amaze me. Now all I had to do was marry my warlord and live happily ever after.

"So you're telling us that Dallas showed up at the photo shoot and blew his top?" Kasey laughed.

Glancing at my betrothed, I giggled when I thought about it.

"Yep. However, it may have had something to do with the kilt. Picture it ladies, the fair-haired maiden was overseeing the photo shoot of her current book 'Highlander's Gift.'"

"Why are you talking in third person?" Angela asked.

"Just go with it for now." I explained.

"Do you talk in third person a lot?" June laughed, looking

around the table at my friends.

"No, I think in third person therefore I tell a story in third person," I huffed. "Do you want to hear this or not?"

"By all means, don't keep us in suspense."

Looking back at Dallas before I finished, I watched as he took a pull from his beer. Sensing I was looking at him, his eyes drifted to mine and then narrowed.

"What?" he asked a little warily.

"Nothing. I was just thinking about kilts."

Shaking his head slowly, he turned his back on us mumbling, "Hell hasn't frozen over yet."

Laughing at the brooding brute, I turned back to the girls and started back with my tale.

"Where was I?"

"The fair-haired maiden was ogling the male model during the photo shoot," June threw out.

"Right. So imagine if you will, for the cover of her new book the fair-haired maiden needed a man who was tall, broad, and very well built. He had to be devastatingly handsome like her warlord and, of course, have great legs to pull off a kilt. Therefore, she hired a dark and dangerous looking fake warlord to grace the cover of her new book. As you can imagine, she would need photos with the handsome warrior to put on her Facebook page so her readers could appreciate her future—"

"This is where Dallas comes in I bet," Kristina laughed.

"Exactly. So the fair-haired maiden was posing with the dark and dangerous fake warlord, just having a bit of fun."

"How much fun?" June asked with a grin.

"I believe he was holding her hair back seductively like he was going to kiss her," I explained.

"Oh, Lord," Kasey laughed.

"Hot," Angela smiled.

"Can I come to the next photo shoot?" Kristina begged.

"I've heard this story already," June interjected, "according to Bill he had his hand on your ass."

"It's possible, but I was in a period gown wearing a corset so I was concentrating on breathing."

"Is that when Dallas walked in?" Kristina asked.

"Wait for it, Kris. So the fake warlord was leaning in like he was supposed to, holding his mouth about an inch away from hers, so it gave the appearance of a kiss."

"Oh, Lord," Kasey mumbled.

"Way hot," Angela agreed.

"Seriously, I want to go to the next photo shoot," Kristina begged louder which drew Dallas' attention.

"She's not going to the next photo shoot," Dallas growled.

Rolling my eyes, I leaned in further and tried to finish the tale without interruption from my dark and dangerous fiancé.

"Ignore him, I do," I laughed. "Anyway, there she was holding her pose while well over six feet of hard muscles held her tightly for the camera, when all of a sudden she heard a deep voice growl, 'You wanna get your hand off my woman's ass?'"

"Oh, Lord," Kasey sighed.

"Protecting his golden pussy," Angela laughed.

"You have all the fun," Kristina complained.

"CAUSING," I broke in loudly so I could finish the story, "the fair-haired maiden to jump. I'll remind you that the dark and dangerous fake warlord slash model had his lips a hairbreadth away from hers."

"You kissed him?" Kristina gasped.

"Technically, it was more of a lip bump. But try explaining that to Dallas."

"No wonder he won't let you go to another photo shoot," June mumbled, looking back at Dallas.

"I tried explaining to him if he'd just posed for the cover in the first damn place none of it would have happened."

"Oh, yeah, he would have been perfect for the cover. Why didn't he?" Kasey asked.

"According to him, he'll do it when hell freezes over," I answered with a shrug.

"So what happened when you kiss "bumped" the guy?" June inquired.

Smiling, I leaned in and whispered, "He may have looked like a warlord, but when Dallas lunged at him, ready to rip his head off, he pulled me in front of him to protect himself from Dallas."

"No way," all four gasped in unison.

"WAY!" I confirmed.

***

"You gonna make it to the wedding?" Dallas asked Parker as he watched Nicola laugh with her friends.

"I'm stuck in Bethesda. The director pulled together a joint task force on The Harvest Killer. He's hoping to get a jump on him before he starts killing again in the fall."

"Your Harvest Killer makes Shockley look like a saint," Dallas sighed.

"He's a sadistic fuck, Vaughn. He hangs his victims in a field like scarecrows, even sews their eyes and mouths shut."

"Jesus."

"There's no God involved with this one, he's been sent straight from hell."

"Right, so send him back," Dallas growled.

"I will, with extreme prejudice," Parker vowed.

"Before we hang up, answer me something, Parker. I asked you once why you pushed my buttons that night at the restaurant. You and I both know you were testing me for a reason and I want to know why."

"I wanted to see your reaction."

"I get that, but why?"

"You know Shockley hacked the firewall, but what I never told you was that he used your ID to get through."

". . . Are you telling me he concealed his identity by hiding behind me," Dallas seethed . . . "Jesus, why the hell didn't you arrest me?"

"I go with my gut. When I met you I knew instinctively you were being set up, but I had to be sure."

"If you were so sure then why did you push my buttons that night?"

"Because after an hour with your future wife I knew Nicola deserved a man who would fight for her, and I wanted to make sure you were that man."

"Christ," Dallas chuckled, looking at Nicola.

She was talking to her brothers now, laughing, her head tilted back as the sun kissed her hair, casting it into a shimmering veil of gold. She was the sexiest woman he'd ever met and she belonged to him. He didn't know what fates deemed him worthy of such a woman, but he'd spend the rest of his life making sure she knew how lucky he was.

"You still there?" Parker asked down the line.

"Yeah, just looking at my wife."

"Future wife," Parker replied.

"Nope. According to Nicola, in medieval Scotland if you agreed to marry someone and then followed it with sex, you were considered married."

"So the wedding in two weeks is just—"

"A formality, Parker. She's mine in every way that matters already."

Dallas ended the call abruptly and moved toward his wife. When he reached her, he turned her around, bent at the waist, and threw her over his shoulder.

"What are you doing?" Nicola asked calmly as he stalked through their house and out to the driveway.

"Exercising my husbandly rights."

"Dallas, we have a house full of people," she sighed.

"We're goin' for a ride on my bike."

"But we have a house full of people," she repeated.

Dropping Nicola to her feet next to his bike, Dallas pulled out her helmet and stuck it on her head.

"Fair maiden, get your ass on my bike."

"And if I don't?"

"Then I'll take you into the bedroom where you'll get my gentle hand and my strong back as I drive into you until you scream my name."

"God, I love it when you quote my books. Now if you'd only wear a kilt," Nicola whined.

"Babe, it's not gonna happen."

"But you promised, Dallas."

Narrowing his eyes, he watched as her cupid lips pulled into a grin.

"You remember?"

"I remember everything. You pulled me from a dark pit, Dallas. I didn't want to wake up because in the darkness, I was safe," Nicola told him as tears started to fall. "Then I heard your voice telling me that you loved me and I knew that the safest place I could ever be was with you, so I woke up."

"Jesus," Dallas responded with a husky resonance as he

leaned forward placing his forehead against hers. He was overwhelmed with possessiveness and the need to own every part of her, to the very depths of her soul. To claim her in every possible way. With conviction born out of a need as ancient as time, he growled, "I want my baby growing inside you. I don't want to wait a year or two. I want it right fuckin' now."

A half-sob, half-laugh broke from Nicolas lips at his announcement. She'd wanted to keep her secret until after their wedding, but decided after that demand by her modern-day warlord, that this was the perfect moment. Staring into Dallas' honey-colored eyes, she saw her own love mirrored in his own. So, with a glint in her eyes and a tremble in her voice she took his hand, placed it on her stomach, and then choked out, "He already is."

And they all drank coffee and lived happily ever after.

The End.

About the Author

CP Smith resides in Oklahoma with her husband, five children, and four dogs.

You can reach Ms. Smith at:
cpsmith74135@gmail.com

https://www.facebook.com/pages/Author-CP-Smith/739842239363610

Other Titles by CP Smith

Reason series:

A Reason To Breathe

A Reason To Kill

A Reason To Live

Standalone

Restoring Hope

FRAMED

Made in the USA
Columbia, SC
19 April 2017